Praise for the Davis W...

DOUBLE ...

"A smart, snappy write

"Archer's bright and si
of Janet Evanovich's
Way and her many mi:

"Slot tournament season at the Bellissimo Resort and Casino in Biloxi, Miss., provides the backdrop for Archer's enjoyable sequel to *Double Whammy*...Credible characters and plenty of Gulf Coast local color help make this a winner."

– *Publishers Weekly*

"Snappy, wise cracking, and fast-paced."

– Mary Marks,
New York Journal of Books

"Hilarious, action-packed, with a touch of home-sweet-home and a ton of glitz and glam. I'm booking my next vacation at the Bellissimo!"

– Susan M. Boyer,
USA Today Bestselling Author of the Liz Talbot Mystery Series

"A roller-coaster of a read. Gretchen Archer has given us enough red herrings to fill the buffet table at the Bellissimo Resort and Casino. The protagonist is smart and sassy with a wise-cracking sense of humor...if you like betting on a winning mystery, then you should be reading *Double Dip*!"

– Cheryl Green,
MyShelf Reviews

The Davis Way Crime Caper Series
by Gretchen Archer

DOUBLE STRIKE

A DAVIS WAY CRIME CAPER

Gretchen Archer

HENERY PRESS

DOUBLE STRIKE
A Davis Way Crime Caper
Part of the Henery Press Mystery Collection

First Edition
Trade paperback edition | October 2014

Henery Press
www.henerypress.com

ISBN-13: 978-1-940976-33-4

Printed in the United States of America

For Laura, for Katie, and for Sam

River deep, mountain high

ACKNOWLEDGMENTS

Thank you Deke Castelman, Stephany Evans, and Kendel Lynn.

ONE

I didn't get married because the lightning protection system at the Bellissimo Resort and Casino failed. Miserably. It's there to intercept bolts of lightning trained on the thirty-story building, then safely conduct them to the ground. It didn't. The call came at three-eighteen, dead of night.

"Davis. Wake up." The man shaking me was Bradley Cole, who also didn't get married because of the lightning strike. "It's Jeremy."

"Who?" I shot straight up, hair flipping everywhere. "What?"

Bradley Cole and I live in a condo on the seventh floor of the Regent, a fourteen-story premier residence on Beach Boulevard in Biloxi, Mississippi. It's a short drive, five miles or so, to and from the Bellissimo, where I work as part of an elite security team. Our bedroom is an entire wall of hurricane-proof glass (plus three normal walls) that looks out over the Gulf, and at this hour, the view was usually a black hole or an astronomy show, but tonight it was a blinding fireworks display. Hundreds of cracked white lines snapped in tandem over the ocean.

I turned to Bradley. "Is my mother here?"

"No, Davis! Wake up! *My* mother is here. Your mother is at the Bellissimo and it's on *fire*." He put the phone to my ear. "It's Jeremy. Talk to him."

So, that was how Friday, the first Friday in October, the day before my wedding, started. With a bang.

* * *

The storm had blown a safe enough distance out to sea by the time I'd splashed water on my face, thrown on clothes, and found my keys. Bradley in his bathrobe and his mother on his heels in hers walked me to the door. Bradley gave me a hug. "Be careful." I fit perfectly under his chin. "I'll be there as soon as I can."

"Bradley." Anne Cole, my future mother-in-law—super short hair the color of ice, Senior Slammers tennis champ, can whip up a gourmet meal from three butter beans and a hot dog bun—petted his arm. "You don't need to go. It's too dangerous."

What about me? Chopped liver? Having spent a few quickie holidays with her, and now a long—and by long, I mean time had come to a complete standstill—four days with her as our houseguest, it was becoming increasingly clear that Bradley Cole's mother would prefer he stay single. Or at least not marry *me*. It was more about the fact that I'd been married before (twice) and that I was from Alabama than anything else. She also had a lot to insinuate about the fact that I didn't know my way around a kitchen, but did know my way around firearms.

I hit the road. My parents, my grandmother, my sister, and my niece were in a burning building. I could worry about my future mother-in-law later.

Beach Boulevard was five lanes of a First Responder Parade. I snuck into traffic on a squeal and several angry honks, then hitched my Volkswagen to a white Crown Victoria, light bar flashing and siren blaring, with MEMA, Mississippi Emergency Management Association, on the driver door inside a black and gold shield. I trailed him to the expanded Bellissimo parking lot, three blocks from the edge of the property and growing. He jumped a curb, parking his front two wheels on the beach. I jumped the curb and parked all the wheels of my black doodlebug in the sand. I grabbed a jacket, hat, and sunglasses, because for the most part, I work in cloak and dagger. I unlocked the glove compartment and got my car gun, a single-action .22 Magnum. I tucked it at my hip. Just in case.

The rain had stopped and the wind had died down. I ran to the waterline and got a good look at the building from behind. Smoke billowed, flames shot out into the night, and three helicopters dangled red water buckets over the roof. Ash floated like snow. The fire appeared to be contained to one corner of the thirtieth floor. The top. The penthouse. Where my boss, Richard Sanders, and his wife Bianca Casimiro Sanders, live.

I ran.

Our team of four—me, my boss No Hair (who Bradley calls Jeremy), Fantasy and Baylor—had just gotten new Bose Bluetooth earpieces. I gave mine a tap.

"Where is everyone?"

"I'm in the lobby." It sounded like Fantasy was in the Superdome. "Baylor's with me, but don't even try to come in the front door because you'll be crushed. The last two floors are being evacuated, and these people are in a hurry."

"Have you seen my parents?" I plowed through sleeping flowerbeds. "Granny? Meredith? Riley?" I'd booked my parents at one end of a suite, my grandmother at the other end, my sister and my niece in an adjoining guest room.

"No, Davis," she said, "but I wouldn't be able to pick my own mother out of this crowd."

"What about Mr. Sanders and Bianca?" I jogged around the south side of the parking garage on the Gulf side. "Did they get out?" It looked like the ocean was on fire with the elongated reflection of the blaze echoing across the water.

"Your family's fine, Davis." No Hair's big voice boomed in my ear. "They're across the street. Everyone find a stairwell and get upstairs."

Upstairs was on fire.

*　*　*

My name is Davis Way. I just turned thirty-three. I'm not all that tall, but when I wear serious heels I can get on eye-level most of the time. I have remarkable hair, in that people make remarks about it all the time. "I love your hair. It's the same color as the brick on my patio." "Did you know that in the olden days, they used to think redheads were witches and chopped off their heads?" "You must be a raging alcoholic with that red hair."

It isn't all that red. But it's closer to red than any other hair color.

I was a police officer for six years in my hometown of Pine Apple, Alabama. After two divorces (from the same man) and more than a year of extreme unemployment (after my own father fired me), I traded Pine Apple for Biloxi and took a job with the Bellissimo.

My three-year employment anniversary is within shouting distance, and in that time, I'd covered most of the nooks and crannies of the three-point-two-million square feet of resort. I know the four sets of common stairwells, all very busy at the moment, and I know one set of uncommon stairs. It's a single-file service stairway, located behind Rocks, the jewelry store in the main lobby. I took off in that direction, which meant swimming upstream through the thick crowd of hotel guests in their pajamas desperately trying to go the other way. A disturbing percentage of the guests had apparently been sleeping in Bellissimo bath towels. I saw a very large man who'd been sleeping in two very small hand towels. Embarrassing. And not just for him.

I'd made it all of ten feet when I heard the honk. Of a car horn. In the middle of a packed-out hotel lobby stampede. It was coming from the casino. Why would someone be driving a car out of the casino and through this crowd? I tapped my earpiece on. "Anyone near the casino?"

"We're halfway up the steps," Baylor panted.

Another long honk followed by two short beep honks.

For three weeks, marketing has had an E-63 AMG four-door gold Mercedes parked in the middle of the casino floor promoting our next over-the-top event: a week long gambling gala called the Strike It Rich Sweepstakes. Please tell me one of the Strike marketing people wasn't trying to get the gold car out of the building through the hotel lobby in the middle of an evacuation.

Honk, honk, honk. Scream, scream, scream.

I wouldn't put anything past the Strike people. They'd been crawling all over this place for weeks, including two behavior analysts and a certified aromatherapist, who believed gamblers emptying their wallets and maxing out their credit cards isn't enough. In addition to going flat broke and living out of a grocery store buggy, our patrons needed a good brainwashing too.

I climbed halfway up a lamppost at the door of Rocks so I could see above the crowd. The lamppost was part of the lobby's indoor street-scene décor. I flipped the hat I was wearing around so the bill wasn't in my way, then looked over the rims of my sunglasses. I hung off the lamppost by the crook of my left arm and got a good look at the driver. Not a Strike therapist. Someone's going to get run over. I should do something.

Four hundred people screamed, "Gun! That woman has a gun!" which gave me some shooting room. Worth noting: When you want people to move faster during an evacuation, wave a gun around.

A headless person sat behind the wheel of the Mercedes. There was nothing above the buttoned collar of a plaid shirt but a tuft of light hair. I made sure I was clear, then took out both tires on the driver side. Now the car was lopsided, and I'd singlehandedly finished evacuating the hotel guests.

I dropped to the floor, smoking gun trained on the car.

"Let's go." I tapped the nose of my gun on the driver window. Fifteen seconds later, I tapped again. "Turn off the engine and get out."

I was hoping, since this guy was driving a car and I was popping off rounds inside an already-panicked public venue, a few Bellissimo Security suits would have shown up by now, but there wasn't a suit in sight. Those big chickens had probably trampled small children and blind kittens to get out the door when they heard the gunshots.

"Fingers laced, hands on your head, buddy. I'm coming in." I yanked open the driver door and was hit with a wave of New Car. The man had torn eye holes out of the fabric of his shirt. Baby blues. "Come on." I waved my gun. His feet came first. New Balance cross-trainers. Then his legs. Jeans. He rose to his full height, a head more than mine, his shirt still over his face. I gave it a jerk and a few buttons flew. I kept my gun on him. He wasn't a man at all. "Are you old enough to drive?" He didn't answer. "Do you even shave?" I flipped him around, slammed the top half of him over the hood of the car and held him down with my elbow in the middle of his back. I had nothing, absolutely nothing, to cuff him with. "What are you thinking, hotwiring a car in the middle of an evacuation?"

His voice was muffled because I had his face planted into the hood of the car. "Dude. I was trying to help."

"Help what? Yourself to a new car? You're not even old enough to be in the casino." I dug my elbow in on *casino*.

By now the lobby was a ghost town, enough so I could hear the drone of a recording over the loudspeaker. It had probably been running on a loop the entire time, but I hadn't heard it over the crowd. *"For the safety of our guests and staff, please exit the building immediately in an orderly fashion."* Whoop whoop, fire-drill music. *"For the safety of our guests and staff..."* Whoop.

"And I didn't hotwire it," he muffled. "It's keyless ignition."

Finally, a line of Biloxi's finest thumped around a corner in a hurry. "Hey!" I shouted. "A little help?"

An officer stopped. He bent, palms-to-knees, and tried to catch his breath and take in the scene. The four officers he'd been with kept going. "What's going on here?"

"Can I have your cuffs?" I asked.

"Can you identify yourself?" The Walkieclip on his shoulder snapped, crackled, and popped with emergency code signals I remembered from my years in blue. Actually, I remembered them from my training. We'd never used codes in Pine Apple, a town of four hundred, except Code Romeo, which meant the town's only bull, Romeo, had hopped his fence and was in someone's corn field.

Or living room. Tonight I heard Code Red (fire) and Code Green (internal emergency). The officer, still out of breath, squelched it.

"Disease Control." I twisted so he could see the big ominous letters on the back of my windbreaker, part of my no-questions-asked disguise, which Fantasy and I had used more than once when we wanted a good booth at Panera. "This kid has bola-bola."

"Never heard of it."

"Do you want to hear about it right now?"

The kid fake coughed.

The officer threw me a Tuff-Tie, then ran.

I zipped the boy's wrists together behind his back. "Stand up." The lady on the speaker was still going with her requests. I tapped my earpiece with a request of my own. "What's going on?"

"Where are you?" Fantasy asked.

"I'm still in the lobby. Long story. Where are you?"

"We just made it to the penthouse. The fire's out," Fantasy said, "and we're going in. Get up here."

"Do we know if the Sanders are in there?"

"No."

"Are any of the elevators working?"

"The building's on generator power, Davis. So, no."

Thirty flights of stairs. With a car thief.

"Come on, Davis. We're waiting on you."

"Go on in," I said, "don't wait."

"If they're here, they're in the panic room. We can't go in without your index finger and your half of the code."

"I don't know the code." I looked at my index finger, something I did know.

"Yes, Davis. You do."

The panic room. It's on the other side of the closet of Thomas Sanders's suite of rooms. Thomas, the only child of Richard and Bianca Sanders, is a boarding student at an ivy-covered-walls school in the northeast, and I'd forgotten all about the room built to keep him safe from his mother and/or kidnappers. I'd forgotten the room, and I'd certainly forgotten the code. Richard and Bianca

Sanders had the whole code, but it was to get *in* the room. Not out. There was no getting out once you were in, a safety feature, so their young son couldn't be bribed out with ice cream. Once in the safe room, you had to be rescued. No Hair had the first four numbers and I had the last four. I'd meant to have it tattooed somewhere discreet when I'd been entrusted with it two years ago, but the son didn't live here, and the subject hadn't come up once.

"I'm thirsty." My prisoner was shuffling his feet.

I gave him a little poke with my gun. "Be still, you little punk."

"What?" (Fantasy.)

"We're in big trouble, Fantasy."

"I agree."

"No. I mean the code," I said. "I don't remember it."

"You have thirty flights of steps to remember it, Davis. Get up here."

"Get me a beer and I'll get you in, lady."

"You shut up. And sit down." I used my gun as a pointer. "You're sick."

"Who are you talking to?" Fantasy asked.

The lobby was eerily quiet except for the lady on the loudspeaker asking us to leave. Whoop whoop.

"A baby car thief who tried to drive the Mercedes off the casino floor," I said. "I've got him with me."

"A baby was driving a car? In the casino?"

I looked at my prisoner. "He's tall for his age."

"Get rid of him," Fantasy said, "and get up here with your finger and that code."

I'm pretty sure I entered the code backwards under the notes app of my phone. Fourteen phones ago.

"I can get you in," the tall baby said.

"I thought I told you to be quiet."

"Look, lady," he said, "I started a car without a key, right?"

That was true.

"I'll get you in."

* * *

I've never been on a stair machine and I'll never get on one. By the tenth-floor landing, my legs were on fire and I was panting like a dog. By the twelfth floor, I had to sit down.

"You should work out," the boy, who had yet to break a sweat, said.

"You should shut up." I didn't have enough air in my lungs to waste any arguing with him.

I made him give me a piggy-back ride for the last eighteen flights of stairs, which was quite the trick since his hands were cuffed and I had no way to uncuff them other than shoot through the plastic.

I was all for it, but using the one ounce of brain he had in his head, he voted it down. He had the nerve to begin negotiations with me, the clock ticking away upstairs, my family, including my eighty-three-year-old grandmother, across the street shivering in a dark parking lot.

"Give me your hat."

"I am not giving you my hat, you little brat."

"And your sunglasses."

They weren't my sunglasses. They were Bradley's. I'd grabbed them out of my car, part of my hurry-up disguise. A part I had no intention of giving this kid. He already had my jacket. I'd shed the dark blue windbreaker somewhere between the fourth and fifth floors, and he'd refused to take another step until I tied it around his waist.

"You're a little kleptomaniac, kid. You want other people's stuff. Don't you have stuff of your own?"

"Dude. It's a good disguise."

"Which is why *I'm* wearing it."

"Who are you hiding from, lady?"

"None of your business."

I work undercover for the Bellissimo, and I look too much like the boss's wife, so for the most part, I hide from everyone. And this brat didn't need the details.

"I'm not carrying you up the stairs if you don't give me your hat."

Had he been any kind of decent criminal, he would have disarmed me, shot me, and left me for dead. As it was, he only wanted my hat. My hair tumbled out of it.

"Nice." His blond head tilted on a leer.

"I'm old enough to be your mother, you pervy little freak."

"Put it on my head."

"I've had about enough of you, young man."

He took eighteen flights of steps, with a hundred pounds of me hanging around his neck, my legs hooked through his cuffed arms, like he was skipping through a field of daisies. When we finally reached the emergency door that would get us through to the thirtieth floor receiving area, he used the backside of me to push against the metal bar, almost knocking my head off, then he tipped back, dumping me on the floor.

"What the hell?" No Hair, my extra-large boss, Fantasy, my partner, and Baylor, the latest addition to our team, all stared at me and the carjacker.

I scrambled to my feet and gave the juvenile offender a shove. "This little punk hotwired the Mercedes in the casino and was trying to drive it out the front door."

The juvenile carjacker grinned at everyone from underneath my CDC hat and from behind Bradley's RayBans.

No Hair growled, grabbed him by the meat of his arm, and pushed him through the security door into the Sanders residence.

What. A. Mess.

There were a dozen firemen, each wearing fifty pounds of gear. There was no fire and the smoke had cleared, but there was a sharp sting of hot electricity in the air, like a hundred toasters had fried, a smell I knew, having been toaster challenged all my life.

Everything was dripping, trampled, not one stick of furniture was where it should have been, and a movie-screen-sized oil portrait of Bianca Sanders and her beloved pooches hung diagonally on the wall by one thread.

I took a second to check my phone, now that I wasn't singularly in charge of an underage joyrider. Bradley Cole had my family and was taking them back to our place.

Your grandmother is wearing a lace top and very shiny short shorts.

(OMG.)

"You're clear," a suited fireman holding his helmet under his arm said to No Hair. "Good luck."

"How do we know they're in here?" I asked.

"Because they're not anywhere else," he said. "It looks like they jumped out of the bed in a hurry. I found their phones on the nightstands." He patted the breast pocket of his jacket, partially obscuring my view of the scissors, dozens of pairs of them in various stages of cutting, on his tie. No Hair only wore a tie once, and at his age (washed up), he'd gone through every normal tie ever made, so he wore increasingly strange neckties.

The hardwood floors were sludgy with what felt like mud. The rain from the ceiling sprinklers had married the dirt from the fire boots, at which point I realized I probably wouldn't be getting married this weekend. This was a mess of gigantic proportions, and it wouldn't be cleaned up before Saturday at seven.

We all stepped into the son's closet. It was the size of my first apartment. My whole first apartment. No Hair and Baylor ripped a tall stack of shelves away from the wall, because there was no electricity to operate the slidey.

The steel door held a keypad and a touchscreen. No Hair pressed a meaty finger pad against the screen and it flew through several fingerprints before it locked on his. He pushed four buttons on the keypad. Beep, beep. He stepped back and waved me forward.

I stayed put.

"Oh, for Pete's sake, Davis." A beam of flashlight was trained on the crown of No Hair's bald head. "You don't remember your half?"

I pushed the juvenile delinquent to the door. "Do it."

The little thief hacked the fingerprint touchscreen in two seconds and the code keypad in three—I was beyond impressed—then pulled open the six-inch-thick steel fire door.

Battery powered can lights illuminated the stunned faces of Richard and Bianca Sanders. Our invasion was also noted by her killer Yorkshire terriers, Gianna and Ghita, by way of piercing, reverberating, diabolical song. Such little dogs, so many teeth. They raced our way. I climbed up Baylor's leg (those dogs hate me), but they flew right past me without their regular attempt at a pound of my flesh and instead, set their sights on the baby carjacker. Who they seemed to like.

Mr. Sanders's head snapped back. "Thomas?"

Mrs. Sanders's snapped up. "Thomas?"

My head just snapped. "*Thomas?*"

The baby carjacker scooped up the dogs. He said, "Hey Mom, Dad."

TWO

The safe room was, as Thomas Sanders announced, "Amazeballs." His and his father's heads grazed the ceiling. No Hair, the size of three men, didn't even try to get one of his big feet in the door.

Thomas studied a built-out Lego space city taking up two feet of shelf that had, at some point, been locked up in here, along with a sofa, emergency supplies, a satellite phone (dead), and more boy treasures. "I haven't been in here since I was a kid."

When was that? Last week? By my count, he was fifteen.

"David, give me your clothes." Bianca breezed past me. "Mine smell."

"It's Davis." She asked for the clothes off my back because we're the same size. We're almost the same everything, and that would make me Bianca's celebrity lookalike, which is how I got this job in the first place. We're all but twins, with a few exceptions: She's blonde with chilly green eyes. My hair is caramel red and my eyes are one shade darker on the caramel side. I wear colored contact lenses and spray my hair Honey Kiss Gold when I take care of business—corporate, philanthropic, monkey—for her. Sometimes it's fun. This year, so far, I've been queen of my own Mardi Gras parade float, sat beside Cindy Crawford at a Save the Dolphins brunch, and ridden on Air Force Two from Gulfport to Jackson. Often, it isn't fun. Bianca insists I be famished and dehydrated, wear bras named Bombshell and Balconette, and looking like her had landed me behind bars. Which was, like, two lifetimes ago. Not that I'd forgiven or forgotten.

I gave her my clothes.

"Where do you shop, David? At a shelter for the homeless?"

I was forced to wear what she'd worn into the safe room, a salmon-colored silk robe that hit four inches above my knees. That was it. A robe. And it smelled fine. Her car-thief son dug deep, found an ounce of humanity, and gave me back the CDC jacket. Now I was wearing a disease windbreaker over an orange silk nightie with Nike Airs.

*   *   *

Fire barriers between the floors had kept the fire from spreading. The sum total of the storm's physical damage was limited to a large corner of the Sanders's residence. The sum total of lost revenue from the hotel and casino being evacuated was through the singed roof.

By eight o'clock that morning, the sun promising a glorious after-storm day, power was restored throughout the building, and the towel-clad guests were ushered back in. Local, cable, and even national news outlets recorded their reentry. The casino wouldn't reopen until the Gaming Commission said so. The front desk was closed to arriving guests, but was very busy with guests checking out.

"This is ridiculous," a lady said. "My only vacation this year. And you people treat me like this?"

"We're very sorry for the inconvenience, ma'am."

This went on until vouchers were issued for future three-night stays, free slot-machine credits, buffets, and spa gift certificates.

Complimentary pastry and coffee kiosks were set up like soup lines all over the lobby. Ambulance-chasing attorneys wove in and out of the crowd passing out business cards. The Mercedes Thomas Sanders confiscated and I shot the wheels off of had disappeared. At the casino entrance, a hundred hotel guests were pressed against the red ropes separating them from their blackjack tables and slot machines, chanting, "Let us in! Let us in!" Suits, hardhats, and badges tried to control the chaos. The whole place smelled like bacon because Plethora, the buffet adjacent to the casino, was trying to minimize the losses by cooking everything immediately.

We convened in Mr. Sanders's office—me, No Hair, Fantasy, and Mr. Sanders. Baylor had been placed on Thomas Sanders patrol.

"Okay," Mr. Sanders, not dressed for success, was behind his desk. "What happened?"

No Hair had a cheat sheet from the hard-hat people. "We have one lightning rod for every ten feet of perimeter. They catch lightning strikes and send the charge down to a rod buried twelve feet in the ground, safely bypassing the building." He flipped his cheat sheet over. "A cable conductor for one of the rods on the roof was cut, probably by a construction worker, allowing a strike to hit the building," he folded the paper, "directly above your head, Richard."

Well, that's terrifying. Even more terrifying, Thomas Sanders would tell his parents I tried to shoot him. I wondered where I'd work after I was fired. Maybe I'd just be demoted. Maybe they'd let me run a cash register in one of the gift shops.

"We have no construction on the roof," Mr. Sanders said.

No Hair cleared his big throat and shuffled his big feet.

Fantasy and I whistled and admired different lofty corners of Mr. Sanders's office.

Mr. Sanders threw down the pen he was holding. "Just tell me."

No Hair ripped off the Band-Aid. "Bianca's having a small pool installed on the southwest corner of the roof."

"No, she's not."

"I'm afraid she is."

Mr. Sanders held up both hands. *Why?*

"For the dogs." No Hair said it to the floor.

Every drop of blood drained from Mr. Sanders's face. "Did you know about this, Jeremy?"

"Not until fifteen minutes ago."

"Did either of you?"

Fantasy and I pointed at each other. "She did."

Mr. Sanders turned to me for an explanation. I'd been at the Bellissimo longer, and was the mouthpiece. Mouthpiece, scapegoat, butt of everyone's jokes.

"I only know about it because Mrs. Sanders asked me to go over a few things with the construction workers." Twice a day for two weeks now, I've had to dress up as Bianca, trek up there, and threaten the crew with their very lives if they didn't get every single mosaic and topiary detail right.

Three days ago she suggested I shoot the air conditioner man. ("You have a gun, right, David? Use it.") He had the nerve to suggest she couldn't "condition" the air without enclosing it. She had me suggest he find a way or die right then and there.

Mr. Sanders closed his eyes and took a deep breath. "I suppose you all knew my son was going to drop in for an unscheduled visit, too?"

We all shook our heads no. We did not.

"My son shows up with no warning and my wife's having a kiddie pool built for her dogs." He looked up. "And those are the least of my problems. Who shot a gun in the lobby during the evacuation? Do any of you know anything about that?"

"What?" (No Hair.)

"What?" (Fantasy.)

"*What*?" (Me.)

"Several hundred guests are claiming shots were fired in the lobby."

"That can't be true," No Hair said. "What kind of idiot would shoot a gun during an evacuation?"

At moments like these, I like to smooth my eyebrows.

"Can someone look into it?"

Smooth, smooth.

"You look into it, Davis."

Smooth, smooth, smooth.

"But first," Mr. Sanders pushed back from his desk, "Davis, you and Fantasy get upstairs with Bianca, settle her down and see what she needs."

Settling Bianca down would take a baseball bat. And what she needed were stronger meds.

"I have Newman waiting," he said, "so you two get going." He gave a nod to door number two, the door he wanted Fantasy and me to exit, so Newman could come in door number one. And not see us. Because we're secret spies.

Newman is Levi Newman, Casino Manager. He's a new fixture at the Bellissimo, but certainly not new to casino gambling. He's a Las Vegas transplant from the Montecito, where he'd been the casino manager for fourteen years. He moved here to be our casino manager, and brought his wild wild west ideas with him, including a huge event just days away, the Strike It Rich Sweepstakes. From what I could see, he worked twenty-five-hour days and didn't have a life, spouse, pet, or concern past the Bellissimo property lines.

"Davis."

"Yes, sir?"

"Put some clothes on?"

*   *   *

Three months ago, Mr. Sanders's private jet, a Gulfstream 650, left Biloxi without passengers. First stop, Cape Town, South Africa, to pick up Dr. Fenyang Itumeleng, the world's top authority in facial fillers and lipostructure. Next stop, Buenos Aires, Argentina, to retrieve Dr. Adolfina Aguirre, renowned developer of the TAME (tool-assisted malor elevation) procedure. Last stop, Beverly Hills, California, where the party of pilots and doctors had Asian Fusion catered by Urasawa while they waited on the tarmac for Dr. Tootles Turney, inventor of the Tootles Lift, rejuvenation without downtime. Dr. Turney said she was late because she'd been tied up with Mel Gibson.

After a week of consultation, it was determined that Bianca Sanders could dodge a facelift for at least five years if she'd give up cigarettes. She wasn't the least bit concerned with her heart or lung function, never used the C word, and she couldn't care less about anyone breathing her secondhand smoke. But once convinced she'd see a dramatic improvement in her skin tone and elasticity, plus avoid going under the knife for several more years, she quit. Cold turkey. And took it out on all of us.

"Let me assure you, David," Bianca had both me and Fantasy held captive, "the remodel of my living quarters will go quickly and smoothly. And I expect the two of you to see to it."

"It's Davis," I mumbled.

She rattled off instructions: secure her jewelry, restock her collections—wardrobe, Rembrandts, cosmetics—and replace her half-million dollar solid rock crystal bathtub by her regularly scheduled bath time. Five o'clock.

Fantasy was taking notes. "Who do we call about the bathtub, Mrs. Sanders?"

She blinked twice. "It's from the rainforest. Ecuador, I believe."

The Bellissimo Resort and Casino, a world-class five-star destination, is a big place. With more than seventeen hundred guest rooms, two hundred of those swanky suites, fifty of those extra-luxurious two-bedroom swanky suites, and two of those were ultra, über, over-the-top luxurious four-bedroom swanky suites, only occupied by Jay Leno and such. Which is where we were. The Sanders would be slumming it here. Here already had two swimming pools. One inside, one out. She could take her five o'clock bath in one of those. Maybe they should move here, give one of the pools to the dogs, and be done with it.

Bianca finished giving us our marching orders, which was more of an extensive shopping list than anything else, so we made a run for it. Her parting words: "David. Get dressed. You look ridiculous."

Fantasy and I shared a weary look in the elevator.

"Think you're going to be able to pull it off?"

"I doubt it."

"It really only takes three minutes to get married, Davis."

I rested my head on the mirrored wall of the elevator and

closed my eyes. "My half-plan is to see when they reschedule the Strike it Rich thing and go from there."

Fantasy and I were supposed to have attended an all-day training session today for our next assignment, the Strike it Rich shindig. To keep an eye on things. We were to have spent today orienting ourselves for it. The building catching fire and the hotel being evacuated at three this morning had nixed the orientation, and we were waiting for word on the reschedule. Which would probably interfere with the wedding. And if it didn't, it would most certainly interfere with the honeymoon. And only the orientation would be rescheduled, not the Strike It Rich bash. It was set in solid rock crystal, and nothing stopped the casino train. This building could have burned to the ground this morning and somehow, someway, the Strike it Rich Sweepstakes would still start next weekend.

"Do you think it's a sign, Fantasy?"

"Is what a sign?" We stepped off the elevator.

"Lightning striking the building," I said. "Do you think it's a sign?"

"A sign of what?"

"That Bradley and I shouldn't get married. This weekend."

"Davis. Lightning striking the building is a sign of weather. And nothing more."

*   *   *

It was a Grand Theft Auto XIV showdown.

Fantasy and I entered the bullpen of our 3B offices (B is for Basement) to find Baylor lost in a big bean bag chair and Thomas Sanders deep in another, neither of which we had room for or I'd ever laid eyes on, with Xbox One all over the flat screen. There were two empty pizza boxes and at least eight empty green bottles. At ten in the morning.

"Where did you get an Xbox, Baylor?"

"Target."

Fantasy stepped over them and went straight to control central, through a door on the right, to start knocking off Bianca's chore list. The list started with La Prairie of Switzerland and ended with a partridge in a pear tree. Fantasy would order the restock of all Bianca's cosmetics and skin care necessities by phone, then send a Bellissimo limo and an armed guard to New Orleans to pick it all up. Bianca wanted the exercise completed within a half hour. New Orleans is ninety miles away.

I picked up an empty green bottle and waved it in Baylor's face. He leaned around it and kept poking his game control thing. "Move, Davis."

"Are you drinking beer while you're on the clock, Baylor, or are you letting this one drink beer?" I waved the bottle in Little Sanders's direction.

"It's O'Doul's, Davis. Non-alcoholic. *Move.*"

I moved. To the wall outlet behind the television. The room went quiet.

"Now." I settled in beside Thomas. "Let's talk." I yanked a non-beer bottle out of his hand and passed it to my co-worker. Baylor, regaining a few of his senses, began a clean-up. Clank, clank, clank. I cleared my throat. "Your dad is very busy, Thomas. There's a lot of damage to the building and the casino is *closed.* Do you get what a big deal that is around here?"

He barely shrugged. Not his problem.

"I need to know how you got here and why you're here. Then I need to relay all this information to your dad." I sat back and folded my arms across my chest. "Start talking."

"Dude."

"Thomas." I held up a hand. "I'm not your dude. Call me Davis."

He was a bundle of energy, sitting on the edge of the cushion, his features animated, his eyes bright and busy, and he looked like he might jump across the room grasshopper-style any second. I truly believe the next generation of gamblers, having cut their teeth on Xbox, will take it to another, higher, unheard of, level of casino gaming, because they'll bring their Xbox energy with them.

"So, dude." He caught himself. "My bad. Davis. It's fall break."

"It's your school's fall break? Didn't your parents know?"

He dropped his chin, then whipped his head up and to the right every three seconds as a hair-grooming gesture. "I do not know."

I rolled a hand between us. Keep going.

"I got a ride."

"You got a ride?"

I can't imagine that he can continue whipping his head around like he does without surely, at some point, breaking his own neck.

"A kid in my residence hall? He was coming and I rode with him."

"On what? A tractor? In a car? Delta?"

"Private." Then, in the space of one second, noises came out of Little Sanders perfectly mimicking jet engines starting, a takeoff, a flight hugging the East Coast, hanging a right along the Gulf, then coming in for a smooth landing in Mississippi. All males are born with these noises. In addition, this male was born with a silver shovel in his mouth. He'd probably never even heard of Delta, unless maybe he owned half of it, which was not out of the question. His maternal grandfather, Salvatore Casimiro, owned half of the Las Vegas Strip.

"What's this kid's name, Thomas?"

"Quinn."

"So his father is Mr. Quinn?"

"No. Quinn is the kid at my school."

"What's Quinn's last name?"

"Jennings."

"Were his parents with you?"

"Negative."

"Do you know his parents' names?"

Also negative.

"Do you know where he's from, Thomas?"

"Down here somewhere."

"Biloxi?" Jennings. Didn't ring any loud bells. "Your friend is from Biloxi?"

"Somewhere close," Thomas said. "Georgia. Maybe Kentucky."

I'd get faster and more coherent answers from a computer than this one, which is what I intended to do before I reported back to Mr. Sanders.

"How long will you be here, Thomas?"

"Till, like, school starts again."

I see. "When does school start again?"

"When fall break is over."

Which was as far as I was going to get with Little Sanders.

I stood, walked behind the television, and dangled the cord. "About this morning."

He traced a line from his right temple to his jaw, where I'd slammed his head into the hood of a car.

"Are we good?" The cord danced.

It was impossible to read little Sanders's face. His discerning smile reminded me of his father. The evil glint in his eye reminded me of his mother.

"You don't remember anything about a gun, do you, Thomas?"

I swung the Xbox cord like a pendulum. He followed it with his eyes. "No, Dude."

I plugged in the game.

*　*　*

I wove in and out of emergency vehicles still parked in quickly abandoned ways down half a mile of Beach Boulevard against five lanes of heavy midday traffic, wearing a creamsicle silk robe that barely covered my butt, running shoes, and Bradley Cole's RayBans. Bianca had confiscated every stitch of clothing I keep at work for her own temporary wardrobe. I had to go home to get dressed, but not before I flagged down three large men to help me get my Volkswagen bug out of the sand it was mired in.

On the short drive to get dressed, I thought about what a

missed calendar opportunity today was; it could have been, should have been, Friday the thirteenth, and it wasn't anywhere near over.

I could hear my home from the wrong side of the door. I snuck in and used a tall potted peace lily for cover. From the open foyer inside our condo, it's one huge room. Three granite steps down lead to the living room and three granite steps up, to the dining room, kitchen, and breakfast nook. My sister Meredith was up, banging pots and pans at the sink. My father was sitting at the breakfast table to her left behind a newspaper. The bulk of the noise was coming from down, where my grandmother and my niece, Riley, were singing along with the soundtrack of *The Little Mermaid* on the television, set at a volume guaranteed to make it through the sands of time filling Granny's ears. My mother was also down, at the desk, in one corner of the living room, and Anne Cole, my future mother-in-law, was sitting in a wingback chair in the opposite corner, as far away from my mother as possible. My mother was staring out the window. Anne Cole was staring at a wall. Both mouths were thin, straight lines, both had a foot going ninety-miles an hour, and all four fists were balled. I caught my sister's eye. She twirled a finger around, pointed, then mouthed, "*Go. Leave. Get out of here.*"

My father looked over his glasses and invited me to join him behind the Metro section. I tiptoed. Meredith scooted over and joined us.

"What's going on?" We huddled. "Where's Bradley?"

"He went to work," my father whispered.

"What's wrong?" I asked.

Meredith spit it out quickly. "Bradley's mother says you can't cook and doesn't think you should wear a white wedding dress."

I felt a growl coming on. "I could cook if I wanted to and my dress isn't white." It's not even a wedding dress; it's just a dress. A creamy off-white bordering on pale-yellow dress. "And why is Mother mad at Anne? She told me yesterday I should be ashamed of myself for wearing white."

"She changed her mind," Meredith peeked over the

newspaper, "when Anne said something. Now Mother's on your side like you're the original Vestal Virgin."

My father shifted in his seat.

"What color does Anne want me to wear?" We were whispering the conversation all over Daddy and all Under the Sea, which Granny and Riley had backed up and were enjoying again. At the top of their lungs.

"Blood red?" Meredith shrugged. "Black?"

I stayed behind the newspaper with Daddy, who tapped my nose and assured me everything would be fine, while Meredith snuck off to my bedroom to get me clothes. I dressed in the pantry, tossing Bianca's orange robe down the garbage chute. I gave Daddy's hand a squeeze goodbye, then snuck out.

THREE

It takes great creative minds to keep it exciting at a casino. Never let your patrons get bored. Boredom leads to thoughts of personal fiscal responsibility. Thoughts of personal fiscal responsibility empty a casino faster than a fire. So ramp up the excitement. The exciting Strike it Rich Sweepstakes was less than a week away, and neither Fantasy nor I was very excited, more than anything else, because it had snuck up on us.

In the past six weeks, we'd chased disappearing liquor shipments by posing as bartenders (I told everyone we were out of mixed drinks; it was beer, wine, or nothing, because making a Three Wise Men #2 isn't anywhere nearly as easy as it sounds), we'd played in a week-long Texas hold 'em tournament (flops and turns and rivers, oh my!), and had busted up a counterfeit Gucci ring operating out of Spikes, the ladies shoe store on the mezzanine level, after which we felt obligated to keep a few pieces of remarkably genuine-looking evidence (two whole sets of luggage) for comparison purposes in case they ever tried it again.

Not to mention I'd been planning a wedding.

We'd been too busy to give the upcoming Strike It Rich festivities much thought and now here we were at the gates. Which, as it turned out, we had to crash.

Casino events come and go, and we were so familiar with them at this point—slot, blackjack, keep your hand on the Dodge Ram the longest—our team was seldom needed. For the most part, we let sleeping casino events lie. Marketing cooked up the crazy contests, they landed on Mr. Sanders's desk for approval, he sent it to us, we gave it a hard look, signed off on it, and for the most part, casino parties ran like clockwork.

The Strike It Rich Sweepstakes, however, skipped all those steps. It's been shrouded in secrecy and the closer it got, the less we knew about it. At first it was annoying, like going to the mall. (What is Victoria's big secret? Just tell us.) Then it was irritating, like a new bottle of Advil. (I already have a headache. After thirty minutes of breaking into the bottle, I have a migraine.) It was approaching downright suspicious. (Like sushi.)

Our old casino manager never blinked an eye when a "temporary" employee showed up to lend a hand. Our new casino manager didn't want a hand, and if we offered a hand one more time, I had a feeling he might chop it off.

Three weeks ago Fantasy and I got the bright idea to sneak in and nose around. (No Hair said, "You two sneak in and nose around.") We'd been turned away. Local features reporters weren't welcome in the new casino; they had their own media person, thank you. We waited a week, then waylaid two faux finish painters (sat them down at slot machines, liquored them up, and gave them free play credits), then showed up at the Strike door as their faux finish replacements in cute painter-girl outfits only to be refused again. Our names weren't on the approved entry list. And just last week, when Junior League Fantasy and I, in Lilly Pulitzer and pearls, had tried to get in with silver trays loaded with lemon bars, the door had been slammed in our faces a third time. At which point we were aggravated, irritated, suspicious, and mad.

What were these Strike people hiding?

One thing we did know was who they were hiding behind—our new casino manager, Levi Newman. Levi began his current reign six months ago, the first month a transition of out-with-the-old and in-with-the-new(man), as the former casino manager, Ty Thibodeaux, who'd come with the first brick, the only casino manager the Bellissimo had known since the ribbon cutting in 1996, was retiring.

Naturally, the new casino manager wanted to bring in his own staff of faithfuls who'd also lost their jobs when—don't know the details—someone had gone on strike, and in the end, the Montecito closed its doors. And Richard Sanders, as good as they come, wouldn't dream of displacing his own staff just because it was a new day. Handily clearing the line in the sand, Levi Newman tossed up pie charts, bar graphs, and earnings projections, selling Mr. Sanders on a fall campaign guaranteed to blow the lid off, with one caveat: It would need a separate staff. And designated space for a second casino, a mini casino Newman would be in charge of. "Let me show you what I can do, Richard." He showed Mr. Sanders how he could sneak his people in the back door to implement the Strike it Rich package. Bellissimo staffers would fill the grunt-work gaps when the time came, but until then, the Vegas transplants were in charge. Total strangers had called the gaming, marketing, accounting, and mini casino-floor shots for Strike. And there had been, to date, exactly zero information sharing. We had no idea what was going on behind the Strike doors.

Mr. Sanders said it was simply a matter of the Strike staff not wanting the details of the gaming leaked before the event. I doubted that. I felt certain they were locked up in that mini casino emptying the Bellissimo vault. No Hair landed in the middle. He understood the Strike staff wanting to keep a lid on the big gaming reveal, but as we were turned away again and again, he too wondered if there wasn't something shady going on. The consensus was the Strike Sweepstakes only lasts a week. What all can happen in one little week?

The one little week was a little week away, we were finally getting in, and the better question turned out to be how many times could our phones ding? Clearly the Strike It Rich Sweepstakes was powered by Twitter. Because we were forced to sign up (@WayToGo) and instantly began receiving tweets. Tons and tons of tweets.

We were deep in 3B when our phones tweeped at the same time.

#StrikeItRich quick meet @5 Employee Training B. Orientation reschedule tomorrow @8 Theatre C. No shows ~NO!WAY!~ DM @ElspieBabie #GameOn

It took Fantasy and me ten minutes to decipher it. We had a meeting at five in an employee training room. The orientation that hadn't taken place today because of the lightning strike this morning was rescheduled for tomorrow. If we couldn't make it, although we'd better find a way, send a direct message.

So far, our only glimpse of Strike It Rich had been the social media blitz of it all. It rolled out eight weeks ago via Facebook, Instagram, Twitter, and Vine, which I'd never even heard of. To earn their way into the sweepstakes, hopefuls had generated forty-seven million social media impressions, including more than fifty thousand likes on Instagram, twenty-two million impressions on Twitter, half a million hits on Tumblr, and seventeen thousand new Facebook fans. It was the buzz, and the Baby Boomers were furious. They didn't even get on the line. How were they supposed to qualify?

The Social Media Director, a fourteen-year-old hipster, was driving us crazy. She spoke in hashtags, dusted glitter over her makeup, wore her long dark hair in a bouncing palm-tree ponytail that burst out of the crown of her head, and she didn't eat, she juiced. She carried a big jug of thick, dark green slush around that she regularly slurped from, and it was disgusting. We received notifications from her around the clock, and had suffered through numerous #StrikeItRich promotional videos she kept posting on Vine and YouTube, all ridiculous, and all requiring a giddy response from us (#DoUsASolid! #WeighIn! #Comment! #Like! #Share!) Her Pinterest page was nothing but baby hedgehogs, Miley Cyrus, and #StrikeItRich propaganda, and she constantly electronically requested we go look at it. She gave me a pingy headache right between my eyes.

She's the Social Media director for Strike It Rich and her name is... wait for it... Elspeth Raiffe. Fantasy and I called her Hashtag. Sometimes we called her Hashtag Elspie. When our assignments had come through a few weeks ago—we'd applied for, traipsed around half naked for, and been hired as, Strike It Rich cocktail waitresses—No Hair had overheard us complaining about Hashtag Elspie's giddiness and I got the lecture again.

"Davis." No Hair scowled at me. "We've been over this and over this. Do not call that girl anything except her given name."

"Her given name is stupid."

"Her given name is Elzbath."

"You don't even know her name, No Hair."

I grew up in a town of four hundred, where everybody knows your name. When I'd landed the job at the Bellissimo, I met more people in thirty days than I'd met in the previous thirty years, and keeping up with everyone's names had been impossible. Easier, for me, was to assign nicknames, and No Hair didn't like it a bit. We'd reached an agreement, after I accidentally called a high-roller Mrs. Claus (total accident, he's a really nice man, who looks just like Mrs. Claus) that he would continue to allow me to call him No Hair instead of Jeremy (old habits and such) if I would agree to call everyone else by their real names. He insisted it made communication between us easier if he didn't have to try to figure out who Cleats and Glows in the Dark were.

Whatever.

"Why are we on cocktail duty, No Hair?" Fantasy had asked. "We'll run our legs off."

"Would you rather empty garbage cans?"

Cocktails it is. Although, I didn't do a very good job of pouring myself a cup of coffee and coming out of it without injuries. This cocktail waitress gig would be a challenge. "Do we get to keep our tips?"

"Davis!" And then another lecture. Yes, we were highly compensated already. Yes, people would line up around the block for our jobs. Yes, Richard Sanders would be very disappointed in my attitude.

Yes.

"Should we tweet Elspie back?" Fantasy asked. "Tell her we'll be there?"

Before I could say no, our phones binged again.

#WaitressWorkouts! #BellissimoBarre! M-Th 6-8 RT to everyone! No shows ~NO!WAY!~ DM@ElspieBabie #StrikeItRitch #BringIt!

"Shoot me now," Fantasy said.

It was a little after two in the afternoon. Fantasy and I were enjoying freshly brewed coffee and a few quiet moments in our basement offices. In other words, we were hiding. From @ElspieBabie, Bianca Sanders, and the world at large.

Rumor had it the Gaming Commission would allow the casino to reopen at eight tonight. I sent a car to the Regent to (get my family away from my future mother-in-law) bring my family back to the hotel, and they were half a mile above me in their guest rooms making revised rehearsal-dinner plans and waiting on updated wedding plans, of which, I had none. Baylor and Little Sanders were off playing squash. (Squashing what?) Bianca Sanders was resting comfortably at Jay Leno's place, surrounded by a three-stuffed-limo delivery of replacement luxuries from boutiques all over the French Quarter, and rumor also had it she'd cleared half the racks at Saks Fifth Avenue on Canal.

"What's Bellissimo Barre?" Fantasy asked.

"Isn't it part of the employee fitness thing?"

"I get that," Fantasy said, "but what's barre?"

"I think it's ballet."

"We're taking dance lessons?"

Hell if I know. So far, the Strike It Rich learning curve had been steep, and we were at the bottom scrambling our way up.

"Maybe it has something to do with the waitress uniforms," she said. "Are we in ballet tutus for this gig? Have you looked?"

When the Strike It Rich waitress uniforms we'd suffered through an afternoon of fittings for had arrived—#SCORE! #STRIKEITRICH uniforms IN! Pick up @uniform dist. ASAP! Probs? Need a refit? DM@ElspieBabie!— right in the middle of Dr. Phil, naturally, we sent Baylor to fetch them. They were still in our dressing room.

"Maybe we should look," I said.

"Go ahead. Bring mine, too."

The hanging bags weighed nothing, even though the paperwork attached said each contained three uniforms. How could six uniforms weigh less than six marshmallows? I lobbed the bags over the sofa back and unzipped. "There's nothing here."

Fantasy peered. "There." She pointed at a dangling string.

Gold bikinis. Between the two hanging bags, we had six shiny gold bikinis.

* * *

To: rsanders@bellissimo.com

CC: bsanders@biancacasimirosanders.com

From: dway@bellissimo.com

Mr. Sanders,

Weeks ago, Mrs. Sanders signed off on a community service project for Thomas's fall break. It was an asbestos removal project at a homeless shelter/soup kitchen in Methuen, Massachusetts. The school reports a confusing computer glitch, in which Thomas's name was removed from the roster. They're looking into it. Thomas met up with a boarding student in Hunt Hall, Quinn Jennings, a senior, whose parents were flying him to the Bellissimo for fall break. Thomas made his own arrangements to accompany him. The Jennings, Missy and Redmond, are from Lickskillet, Alabama, checked in on Wednesday afternoon, and this is their first trip to the Bellissimo, although they're former Montecito players, so it's possible that someone formerly with the Montecito knows them. They both qualified for the Strike It Rich Sweepstakes through Google+. I'm in the process of background checks on them, and I'll let you know ASAP. Mr. Jennings is a farmer, and the wife, Missy, runs a ballroom dance studio in Fort Payne, Alabama. Thomas's plans include returning to school on the Jennings' private plane, a Pilatus PC-24 with 214 hours on the engines, spotless record, qualified and dedicated pilots (2), tail numbers 0821MS, next week.

Late Wednesday. Classes resume on Thursday morning. I'm striking out on any news regarding the alleged gunfire in the lobby this morning. Security video is inconclusive. It's probably just a vicious rumor. Let me know if I can be of any further assistance. DW.

Ten minutes later there was a reply.

To: dway@bellissimo.com

From: bsanders@biancacasimirosanders.com

David. Set up dinner with the Jennings for me (you) and express my gratitude, etc. Dress appropriately, no commitments.

Two minutes after that, Mr. Sanders weighed in.

To: dway@bellissimo.com

From: rsanders@bellissimo.com

Davis, let's get all we can on the Jennings. Get back with me as soon as you can. I see you were scheduled for a few days off, and I'm hoping with the complications and aftermath of the storm, you can reschedule. Have Baylor keep an eye on Thomas until I can wrench myself away from my desk. Get word to Thomas to be in our suite at 7 for dinner. Security has taken forty eyewitness reports on gunshots in the lobby this morning. Keep digging. We will be pressing charges. RS.

*   *   *

Fantasy and I hit the door of Training Room B three minutes late, signed in, got individual packets of information, had employee photo badges made, then snuck in and sat in the back row. I'd been on the clock since three that morning, and I was ready to end my work day so I could get with Bradley and tell him that I could possibly marry him tomorrow after my Strike It Rich orientation, if we made it quick, but I wouldn't be honeymooning with him.

"If you'd go ahead and tell Mr. Sanders and No Hair you were going to get married tomorrow, you know they'd help you work it out."

"It would get me out of ballet."

We wanted a quick, quiet, small ceremony, family only, then squeeze in a quick honeymoon before I had to be back for Strike It Rich, and I'd never gotten around to telling Mr. Sanders or No Hair I was taking four days off because I was getting married. There was entirely too much going on for me to bring it up now.

Hashtag Elspie was at the front of the room, clapping her arms above her head, chanting, "Strike! It! Rich! Strike! It! Rich!" and most of the room's occupants were chanting along with her.

Gold Bikini waitresses Fantasy and Davis weren't chanting.

Our disguises were low-energy, on purpose, because we had to look this way every day for two straight weeks and didn't want to endure fourteen extreme makeovers. Fantasy had gone from shoe-polish black pixie to dark brown extensions that hit between her shoulder blades, and from bright blue eyes to hazel. (Think Halle Berry.) I'd sprayed my hair Hot Toffee, which sounded delicious, and would be easy, because it only took one can of temporary color to cover my red. I went Jade Green on the colored contact lenses, which I poked in on the run in the elevator, and might have been a mistake. My new employee ID had a creature-from-outer space glow about it. The lights were going down for a Strike it Rich movie (produced by Hashtag Elspie) when Fantasy said, "Yow, Davis. Your eyes look nuclear." The Jade Green was one of several new colors I'd ordered. Keeping it fresh. "Good grief," she backed away from me, "those contacts are the color of slime."

The movie began with the construction of the little casino. Salsa, the Mexican restaurant, had been moved from the back of the house to the front, renamed (Nachos), and scaled down. A ten-foot tall sheetrock mural of gigantic winning faces had been placed in front of the former Salsa six weeks earlier to hide the transformation from enchiladas to casino-in-a-casino. It was now Strike it Rich. And we were getting the first peek. Set to rap.

One minute in, my phone buzzed with an incoming message. My future husband's face filled the screen and the accompanying text message read *911*. I let Fantasy see it for a millisecond before I ran out of the room. All but screaming.

"Bradley? What? What's wrong?" In the three seconds between receiving the message and getting him on the line, I ran through every horrible scenario imaginable, all involving sirens.

"Davis."

He sounded perfectly and completely defeated.

"Are you okay, Bradley? What's wrong?"

I waved a concerned passerby off and ducked into a restroom. Which turned out to be a men's room.

"You need to sit down. I have some news."

I had three sit-down options. I stood.

"Say something." I could hear him breathing. "Just tell me."

"I stopped by the court clerk's office to pick up our marriage license."

"And?" My brain flew to court-house shootings. Killer bees. Volcanoes.

"It was denied."

I sat down.

"Davis, you're still married to Eddie."

FOUR

Bradley Cole grew up in Texas. His Texas heritage was never more on display than during football season, when his weekend wardrobe either said Hook 'em Horns or Go Cowboys. And Bradley Cole looked like a Texan—broad shouldered, sun-bronzed, sandy-blond. If he wore a Stetson with his lawyer suits, you'd swear he was an oil baron who'd just climbed off his Appaloosa after checking the rigs on the north forty. His real Texas tell was the hot sauce; Bradley doused chocolate cake with Texas Pete hot sauce.

Smart guy that he is, Bradley's final year of law school had him twiddling his thumbs. He was down to two required courses to finish his law degree, so he filled his schedule with bar-exam prep things and electives. He took a Taxation of Financial Derivatives class, which turned out to be a hard look at how the gaming industry wove in and out of the overall body of tax law, and how gaming corporations capitalized on mark-to-market, constructive sale, straddle, wash sale, and short-sale rules to their bottom-line benefits. Included in the course syllabus was a trip to Las Vegas, where he spent four days at the University of Nevada at Las Vegas in the Konami Gaming Lab, just a few miles off the Strip, and four nights at the Grand Palace, where his law professor had arranged a meet-a-casino-mogul reception. The president of the casino, a Dallas Mavericks fan, took the empty seat next to Bradley. One drink turned into two, then four, and when twenty-four-year-old Bradley left Las Vegas, he'd signed up for more school and had a job. Upon completing his law degree, Bradley moved to Las Vegas to get a quickie degree in Gaming Management from UNLV during the day while working the casino trenches at night. After obtaining the additional degree and passing the bar, Bradley joined the Grand's legal team. Two years later, when Grand Palace Biloxi opened its doors, Bradley Cole, lead attorney, was one of the ribbon cutters.

None of this sat too well with his mother, who'd wanted him to move back to Texas, hang his shingle a block from the house he'd grown up in, practice family law, marry a nice Texas girl, give her grandbabies, and so forth and so on. How she managed to blame me for this dream not coming true was a puzzle. I didn't have a thing to do with it, because Bradley and I met three years ago. And in those three years, my ex-ex-husband has caused us immeasurable grief. He just wouldn't go away. And I'm still married to him? How? Why?

We couldn't talk at home because his mother was there. Bradley had no desire to leave the casino where he worked to meet me at the casino where I worked, nor did I, so we split the difference and met in the middle.

He was waiting for me in the Lucky Lady bar at the Belle of Biloxi Casino, built out like a riverboat, with a Scotch neat and a water back, at a small round table in a dark corner. He looked up, and stunned, when I walked in the door. A Keno runner girl almost knocked me down with her tray of tickets and mini pencils as I made my way to him. "No, thanks. I don't understand Keno." (True.) My purse thumped to the floor; I fell into a chair. I held out my hand, he passed me the envelope.

It was arbitrarily rubber stamped near the middle, with the word DENIED. Beneath it, the second item on the list had a check mark in the box to the left. PRIOR EXISTING MARRIAGE. It didn't say which one of us had a PRIOR EXISTING MARRIAGE, but Bradley had never been married, so I was it.

To issue a marriage license, Mississippi doesn't ask for proof of prior marriage dissolution, unless it'd been less than six months. I was only asked to list the month, year, county and state of all divorces on record. (So embarrassing, to have been married twice already at the ripe, old age of thirty-three. The first one had been annulled when I was sixteen. So I didn't count it, but everyone else in Wilcox County, Alabama did. ("She's been married *twice* already. It's shameful.") At issue, apparently, was my second divorce. From the same man. Eddie Crawford the Snake Rat Pig and many other Chinese Zodiac offerings.

I blinked back tears.

Bradley ordered another for himself and a glass of wine for me.

Five more minutes passed, with me, several times, sucking in air to speak only to chicken out.

"It could," Bradley broke the horrific silence, "be a simple paperwork error." He looked in his empty glass for answers. "You know you went to court." I nodded along. "You paid your attorney. You received a judgment." I remembered every precarious step. "It could simply be a matter of the court not filing the paperwork."

I was a snapping turtle. No words would come out.

The Keno runner bounced to the table in her short skirt and big grin. Finally, I found my voice. "No!" I barked. "Go *away!*"

"Davis." He pulled me in. "It's not her fault."

An hour later, we sat at a long table overlooking the bay at Mary Mahoney's Old French House Restaurant. Everyone had a glass of red wine except Bradley, who was still on the Scotch, and my niece Riley, who was on Cherry Coke. My mother kept lobbing ice cubes into Granny's glass of wine. Granny got a little goofy when she drank too much. Or at all.

"We're all here, good grief, I think you two should go ahead." My sister Meredith reached for the bread basket. "Let's all get up first thing in the morning, go to the courthouse, get you two married, then you can go to work, Davis. Be done with it, already."

"There's no need to rush." Anne Cole, after four days of being wound tighter than a tick, was relaxed, chipper, and even trying to make small talk with my mother. "I think they should wait," she said. ("Forever," she didn't say.)

Bradley shared our news while I studied the stitching of the napkin in my lap. "We've decided, with the unexpected events at the Bellissimo this morning, since Davis can't take even a day off, to wait."

His mother hooked a possessive arm through his. "It's for the best." She wore the only smile at the table.

My father, from the other end of the table, eyed us both. Back and forth.

* * *

"We're the future of gaming." Levi Newman welcomed us to the rescheduled Strike orientation in Theatre C wearing a dark suit, red silk shirt, shiny shoes, and a headset microphone. A spotlight followed him. It felt like a Get Rich Quick motivational seminar. A flashing screen display behind him said, *futureGaming*, in monster-sized letters.

"We're a casino within a casino, completely self-contained, and the gaming industry hasn't even thought of, much less seen, what we're about to unleash." He crossed the stage in the small amphitheater auditorium. "The software for the gaming has been six months in development, and it's guaranteed to blow you away."

Hashtag Elspie hopped up and led the crowd in a cheer, clapping her arms above her head. "Blow! You! Away! Blow! You! Away!"

"The goal is to keep the Strike players in the Strike casino for the twelve hours we're open, each and every one of the seven days." Mr. Newman was a big man, with a mop of chestnut hair and very sun-damaged skin. He wore a thick gold chain around his neck and a square gold pinkie ring on his right hand. "And we believe we can do it, by offering unparalleled gaming, amenities never before even heard of, and if that doesn't work, we'll lock the doors and not let them leave."

("Lock! The! Doors! Lock! The! Doors!")

"We want the players addicted to Strike, and returning again and again for the thrill. Even after the players are eliminated from the competition, we want them glued in their gaming chairs." He waited until you could've heard a feather floating to whisper his next words into the microphone bud: "On. Their. Own. Dime."

("Their! Own! Dime! Their! Own! Dime!")

Fantasy and I sat on opposite sides of the room and texted each other.

WTH?

We think it's just a paperwork problem. Don't breathe a word of this to anyone.

You didn't tell your dad or Mer?

NOOOOOO!

You should tell NH.

No Hair didn't even know we were getting married. Why would I tell him this? No!

"Let's say a Strike guest needs a spa appointment rescheduled, the bottled water in their guest room switched to another brand, or maybe   a   little..."   Levi   Newman   paused   for   effect, "...companionship."

Did he really just say that?

OMG, he's so slimy.

"You'll direct all these inquiries to our Strike Concierge, Bret Renfroe. Stand up, Bret."

Bret stood and took a bow.

Does Eddie know?

NOOOOOOOOOOOOO!!!!!!

You're going to have to tell him.

I realize that, Fantasy.

Levi Newman wandered up and down the main aisle speaking into a headset microphone. "Credit lines for all qualifying players have already been established with a twenty-percent cushion. Which means," Levi Newman said, "if a Strike player asks you for an increase on their credit line, you direct the player to this young lady. Stand up, Rachel. Ladies and gentlemen, Rachel Logan, Strike Casino Credit Manager."

How's Bradley taking the news?

Not great. He thinks we'll have problems with E the Ass.

"All banking will be handled within Strike. Advances, transfers, wires, deposits, ATM transactions, and markers happen right then and right there. Let me introduce you to our Strike Cage Manager, Cassidy Williams. Cassidy?"

Like what?

Like him not cooperating.

"And your name?"

OMG.

"Your name, young lady?"

Or demanding some ridiculous amount of $$$. I haven't had time to put a plan—" my phone flew out of my hand. Levi Newman waved my phone in the air. His rear end in my face, he spoke to the assembly. "Does it not go without saying you all need to silence your phones?"

There were beeps.

Just then my phone pinged with an incoming text. Levi Newman read it to the class. *"The only way to fix this is to kill him."*

There were gasps.

Levi Newman dropped my phone into my lap, then pushed the microphone bud of his headset to his lips with a finger. "You. Are. Fired."

("You! Are! Fired! You! Are! Fired!")

*   *   *

My grandmother had buried two husbands and was divorcing a third. There weren't many man problems she hadn't dealt with in her eighty-three years. Already in disguise, and suddenly semi-unemployed (No Hair was going to have a fit), I hit the casino, where I thought I might find Granny. I needed to lay a little groundwork on my way to Pine Apple to kill the attorney who'd mishandled my divorce.

I tracked her down at the most irritating slot machine in the building. Kitty Galore. She liked it, she said, because she could hear it. Which meant the volume on the machine was cranked to Ear Splitting. She played the one-cent denomination, and kept her little bird hand going on the spin button full speed. The screen would hold up to fifteen screeching cats, and Granny hit the play button so quickly, switching hands when the one grew weary, it was nothing but a huge cat fight on a loop that could be heard next door. The trick to the game was to line up the same breed, which made the cats purr, and rarely happened. When they didn't line up, they wailed, which was happening non-stop. The bonus round was called Caterwaul. And it meant it.

"Granny, let's play something else," I said. "It doesn't look like you're winning on Kitty Litter."

"Are you kidding me, Davie? I have twenty-seven dollars in this thing." She gave the screen a whack. "I'm not leaving until I get my money out of it." The game began meowing from inattention. "What is wrong with your eyes, honey? They're the color of snap peas."

I dug in my bag for sunglasses. I wasn't feeling very eye-contacty anyway.

"I thought you were working all day."

"I took a little break." I got fired. "And thought I'd come visit with you for a minute."

She grabbed me by the chin. "Spill the beans."

"Walk with me, Granny."

She gathered her things: a player card in the Kitty Litter machine attached to a plastic coil rope that was clipped to the collar of one of her sweaters, her pocketbook, which was more luggage than handbag, two extra sweaters, and an array of good luck charms she had scattered around the flat surfaces of the machine: a rabbit's foot on a keychain, a naked purple-haired troll doll, and a 1964 Kennedy silver half-dollar coin. It took her ten minutes to pack. "Where to?"

"Let's go see the new casino in the back."

"Oh, yeah," Granny said. "The Strike thing." She shuffled. "I tried to qualify for that, you know. Didn't even get this close." She spread her arms wide, hit three people, and dropped everything she was holding. "Can you get me in?" Ten minutes later we got going again.

"Tell me why you're getting a divorce, Granny."

We'd covered two feet of casino floor. "Same reason everyone else gets one," she said. "Unreasonable differences." She stopped. "Is this what you want to talk to me about? Divorce?" (Yes.) "Honey, you're not even married." (Debatable.)

Granny used the slot-machine seats along the aisle instead of a cane or walker, and she didn't care if anyone was sitting in them or not. A woman yelled, "Hey!" when Granny got a handful of her long hair. "I'm Price is Right, he's Let's Make a Deal. I'm Polident, he's Fixadent. He's taken up with a mangy dog, and you know I won't live under the same roof with a dog. He lost my good gravy spoon, and he farts." She knocked a guy playing Billionaire Sevens in the back of the head with the corner of her suitcase pocketbook and kept on going. "The worst?" She stopped in front of a bank of very busy Monopoly slot machines and raised her voice to be heard over a Go to Jail bonus round. "HIS GET UP AND GO HAS GOT UP AND WENT." Granny twerked. "IF YOU KNOW WHAT I MEAN." The Monopoly players knew exactly what she meant. The cocktail waitress going the other way who stopped cold with a tray full of drinks knew what she meant. The four people who ran into the cocktail waitress who stopped cold holding a tray full of drinks knew what Granny meant. Every player in a five-foot radius showered with glass, ice, and alcohol from the cocktail waitress's tray knew what she meant.

Granny shuffled a few feet, then turned. "But mostly," she said, "it's that dog. Are you coming?" Leaving destruction and ruin in our wake, we rounded a corner to torture a whole new set of Bellissimo patrons as we made our way to Strike.

"Have you said anything to Cyril about the dog, Granny?"

"Three hundred times."

As a young girl growing up in Pine Apple, Granny had walked

a dusty Alabama path to school, as did the other four or five students, and her fear of dogs was rooted on the two-lane to the schoolhouse. She tells the story about once a week. "I was in primary school. I had my book satchel and my lunch tin. The big dog came out of nowhere." Granny's left arm still bore the scars, and to this day she remained terrified of dogs—all shapes, all sizes, she should meet Bianca's little rats—and everyone in Pine Apple knew it. Cyril surely knew it at some point, but at this point, Cyril didn't know what day of the week it was. Obviously, he'd forgotten that Granny could hardly carry on a conversation about dogs, much less live with one. A dog, much like a prior-existing marriage, was a deal-breaker. I'd give old Cyril a call and remind him, but he had the hearing capacity of a rock, and I'd just been fired, so I didn't feel like screaming into the phone.

"Who's your lawyer, Granny?"

"Smerle."

Good. Smerle T. Webb was the only attorney in Wilcox County, Alabama, and he'd been my attorney of record when I'd (apparently not) divorced Eddie. The second time. He was Granny's attorney, too, so me paying Smerle a friendly visit under the general heading of my grandmother's behalf wouldn't stir it up. Of course, sneezing stirred it up in Pine Apple. ("Where's she been to catch a cold? Out honky-tonkying probably.")

"And how's it going?" I asked. "Divorce can be tricky." And ineffective.

My grandmother came to a stop. "We don't have kids, you know."

I knew this.

"So it's pretty run-of-the-mill divorcery," she said. "Other than him wanting spousal support." She shook her blue curls. "Can you believe it? Cyril wanting me to support him?" She moved an inch. "So I'm countersuing him to support me."

"Does Cyril have any money, Granny?"

"Not a stinkin' dime, honey. It's a strategic move on Smerle's part to pressure Cyril into dropping his suit against me." She caught my eye. "Personally, I think Cyril will drop dead before any of this comes to pass. He's old as the hills you know."

Yes, I know. "I was thinking, Granny," Strike was, mercifully, in sight, one hundred yards ahead, "that since my wedding is postponed and I have a few extra days on my hands, that I might check in with Smerle for you." Her bright eyes found mine. "Just to look over everything. You know. Protect your assets."

"Lookie." Granny pointed. "The little casino. Let's get our assets in there."

"Why don't you wait here, Granny," I led her to a Triple Double Five Times Pay Deluxe Diamond Doozy slot machine, "and let me make sure the coast is clear."

Granny dug in her suitcase and met up with a five-dollar bill. "Okey-doke."

I tiptoed behind the Pardon Our Progress partitions and pushed right through the front doors. So much for security and secrecy.

The smell almost knocked me down. What in the world? It wasn't necessarily a bad smell; the problem was there was so much of it. I yanked my shirt over my nose and mouth to diffuse it, then google-eyed the Strike Casino. It wasn't a casino at all; it was a futuristic nightclub.

Salsa, the restaurant, had been 11,000 square feet, sixty percent of that dining room. The rest had been kitchen, service, and storage. The Strike it Rich mini casino replacing the restaurant looked to have been remodeled much to the same floor plan, at about the same proportions: nightclub in front of me, staff areas behind several doors. The walls were cold, black granite, at least thirty feet high, the furniture black leather, and everything else was gold. Ah. A gold mine. As in strike gold.

The centerpiece of the room was an elevated bar. It was long, oval, and solid black granite. Above it, one of the most breathtakingly beautiful sights I've ever seen: a blown-glass chandelier suspended from the ceiling, at least fifty feet long and ten feet wide, made up entirely of individual gold glass icicles. It was absolutely celestial. Thousands of illuminated gold spikes in varying circumferences and lengths each pointed to one of the three hundred and sixty degrees possible. They had pinpoint stiletto tips. There's no doubt, if you could reach it, you'd prick your fingertips on the needle tips.

I bet you could perform micro-surgery with one of those things. I wondered how in the world they'd installed it. It was gorgeous, and there was absolutely no telling what it had cost. I would be scared to death to sit under that thing.

The bar seating, forty or so black leather stools, were just outside of the perimeter of the chandelier (still too close for comfort), but the bartenders would be working directly under the golden spikes, and far enough below it that should one of the golden stalactites break free, it would have a good running start before it split you in two. I'd be demanding hazardous duty pay.

It twinkled.

When I finally tore my eyes away from it, I counted two small cafés, bistro tables and settees on opposite ends of the room, a banking center, his-and-hers lounges, and two sunken conversation pits on either side of the bar, black leather loungers around circular black granite tables.

The actual gaming floor was fifty empty spaces. *future*Gaming was so secret, its installation was still days away. The whole place was other-worldly, as quiet as a library, and empty. It was a perfect time to sneak a peek, because everyone who had anything to do with Strike was in the meeting I'd been kicked out of.

"Excuse me. How did you get in here?"

Except her.

"Is there something I can help you with?"

"I, uh..."

"You were in the orientation meeting," she said, "and you were fired." The woman behind the accusations was also behind the cashier's cage, and she was one of the Strike managers introduced by Levi Newman. Cassidy Banking. "You need to leave. Right now. Or I'll have to call security."

"Wait." I took a step in her direction. "I really need this job. I really really need it."

She stepped from behind the counter. "Then you'll really really need to speak to Mr. Newman."

If I were still allowed to assign monikers, I'd call this one Vogue. As in on the cover of. Cassidy Banking was tall and so thin I could see her bones. Her gold hair was slicked back and tucked somewhere, and her eyes were black. She matched the room. She wore very little, or very good, makeup, and all black clothes, including several feet of black boots that flared out above her knees. Her only accessories were a collection of bracelets halfway up her left arm.

"Let me help you out here," she said. "I've worked with Mr. Newman for years. It's no three strikes and you're out. It's *one* strike and you're out. He won't hire you back."

Shoot.

"This is a big casino." She gestured beyond the doors I'd snuck through, bracelets jangling. "I'm sure you can get a different job, just not in Strike. This," she presented the immediate area, "is a machine. A lot of work, money, and effort have gone into it, and its success hinges on seven days of gaming. There's no room for error." She dusted her hands together. "Now, if you don't mind." She showed me the door, bracelets jingling.

I skedaddled. No need to stand around and let her get a really good look at me, because there was no doubt I'd be back in some form or fashion.

It was time for Granny's nap, and when her naptime rolled around, it didn't matter who, what, when, or where. I rubbed through three layers of sweaters. "Granny?" She woke with a bark and a start and tried to kill me with her suitcase. "Granny, it's me!" I blocked the blows.

"I thought you were trying to rob me blind!" She adjusted. "Did I mess my hair up?"

I'm just over five feet tall and Granny's an inch shorter than me, but her hair, colored, shampooed, and set (in stone) every single Thursday morning of her life for the past five decades, was cornflower blue and towered over both of us. For every millimeter she lost in stature as the years rolled by, she made up for in hairdo, which at this point, erupted from her head a full seven inches. She would soon have Marge Simpson's hair, and right now it was a nightmare, leaning way starboard. "Your hair's just fine, Granny."

"I'm going to see that little casino later, honey. Right now I need to take a power nap." She wobbled up. "Let's bounce." She shuffled in the direction of the main aisle that led to the casino entrance. I snatched her good luck charms off the Diamond Doozy slot machine and caught up with her, just in time to stop dead in my tracks. At a blackjack table to my right, sitting at third base, was my coworker, Baylor, hiding under a Braves baseball cap and sunglasses. Beside him, on second, under a Center for Disease Control hat and silver reflective Costa Del Mars, was none other than fifteen-year-old Thomas Sanders. Chewing on a toothpick. Tossing out hundred-dollar chips.

I snuck up between them. "Never split tens." I grabbed Little Sanders by the ear and dragged his happy ass out.

FIVE

No Hair paced in a threatening way. He planted each foot slowly and deliberately, like he was rubbing out a scorpion with every step. He tapped his chin, occasionally studying us, and when he turned to pace the other way, I could see the bulge of the butt of his gun beneath the fabric of his jacket stretched across his wide back.

"Let's see if I've got this straight."

Baylor, Little Sanders, and I were lined up on one of the sofas in our basement office. The one at the receiving end of No Hair's wrath.

"You." (Baylor.) "Are supposed to be taking care of Thomas."

We all heard Baylor swallow.

"Do you need to be reminded there are surveillance cameras in the casino? Five dedicated cameras trained directly on every single blackjack table? Recording everything?"

"Yes, sir."

"Yes, what? You need to be reminded?"

"No. I remember. I knew. I know. I didn't know there were five cameras, but—"

I leaned past Little Sanders. "Baylor, shut up already. The whole thing is rhetorical. Sit there and take it like a man."

No Hair turned on me. "I'll get to you in a minute."

I zipped my lips.

"And are you aware, Baylor," No Hair was fists on hips, "that it is against the law for a minor to even *be* in the casino unless accompanied by security and passing through?"

"He was accompanied by security," Baylor said. "I'm security."

"You were." No Hair let that sink in a minute before he moved over a spot. "And you, young man."

"Dude."

No Hair inhaled sharply.

"If the Gaming Commission, who happens to be crawling all over this place at the moment, caught you in the casino, they'd close the doors. The fines would be through the roof, which you might remember has a big hole in it right now, and not only would your father be extremely disappointed in you, he'd probably fire Baylor." He cut his eyes back to Baylor. "Not that I'm not going to."

Baylor assumed a fetal position.

(No, he didn't.)

"And you." (Me.) "Somehow managed to get fired before the job even started."

I shrugged. "That guy's a real hard ass, No Hair."

"Yeah? So am I."

"Baylor." No Hair whipped around. "You get the waitress job for Strike it Rich."

Baylor's eyes popped. I snickered. Thomas said, "Dude."

"Get to uniform distribution, get yourself fitted for a uniform, and I hope it's the most ridiculous, humiliating getup you've never even dreamed of," No Hair said. "Then go sit through orientation for the rest of the day."

Baylor whimpered. I snickered. Thomas said, "Dude."

"You." (Dude.) "Get upstairs with your father. Grab a book or a laptop or just sit quietly in the corner." Little Sanders's left leg started going a mile a minute. "Spend an afternoon seeing what your father deals with all day every day and see if you can't drum up a little respect for how much is at stake here."

"And you." It was my turn. "You're the new Social Media assistant. You'll be working with Elzbath. Get ready to do twitters."

Oh, no. Hashtag, no. No, no, no.

"MOVE."

* * *

"You've reached the Wilcox County Court's clerk's office. We're sorry we're unable to take your call—"

I hung up. It was Saturday, government offices closed. I'd have to hack into the court's records. I'd known about my legal troubles, which is to say I'd been sick, for twenty hours now, and had not been able to make myself look into it. I was hoping it would just go away. (Ooops! Nevermind!)

Bradley Cole, bless his heart, who'd known for twenty-one hours, was entertaining the troops on this, what was supposed to have been, our wedding day. Other than Granny, who was upstairs in her Bellissimo guest room napping off her morning gambling, everyone was touring Beauvoir, the plantation home of Jefferson Davis. Which took all of three minutes. Bradley said he'd drag it out, then we'd all meet up for dinner. Tomorrow, thankfully, everyone would go home. And by everyone, I mean his mother.

Dinner with the fam at six-thirty would be dinner one for me. I (Bianca) had a dinner date with the Jennings, who'd given Little Sanders a ride on their little plane, at eight. They were next on my list. After the Wilcox County Records Department's database.

I had 3B to myself. Our offices are made up of three large hard-to-get-to rooms below sea level. I was in the room I call control central amid an assortment of computers, monitors, and other power-hungry electronics, and where I generally did my best work. I'm a degreed criminologist (University of Alabama at Birmingham) and a degreed computer information scientist (same school). When a cyber-digging is necessary, this is where I hole up.

I'd received, without responding to, several texts and tweets. Hashtag Elspie was #PUMPED! at having a virtual assistant, and couldn't wait to #HOOK! with me. Baylor texted instructions to organize his going-away party, because he wasn't wearing "this shit" for a whole week. And Fantasy regaled me with quick pictures of Strike Orientation funnies I was missing after being fired. Most featured Hashtag Elspie, who had to be on crack, and several were of Levi Newman. "*Check it out, D. He wears a rug.*" Fantasy snapped the casino manager's wavy chestnut mane slipping sideways. "*Do we know these people?*" She zipped over a picture of Cassidy Banking, who I'd had so much fun with when I ran into her at the Strike casino earlier today, huddled with two well-dressed backsides, one male, one female. I couldn't see them. So I couldn't tell her if we knew them or if we didn't.

Seconds later, a second photo popped up of all three faces, Cassidy's and the two strangers, all very serious and all studying something in the distance, and no, we didn't know them. That I knew of. "*Something's off here, D. These people aren't part of Strike and she shouldn't know them.*" The messages had come in right and left, so when my phone actually rang, I almost jumped out of my skin.

"Daddy!" I patted my chest. "You scared me."

"We're back at the hotel, Punkin'. Can you spare a few minutes for your dear old dad?"

"Of course I can. I'm in my office. I'll meet you behind Shakes and bring you down." Only a handful of people could actually waltz down here, and only a handful of people, myself excluded today, wanted to waltz down here. Super Secret Spies have Super Secret Inaccessible Offices. If you weren't us, you had to be escorted by one of us.

"Ten minutes," he said.

"Great." I wasn't in the mood to hack into Alabama's Vital Records anyway, because I'd have to type my rat bastard ex-ex husband's name when I did.

My phone beeped in another message as I was rising from my chair to go fetch Daddy. Fantasy zipped two more pictures to me. The first a tight shot, showing a hidden handoff behind a handshake—a thin slip of white paper. The second picture was wide, and all you could see was the handshake. It was Cassidy Banking slipping something to the people we didn't know. *We should track these people down, D.*

My phone kept dinging until I muted it. Hashtag Elspie, tweet,

tweet. Davis, delete, delete. I couldn't ignore her forever, but I couldn't deal with her right now, either.

My father is in his late fifties. He's the Chief of Police and Mayor of Pine Apple, my Alabama hometown, population just over/under four hundred. Two years ago, he'd had a heart attack and bypass surgery, which had taken away his spare tire but hadn't diminished him in any other way. Honestly, he felt better, looked better, and was healthier all the way around than in the years before the heart trouble, and I loved him with all my (at the moment troubled) heart.

He made small talk in the elevator and down the long hall. It's been a nice visit, but he's ready to get home; the paperwork is surely piling up. Granny's a little hard to handle when there are slot machines and hot toddies nearby. My young niece is getting restless with no other little ones to play with. Mother doesn't know what to do with herself without a kitchen.

We had one foot each inside the door. "Why have you postponed the wedding, Davis?"

I burst into tears. He pulled me into a big hug, and let me cry it out. When it was all over but the hiccups, he asked, "Does he just want to wait awhile, honey?"

"Who?"

"Who?" Daddy held me at arm's length. "Bradley."

"Neither one of us wants to wait."

My father tapped his right temple. His thinking move. "Then which one of you postponed the wedding?"

I hiccupped. "Neither."

"So why aren't you getting married today?"

"We don't have a marriage license, Daddy. It was denied."

"What in the world? Why?"

"Because," (hiccup) "I'm still married to Eddie."

Daddy slapped a hand over his heart.

* * *

Anne Cole, who may or may not end up being my mother-in-law, didn't know a thing about (me) my job, and when I showed up for our family dinner dressed as Bianca so I could zip straight to my second dinner with Mr. and Mrs. Jennings, she was a little stunned.

"Those are the largest sunglasses I've ever seen in my *life*."

Going outside the confines of the Bellissimo property all dolled up as Bianca was a gamble, and I tried my best to avoid it. First, if she knew I was out dressed as her and she hadn't sanctioned it, she'd have a fit. Second, people recognized her and wanted to rub elbows. To avoid anyone interrupting our dinner by approaching Bianca (me) and asking for Bellissimo favors at Outback Steak House (my grandmother's all-time favorite fancy restaurant), I was wearing Heidi London metal studded sunglasses that were so big, it looked as if I was wearing two metal-studded personal pan pizzas on my face.

When Bianca had tossed them to me, because it looked as if I'd been "weeping" (I had), I asked if they were for Halloween and she'd answered, "Certainly *not*." Then suggested I acquire some *style* sense. I suggested she acquire some *common* sense. (No, I didn't.) "And no smoking," Bianca said. "It was hard enough to quit once. I'm not putting myself through it again."

"Your headdress is very Jackie-O." Like the sunglass observation, Anne Cole didn't mean this one as a compliment either. I'd covered my Bianca blonde French twist updo, which looked more like an eagle's nest on my head, with a red silk scarf I tied beneath my chin. Under the scarf and pizza glasses, my lipstick was high gloss blood-curdling red.

I haven't even gotten to the good part of my outfit.

Bianca had me in all white, the same color neither my mother nor Anne Cole thought I should be wearing today, and they were right this time: no one should wear this on any day. The dress was your basic sleeveless pencil, two sizes too small for me and three sizes too small for Bianca, but it was the just-arrived beast she'd snagged from the Fur Salon at Saks today that sent this getup over the top.

It was seventy degrees out.

She had me in a white mink hooded cape with dyed ermine tips that looked like mutant beetles crawling all over it. The fur was buttoned at my neck and flared out six feet just past my butt. The hem of the dress hit a smidge below the fur, and Bianca's a big believer in the bare leg look. I was wearing a mini dress and a massive fur coat that could barely clear a doorway on top of bare legs. On my feet, solid white six-inch platforms. It was nothing short of mortifying to be ordering a blooming onion in this blooming outfit.

I shed the coat, but wouldn't let the waiter hang it (Bianca would kill me if a waiter breathed on it before she got to shock the public wearing it), so I climbed out of it, rolled, then wadded the thing and held it in my lap, which was about as comfortable as trying to sit at a long, skinny dinner table with my arms wrapped around a bale of hay.

"What is it you do, exactly?" Anne Cole's tone was suspicious and accusatory. "I thought you were on the casino police force."

And that's when my niece Riley, sitting directly across from me, sent her large glass of chocolate milk flying.

*   *   *

"It's so nice to meet you? Right? This place is perfect for us? And you're, like, Head Bitch? Right?" Missy Jennings ended every statement on a lilt, so everything sounded like a question. And she was the second person I'd met in one day with ink-jet black eyes. "Red plays the tables? And I like the slots? Right? And this is way closer to home than Vegas? So we went online and here we are?" Jazz hands, and a totally veneered smile. Her husband, Redmond Jennings, also totally veneered, plus pickled in aftershave, paid absolutely no attention, but knew to smile in agreement when his wife took a breath. Like just then. Bianca would have picked up her steak knife and gone for the woman's jugular. Like just then.

"And where is home, Missy?" I asked.

"Girl?" she waved a hand through the air. "We're from a spit in the road in Alabama? Right? You've never heard of it?"

(Try me?)

They looked too young to be parents of a high school senior, and they looked too young to have the kind of money they were wearing. Missy had ten pounds of jewelry on her person, Red, fifteen. Honestly, they looked like they'd just had talk-show makeovers, everything mannequin matchy-matchy. He wore designer jeans and ostrich cowboy boots, a silk sports coat over a stiff, starched tuxedo shirt unbuttoned for as far as I was willing to look, with ropes of gold chains resting on a shag carpet of wiry chest hair. (Totally grossing me out.) She wore everything, I mean everything, she could get on her person. There was big hair, false eyelashes, double-pierced ears, and a charm bracelet with seven hundred noisy charms. She wore four layers on her top half—silk teddy, oversized designer T, cashmere scarf, and matching cardigan sweater—all tissue thin and the same shade of olive green. And on her bottom half, a short, bouncy (olive green) peplum skirt over olive green leggings, and olive green suede booties. I had the feeling there might be a price tag somewhere between them they'd forgotten to snip off ten minutes ago.

We were in Chops, the steakhouse, one of the twelve eateries at the Bellissimo. We had reservations at the fanciest of the Bellissimo restaurants, Violettes, but I'd changed it last minute, needing a darker and less populated venue, one where the chances of Bianca having her picture snapped was less likely, since I was wearing chocolate milk all over her new fur. And speaking of price tags, Meredith had poked on her phone while I'd smashed the chocolate milk deeper into Bianca's fur with a stack of Outback Steak House napkins. When she found it on Saks's website she flipped her phone around, showed everyone, and gave us the good news. "Thirty-eight thousand dollars."

I let go of my thirty-eight-thousand-dollar chocolate-milk

panic soon enough. When I met the Jennings, in fact. (Right?) I was already seated in a dark corner and on my second glass of Calm Down Chardonnay when the waiter led Missy and Redmond Jennings to the table. They were ten minutes late to dinner, but had already arrived on my phone. I had four photos of them huddled up with Cassidy Banking. These were the people Fantasy suggested we take a look at. (Check. I'm looking.) And that trumped the chocolate milk panic. Not that there won't be hell to pay on the fur coat business.

"Please," I said over salads. "Tell me about yourselves."

"Red has a little farm? Right?" Missy flagged down the waiter and asked for more Ranch dressing. "And I'm a dancer? I have a dance studio?" Jazz hands.

"Lovely." I smiled. "What do you grow, Red?" Other than hair on your chest.

"Trees," he finally spoke. "Christmas trees."

I had no idea there was that much money in Christmas trees.

Quinn was their only child. Missy willingly volunteered between bites of a well-done petite filet that her son was a slip-up after a high school football game, which I knew first-hand was just part and parcel of an Alabama heritage. "That game went into overtime? Right? And next thing we knew? A bundle of baby boy?" Jazz hands. They traveled often, mostly to Vegas until the Montecito closed, so boarding school was the right place for their son. "Can't leave them home alone? Right? And we still act like teenagers? Right, Red?" Red winked at his wife. "There's nothing for Quinn to do in Alabama but get in trouble? Right?"

According to his school records, Quinn had found plenty of trouble in New Hampshire, and according to the school's annual report, Missy and Red Jennings weren't too offended, because they were Diamond Donors. Their hefty donations fell in line right behind Quinn's misconducts.

At the end of my second dinner on what should have been my wedding night, I thanked them again for giving Thomas a ride, wished them luck with the Strike It Rich Sweepstakes, and as we stepped out of the restaurant, I casually asked them if they'd bumped into any old Montecito friends who'd transferred to the Bellissimo.

"No." The first word out of her mouth without a question mark. "We don't know a soul who works here."

SIX

My family checked out of the Bellissimo at seven Sunday morning, stopped by our place for coffee, a light breakfast I did not cook (croissants from Dunkin Donuts and fresh frozen fruit from Dole), and to say goodbye to Bradley's mother. Anne Cole's car was gassed up and her packed bags were loaded. If it were up to me, it would've been running with the driver door open. We wished the whole lot of them happy trails and safe travels at 8:30. We locked the door behind them and agreed the dishes could wait.

SEVEN

The biggest difference between Bellissimo Ballet Barre and every other workout since the beginning of workouts was you do this barefoot and the instructor has a foreign accent. Otherwise, it's every yoga move you've ever seen plus seven thousands squats, all assumed from a standing position, hanging on to a waist-high bar for dear life, and at a mirror. The music is nice, if you can hear it over the British woman yelling, "Extend! Lift! Point!" She also said things like, "Relevé plié! Parallel plié pulse!" and "Embrace your inner ballerina!"

Watching Baylor embrace his inner ballerina was well worth being here at six on a Monday morning. I doubt Baylor would ever, ever, ever let Little Sanders talk him into anything else. Ever.

He was way overdressed in running tights and a long-sleeved microfiber shirt, and as a result, he was sweating like a boy pig. He was the only male in the small, hot room with fourteen small, hot cocktail waitresses, the British instructor, Hashtag Elspeth, Fantasy, and me. Fantasy rose above it all. At almost six feet, she was a head taller than the other waitresses, and when she went to "*Extend! Extend! Extend!*" she extended halfway across the room. She smacked the girls in front of and behind her a dozen times. "Sorry, honey. My bad."

I was Amy Medina, Social Media Virtual Assistant. My hair was sprayed Chocolate Covered Bing Cherry and my colored contact lenses were amethyst. "I've never met anyone with, like, purple eyes." Elspeth's ponytail bobbed. "Mind if I Instagram you?"

When she adjusted to the odd combination of my black/red

hair and violet eyes—I really need to slow down and invest a little more time in my disguises these days—and I adjusted to her thirteen-year-old speech patterns, I stuck my neck out and questioned the wisdom of the grueling workouts. For one, everyone in the room already had abs of steel, and for two, working out every day this week couldn't possibly have much impact on next week.

"Oh, we've been at it for, like, five weeks already," Hashtag said. "Except for, like, the two new ones. Who just landed in my lap." Her lap held fictional personnel files on the two new ones. Right then, one of the new ones, the Baylor new one, busted his ass when he fell out of a rond de jambe and slid across the floor. The other new one, the one who kept kicking everyone else, doubled over laughing.

"So you didn't ask for two more waiters?"

"Not at all," she said. "It came down from the president's office that there wasn't enough diversity on the waitstaff."

Hashtag cared nothing about personal space. She was so, like, in my face.

"I would have never thought to hire a man to serve cocktails at a casino," she said. "He's, like, clunky." Hashtag slurped her pink lumpy breakfast from a big plastic bucket. "Cute," she said, "but a clunk."

Clunk stripped off his shirt, tossed it, and, like, hit me in the head with it. Clunk had abs of steel, too, which didn't escape the short waitresses.

"And she's black." Hashtag tapped Fantasy's fake folder. "So we're diverse."

Fourteen Barbie dolls, six-foot dark-skinned Fantasy, and a clunky man child. Yes. Diverse.

"These workouts are more about, like, media than fitness," Hashtag said. "The waitstaff is the face of Strike, and if they didn't, like, look fab, they wouldn't be here in the first place." Hashtag Elspeth and I were on short stools in a corner of the room. As her virtual assistant, I would be running her electronic errands for the next two weeks, because she was going to be, like, very busy (doing what?) and, like, she was training me. "They'll have more overall media coverage than anyone else," she said. "Having them here this early keeps them in shape and in line. Hey," she placed a camera, no larger or thicker than a credit card, on my thigh. "We need to shout out."

She wanted me to scream?

"Tweet a pic," she said. "Shout out to the Strike team."

She picked up the camera, tapped it several times, then passed it back to me. I looked through the small screen and found Fantasy, who had a leg wrapped around the back of her head, teeth bared, and a childbirth expression on her face. I thought she made an excellent shouting subject. Shoot. Shout. Send.

When it was over, Baylor spread eagle on the floor and threatening to throw up, Hashtag Elspie sent me on a shoe mission to New Orleans, since Baylor wouldn't look good in gold stilettoes.

"I don't know," I said. "Have you had him try any on?"

Baylor raised one finger off the floor.

Hashtag Elspie punched me in the arm and laughed. We agreed to meet again at seven that evening for Waitress Dress Rehearsal at Strike, which gave me the rest of the day. Baylor could find his own shoes.

"Amy, before you go," Hashtag said, "stop by Strike. The gaming installation is underway. Check out the chairs. Take a peek at the game and take a ton of pictures. You'll need them."

* * *

To see the future of gaming and have a shot at striking it rich, contestants had to qualify by playing a cyber scavenger hunt, bouncing around Google+, Facebook, Twitter, Vine, Instagram, Snapchat, Vimeo, Pinterest, Flickr, and Tumblr gathering clues. Of the fifteen thousand registered participants, seven thousand were successful. The seven thousand were allowed access to the virtual casino—strikeitrich.com—where a week of competition point play narrowed the field to two hundred. Forty-two thousand concurrent viewers attended the four-hour webcasted finals event that got down to a single hand of blackjack, seventy-two players against the house, and the fifty who didn't bust against the house's eighteen were the final contestants.

The Bellissimo was feeling the buzz. Occupancy, gaming revenues, tempers, and without a doubt, social impressions were up. We were Internet Darlings.

All anyone really wanted to do was sit in the chairs. The closer we got to Strike, the more we heard the word "chair." Chair, chair, chair. Time for me to see the chair.

No less than six hundred pounds of security stopped me at the door. "Ma'am," the first three hundred said, "this area is closed." The gold-icicle spike chandelier looked like the sun blazing behind him.

"I'm an employee." I flashed my new purple-eyed Amy Medina badge. "I'm here on behalf of social media." They parted; I choked.

What was that *smell*? For the second time, I pulled my shirt over my nose.

"Yeah, it's strong," the other three hundred pounds said. "It'll calm down when this place opens and the players light up."

"Let's hope."

I joined a roomful of people—technicians, construction-types, suits—all heads bent, all working. Levi Newman looked up from a clipboard. "Can I help you?"

"I'm here to shoot you. Pictures of you. Pictures of the casino. I'm Amy Medina. I work for Elspeth."

His eyes wandered to my employee badge. Then back up to my purple eyes. "Have we met?"

"Today's my first day."

He looked at his Bedazzled watch, and told me he had five minutes. Which was fine, because I had four. "We have one kiosk up. This way." I followed him through a maze of crates and cords, up three steps, then stopped cold. No wonder people were willing to stay up all night gathering cyber four-leaf clovers. It *was* about the chair.

"Have a seat, Miss Medina."

It was a black leather recliner with wide arms and a wraparound headrest. I sat down and as soon as I did, the chair started moving.

"You're sitting in a chair made of full-grain European leather. It's designed for every seating position from upright to fully reclined, and it knows you."

It must have known I needed a hug and that I was short and cold. It adjusted to my height, it closed in on pressure points on my back, and it radiated heat.

"Lay your head back," he said, "as if to rest."

The chair stretched me out like I was on the beach. The canned lights trained on the chair dimmed.

"Say music."

I said music, and Bruno Mars came softly out of the headrest.

"It's equipped with THX surround sound," he explained, "and an air filtration system to eliminate all traces of smoke for those who do and for those who don't, and it has a built in light-therapy system, delivering full doses of Vitamin D at regular intervals."

Hashtag impressed.

"It has a heating and cooling system that responds to body temperature and spa features from a low vibration to deep-tissue massage."

"So, where's the game?" I got the chair. It's a beaut.

"Take your right hand," he said, "and rest it comfortably on the arm."

As soon as I did, I felt four buttons at my fingertips.

"Push the first button."

Goodbye, cruel Earth.

Three 24-inch LED touchscreens dropped from the ceiling to land almost in my lap, and my jaw dropped all the way to the floor.

He put the game in to demo mode. The screens tilted to wrap around me, then came alive. Millions of *future*Gaming logos swam in and out of all three screens. Who wrote the programming for all this? I turned my head to speak, and the screens automatically backed away. I was in my own personal gambling robot. "One last question, Mr. Newman. What is that smell?"

"The human brain is manipulated by fragrance." He tipped his toupeed head back and sucked in two lungs full. "Our take on these gaming stations will be forty percent higher as a direct result of aroma branding," he said, "and these players will return to the Bellissimo again and again, after the Strike sweepstakes is over, just to get another whiff."

"Where's it coming from?"

"The chair."

"What is it?" I asked. (Legal, I hoped.) It wasn't vanilla. It wasn't cinnamon. It wasn't gingerbread.

"It's chocolate chip cookies."

* * *

We left my car at home. Bradley's legs didn't fit in it.

"Are you ready?" His hand was on the gearshift.

"No."

"We'll get to the bottom of it, Davis." He tucked a lock of my chocolate-covered-cherry hair behind my ear. "Have faith."

"I have hives, Bradley. I have heartburn. I have the heebie-jeebies," I said. "Everything but faith."

And we were off. Destination: 4th Judicial Circuit of Alabama, Wilcox County Courthouse, Camden, Alabama. Somewhere between the Municipal Court on Walter Street and the Judicial Court three blocks over on Broad, my divorce had fallen through the cracks. We were on our way to walk the same path, find the crack, and dig my divorce out of it. Our goal is to take care of this matter without my ex-ex-husband, or anyone else who didn't already, knowing. Bradley Cole is an attorney; he knows the law and his way around a courthouse. I'm a former police officer, current Super Spy. Between the two of us, surely we could get this done.

We hit the drive-through of Starbucks.

"When do you need to be back?"

"I have to be in the new casino at seven." I blew across the top of my tall skinny double-shot pumpkin spice latte with easy whip.

"Where are you supposed to be now?" We were on I-10 east, headed for Mobile. I knew every bump and grind of this road, having traveled this route from Biloxi to Pine Apple, Pine Apple to Biloxi, at least once a month for three years. Sometimes more often, depending on what was going on at home. (My mother and my niece had birthdays that were just days apart. Could we celebrate them together? No.)

"I'm supposed to be buying Baylor shoes."

"Why can't Baylor buy his own shoes?" Bradley asked.

"That's what I said."

We crossed the state line into Alabama and I started getting twitchy.

"You're not going to have any eyelashes left if you keep trying to pull them out, Davis. Think about something else."

I doubt he wanted to think about what we might find up the road either. We'd managed to spend the entire day alone yesterday without discussing it once. Not that I'm complaining.

"Talk to me," Bradley said. "Tell me about Strike."

"I told you I was fired, didn't I?"

"What? Who would fire you, Davis? The nerve!"

"Exactly!"

My job had me working in tons of positions within the Bellissimo, always in disguise, and I got fired from them all the damn time. A few months ago, right after Fantasy and I graduated from cyber blackjack school (I might have skipped a few lessons. How hard can it be?) I was fired on my second shift of dealing blackjack. "Lady," the pit boss said, "you just can't *count*."

"I've already been hired again," I said. "I'm the new social media assistant."

"Congratulations."

"Thank you, Bradley."

He pushed a button, the sunroof noiselessly slid back, then

falling-leaves, chili-supper, football-crisp air filled the car. "What, exactly, Davis, does a social media assistant do?"

"I'm not sure."

Which entertained Bradley.

"Have you seen today's paper?" he asked. "There's a big write up about Strike. Countdown to the casino of the future." He shifted in his seat to a more comfortable position and offered a hand my way. I took it. "With a big picture of everyone standing under the sun."

"That's a glass-blown light fixture in the little casino," I said. "Very pretty."

"The new casino manager? Levi? Looks like David Hasselhoff."

Bradley nailed it. *"Baywatch* David Hasselhoff?"

"No," he said. *"Knight Rider* David Hasselhoff."

"Maybe he *is* David Hasselhoff." For some reason, right then, on the interstate going ninety, we met over the console and kissed. Just a peck. It felt good to be away from the Bellissimo, out of Biloxi, with Bradley. "Did you see my new boss in the picture?"

"I don't know," he said. "Who does he look like?"

"It's a she," I said, "and you can't miss her. She wears a ponytail that looks like a fountain coming out of her head, lots and lots of glittery makeup, and crazy clothes. Her name is Elspeth."

"It is not."

"Yes it is."

"There was no one in the picture with a fountain head." Bradley passed a motorhome that had a Twitter address and invitation to follow their travel tweets painted along the driver side. "There were women," he said, "but I didn't notice any glitter or crazy clothes."

"My new boss Elspeth is in charge of social media," I said. "Actually, she was my old boss, too. She's in charge of social media and the waitstaff. No Hair had me waitressing for this gig, but now I'm her virtual assistant because I was fired from waitressing."

"Why is the same person in charge of both social media and the waitstaff?" Bradley asked. "I don't see the connection."

And with that, I didn't either.

"It sounds like Jeremy *wants* you working for Elspeth the whole time."

A good point I'd been too busy to make. No Hair had me working for Hashtag Elspie twice. Interesting. No Hair generally knew a lot more than he let on, and he generally threw me in the fire without a briefing. The method to his madness was this: Let Davis figure it out.

"Davis?"

"You're right," I said. "No Hair wants me on her."

"Why?"

"Why, indeed."

"Okay." Bradley said. "Get a step ahead. What's so interesting about Elspeth?"

"I can tell you one thing about her, she's on Red Bull. Seriously. I haven't seen her when she wasn't bouncing off the walls."

"Not necessarily a bad personality trait for someone in her chosen profession," Bradley suggested. "What else?"

"She's gay."

"Did she tell you that?"

"No."

"Then how do you know?"

"I just do," I said. "We didn't discuss my sexual orientation either, but she knows."

"How does she know?"

"She just does."

"Okay, Davis. What does this have to do with anything?"

"Nothing."

He raised an eyebrow.

I raised two. "Since when do I care what people do when they're not at work?"

"Davis, there's a reason Jeremy wants you glued to her, and I doubt it's so you'll become a Twitter expert. You might want to care what she does when she's not at work."

EIGHT

"Davis. I don't care what you do when you're not at work."

Our phones—mine, Fantasy's, Baylor's, No Hair's, Mr. Sanders's—had locked interfacing GPS. There were times when we needed to find each other fast. No Hair let me get all the way to AL-28, the Welcome to Camden sign, before texting instructions to see him the minute I got back. Hours later, when Bradley and I were ten minutes from back, he texted instructions to meet him at his car. *We're going for a ride.*

The first thing he said was, "That is not a natural eye color, Davis, or hair shade, either. What were you thinking? Cover up some of that or I won't be able to talk to you."

I could skip this talk.

He backed into a parking space under Sharkheads Souvenir City, four miles west of the Bellissimo on Beach Boulevard. We were under the store because it was built on huge pink stilts. Having been drowned by Hurricane Katrina in 2005, it built back with an eye on staying above future storm surges. Early Monday evening wasn't primetime souvenir shopping, so we had the understore parking lot mostly to ourselves.

"With all the irons we have in the fire, Davis, I'm not sure why you'd take off for Alabama for the day and not say anything." We faced each other, our backs against the car doors, but as large as this mother was, there were still five feet of air between us. "And I don't understand why you didn't tell me you were getting married."

"I couldn't. I just couldn't."

"Yes," he got snippy, "you could have."

"Do I need your permission?"

"Of course not."

"I didn't get married."

"I know that."

No Hair drove a big Cadillac Escalade the color of aluminum foil. The interior was Sag Harbor gray leather and it always smelled good. Whatever it was, they should replace the Essence of Chocolate Chip Cookies in the *future*Gaming chairs with it. I tapped a finger to my nose. It was a spicy smell. Not pepper spicy. Man cologne spicy.

"Why do I make more money than Fantasy?"

Frustration knotted No Hair's brow. As time marched on, he had an easier time with the pogo stick that was my thought process and only asked me to back up and explain myself several times a day instead of every time I opened my mouth. "Because you're the lead, Davis, you have seniority. And because Fantasy isn't on the Bianca detail."

"There's no other reason?"

"There's no other reason, Davis."

"And then there's the Baylor in Tunica business."

"Yes." He cleared his throat.

Tunica, Mississippi, was cattycorner to Biloxi on the Mississippi map. Before dockside gambling was legalized by Mississippi in 1990, Tunica County was the poorest county in *America*. Not in Mississippi. Not in the South. In *America*. Now it's second only to Biloxi as a Mississippi gambling venue. Mr. Sanders had wanted to know what was going on at Lost Fortune Casino, a privately owned little place making huge waves, and by huge waves I mean big bucks, which, in my opinion, might be huger waves and bigger bucks if they changed the name. Maybe Found Fortune Casino. Baylor drew the short straw on the fact-finding mission. (It was rigged. Neither Fantasy nor I wanted to go to Tunica.)

"He was arrested with three hookers, No Hair. I had to bail his drunk ass out of jail."

"What's your point?"

"Why wasn't he fired?"

"Please put some sunglasses on, Davis."

"One of those prostitutes was fifteen years older than him."

"What does that have to do with anything?"

"Bad judgment!" I threw both hands in the air. "Surely he could have found three hookers born in the same decade he was!"

We watched traffic for a full five minutes.

"What does any of this have to do with you not telling me you were getting married?"

Of five cars that passed in front of us on Beach Boulevard right then, four were white.

"Are you asking me to fire Baylor, Davis? I know he's young and impulsive, but he's on our team because believe it or not, he's got your back."

I didn't see it. I liked Baylor, I liked him a lot. He'd partied himself out of an LSU football scholarship, but he was a smart kid. He was quick on the draw, he was big and burly, he was cute as all get-out, and we needed him. He did all sorts of Bianca chores—carried her bags, fluffed her ego, held his hand out for the chewing gum she'd grown tired of—and he was essentially reliable. For a man his age. (Twenty-five.) Who lived life to the fullest. And strongly ascribed to the Love Thy Neighbor business, especially if the neighbor was female. As far as him having my back, I wasn't so sure.

Three tour buses passed in front of us, no doubt full of senior citizens on their way to the Bellissimo.

"Are you suggesting, Davis, that Fantasy makes less money than you because she's married?"

A big Harley.

"Fantasy's job is as big as she wants it to be, Davis. If she wanted a larger role, she'd have one."

I knew this. Fantasy had one husband, two dogs, and three sons. She'd been with us almost two years. In the beginning she kept up with me, working round the clock when duty called, but it wasn't long before the job began jeopardizing her home life. She deliberately took a backseat, and now worked a forty, sometimes fifty-hour week. Special occasions, like next week, she'd work more. It was all hunky dory.

"And I'm not keeping Baylor around so he can have your job."

I didn't know this. Baylor had screwed up and screwed up and screwed up. He'd been forgiven and forgiven and forgiven, just two days ago, for letting Little Sanders *gamble*.

"I'm married, Davis. I've been married twenty-five years, and I've done one or another version of this job the entire time. I do this job every day of the week. Being married won't keep you from doing your job, and I don't know how you even cooked that up. Fantasy's job isn't any less because of the fact that she's married, and I'm not grooming Baylor for your job."

No Hair had never, ever lied to me. Not once. I doubt he'd start now. But the pervasive belief that married women are less dependable, less focused, less available than single unencumbered career women was such a deep-rooted mindset—so ubiquitous, so subconscious—I'm not sure No Hair, or any man, would be able to identify, much less acknowledge, their free-floating discrimination of married women in the workplace. So subconsciously, the powers-that-be (Mr. Sanders and No Hair) scoot the responsibility away from a married woman (which would be me) to a man who could barely dress himself (and that would be Baylor). If I were under-the-radar married, I could put the power shift off until I was ready. Or at least until Baylor was ready.

I blinked back the stress and emotion of the day that threatened to roll down my cheeks.

No Hair fired up the Cadillac. "What happened in Alabama?"

"I don't even know where to start," I said.

"I had coffee with your dad Sunday morning, so you can start with today."

Daddy. Greasing the gears. "So you know?"

"Yes, Mrs. Crawford. I know."

I swung. He ducked.

"The divorce went from Municipal Court," I said, "where it was ruled on, to Judicial Court, where it should have been filed." The words hurt. "When it got to Judicial, someone noticed that Eddie wasn't a legal resident of Alabama, which he'd filed as."

"Was he living in Mississippi?"

"No. He had moved back to Alabama." So close to me I could've reached out and slapped him. "But he didn't get a job. He lived in a trailer his parents owned and still had a Mississippi driver's license."

The Bellissimo loomed in front of us.

"So he hadn't established residency when you filed."

"Right. The court notified him to show up with a current piece of mail addressed to him in Alabama within ninety days or we'd have to file again."

"And he didn't?" No Hair asked.

"And he didn't."

We pulled into No Hair's parking place. I had one leg out the door, bracing myself for the drop, when No Hair said, "For the record, Davis, I don't think anything you said just now has anything to do with why you didn't tell me you were getting married. It's not about your job. There's something you're not saying."

Both of my legs dangled in the air.

"Just think about it. And fess up to Richard about shooting the Mercedes in the lobby."

Dammit.

*   *   *

"Girl." Hashtag Elspie and I were under the gold icepick chandelier in the Strike casino. "I thought you, like, were head of marketing for a software developer." She was drinking her juice dinner through a straw from a clear plastic bucket with a dome lid. It looked like tar. "How did you, like, market without social media?"

"They were old fashioned," I said. "Very trade-magazine focused."

"No wonder they went bust."

The installation of the *future*Gaming chairs was complete. The room now looked like an upscale Fifth Avenue nightclub with fifty black space capsules. Or a very cosmopolitan science lab.

"Do you ever eat food, Elspeth?" I asked. "Cheeseburgers?"

She laughed. "Girl!" Her palm-tree ponytail bobbed.

We were with the rest of the Strike casino staff for this dress rehearsal, waiting to be waited on by the Strike waitstaff. Elspeth said they'd gotten hung up in spray tan. The new waitress, Toni, the tall black girl, had a fit and refused to get in the spray tan booth. (I'd like to have been a fly on the wall for that.) They'd worked it out, and everyone would be along shortly. In the meantime, Hashtag said, "We've got to talk microblogging."

"Did I not do it right?" I'd tumbled and retwitted and liked stuff every hour when my phone dinged to remind me, even from the clerk's office at the courthouse in Camden, which is what she'd asked me to do.

Elspie had a Monroe lip piercing I hadn't noticed before, with the tiniest of diamond studs in it tonight. (#Painful) Her dark eyeliner was thick and glittery. This must be her after-six look. (#Impressed) She said never, ever, ever again type the word *hashtag*. Use the pound symbol. And no spaces or punctuation. To separate words, use capital letters. (#GotIt) Don't type *shout out*. It's a capital S, capital O, preceded by the pound symbol. (#WillDo) Use Emojis. Emojis are little picture icons—dancing ballerinas, fried eggs, palm trees. Sneak them in. (#FriedEggs) She was nice about it, but at the end of the tutorial she asked, "How old did you say you were?"

I have yet to meet a firewall I couldn't wiggle through. I write computer code almost to the point of operating systems. I can take out a long-range moving target like a SWAT sniper. Have I really missed this social media boat? (#MissedBoat?)

"You'll catch on," Hashtag assured me with her signature friendly punch. Conquer-the-world Katy Perry music came blaring out of nowhere and she cartwheeled off her barstool squealing, "Here they come!"

The energy level with this one was exhausting. (#Exhausting)

With great pageantry, the waitstaff appeared, one at a time, from behind a dark corner that led to the service area. They were stark naked. (#Hypothermia) Honest to Pete, the gold bikini tops were teeny triangles hanging on by threads, the bottoms barely there. Their skin had been sprayed so gold, they looked like Oscar trophies, and until you looked closely, they looked like they were wearing absolutely nothing. (#Naked) It was hard to see where the gold skin started and the gold bikini ended.

Elspie turned back to me and mouthed, "*O, M, G!*"

The lean, gold Bellissimo Ballet Barre bodies scattered through the room and passed out champagne flutes full of bubbly. Fantasy was the fifth waitress to turn the corner. I barely recognized her. Miss Brazil. She was spectacular. She got two steps in, then stopped dead in her tracks and sneezed all over her champagne. Then again. Then four more times. The waitstaff continued to spill out, weaving around her, while she sneezed at her champagne. Six waitresses later, Baylor appeared. Mr. Chippendale. He was wearing skin-tight gold lamé stripper pants, gold cuffs on the wrists of his bare golden arms, a gold bowtie at the top of his bare chest, and the most ridiculous gold cowboy boots I'd ever seen in my life.

Fantasy turned around and ran back to the service area, sneezing and screaming simultaneously.

I let Elspie spread her giddiness halfway across the casino floor before I slipped my hand into the black leather tote she'd abandoned. I dove in, thinking (a) nothing would bite me, and (b) I wanted her phone for thirty seconds to send a code to the sim card and clone it, so I could get a grip on this twittering business before I got fired again, but (c) got a handful of cold, hard, trouble instead. It felt like a Glock.

Not one piece of Strike was falling into place for a smooth run. Not one piece. At this rate, I may be single for the rest of my life.

* * *

On Tuesday morning, I hung a Do Not Disturb sign on the doorknob of control central in our basement offices, then locked myself in. I had serious work to do. Before I went downstairs, I went upstairs and snagged Little Sanders. He was my ward for the morning. (#FallBreakFail) I parked his butt outside the office with a laptop stuffed full of Strike pictures from the night before and told him he'd better not move a muscle or I'd deliver him to his father for another day of watching him work. Or worse, to his mother, for a day of watching her watch herself.

He said, "Duuuuude."

He complained because he couldn't play with the Baylor dude, and asked what he was supposed to do all day.

"You're going to tweet, post, and make little movies."

"And do what with them?"

"Give them to me, so I can stop what I'm doing every hour and send them out for the next ten days."

He said, "Dude, HootSuite them."

"Who?"

HootSuite is a social media manager. Somehow Little Sanders knew all about it. For a small fee, it would manage all the social media sites, integrate them, track them, analyze them, and best of all, it could be loaded up with scheduled posts and tweets well into the future. HootSuite would do for me what I was supposed to be doing for Elspeth. Which would free me up. "Do it, Thomas," I said. "Load me up with ten days' worth of stuff."

Baylor and Fantasy were recovering from their morning Bellissimo Ballet Barre at Fantasy's allergist's. Fantasy is allergic to all the usual suspects. In addition, she's allergic to nickel—her gun is solid steel, her personal electronics all in OtterBox cases, and she never touched coins—red dye #40, and fingernail polish. Today she was welcoming the newest member to her allergen family—Aroma Brand, Chocolate Chip Cookie flavor.

We'd already seen a sneaky exchange between Cassidy

Banking and Missy and Red Jennings. (Right?) And now Hashtag Elspeth was, for whatever reasons, packing heat and carrying concealed. Our team had gone from Code Let's-Get-This-Over-With to Code Uh-Oh to Code High-Alert.

Fantasy's doc needed to fix her up and fast.

I settled in at the computer with a large cup of coffee and blueberry frosted Pop Tarts. The most pressing question on my mind was, did he know? Had he been waiting for this day to come? Or had it, like most things, slipped right by him without registering in his pea brain?

My ex-ex-husband, Eddie the Ass Crawford, looked and moved like Rhett Butler, but he did it with the mental wherewithal of Pee Wee Herman. The reasons I married him twice are blurry, painful, and well behind me. They can be attributed, for the most part, to me having been born and raised in Pine Apple, Alabama, population two: me and him. I truly, at the time (times), didn't know any better.

The court's clerk in Camden told us we couldn't see the docket, because she had no idea where it was. The filings, proceedings, and rulings for my old divorce were in off-site storage, with seven off-site storage facilities to choose from.

"We hired this company out of Montgomery to scan everything into our system and all they did was rip us off." She dropped her mouth wide open and slid her lower jaw back and forth. Pop, pop. "So we dumped it all over town. We don't have room to keep it here, except murders and stuff." She cracked her knuckles, one hand, and then the other. Crunch, crunch. "All's I can tell you is the divorce never was finalized because your husband didn't live in Alabama." We got out of there before she could ask one of us to walk on her back. Snap, snap.

The bad news was, I couldn't break into seven different storage facilities and track down the divorce docket. The good news was, neither could they.

I had to cook up and backdate evidence proving Eddie the Rat lived in Alabama at the time of our divorce, then cook up and backdate evidence of him responding to their original request. Then I had to go back to Camden, slap down the proof, and get my divorce. So I could get married.

From Alabama Power's web site, I recreated an image of a four-by-six manila card payment-due notice. It was the same goldenrod postcard that I'd pulled out of my Pine Apple mailbox a hundred times. I downloaded the old dot-matrix font and produced an electric bill in the amount of $37.14 for March of 2008. I didn't need to track down the perforated card stock to print it on; I only needed a copy. Next, I imaged a cashier's check drawn off Pine Apple Savings and Loan and dated it three weeks later than the date on the postcard invoice. I stamped it PAID by overlaying a grainy stamp image. Last order of business, I downloaded and used a sloppy, masculine, handwritten font to address a #10 envelope to the Court Clerk, Camden County, from Edward Meldrick Crawford, Shady Acres Mobile Home Park, Slip 18, Pine Apple, Alabama. I overlaid the appropriate postage and USPS processing imprints for the day, then gave everything a seven-percent blur for age. Print.

Like falling off a log. It took longer to eat the Pop Tarts than it did to prove Eddie the Rotten Snake in the Grass lived in Pine Apple at the time of our divorce. The difference is it's perfectly within my legal rights as a tax-paying citizen to eat Pop Tarts. Making Eddie Crawford a former Alabama resident who responded to a court summons took breaking several federal laws.

And that's when I smelled someone else breaking the law.

I threw open the office door to let Little Sanders have it, but slammed it closed faster.

Honestly, I might kill Baylor myself.

NINE

There's Lick Skillet, Alabama, and then there's Lickskillet, Alabama. Let me apologize on behalf of the state I was born and raised in for the confusion.

There's a place called the Lick Skillet Pizza Barn and Auction House at the intersection of Butter and Egg Road and Charity Lane in Hazel Green, Alabama, in Madison County. Alabamians mistakenly call the location Lick Skillet. It's not. It's Hazel Green. So it gets confused with the real Lickskillet in DeKalb County, about ninety miles east. The one I'm interested in is the latter, the home of Red, Missy, and Quinn Jennings. Lickskillet is so northeast, it's a jump and a hop from both the Georgia and Tennessee state lines. The closest grocery store is seven miles of mountain pass down to Fort Payne, home of the Country Music Hall of Fame sensations, aptly named Alabama. Surely those guys are retired by now.

Lickskillet is listed as a "populated place," as opposed to a city or township, and backs into the Little River Canyon National Preserve. The area is dense, woodsy, mountainous, almost uninhabited, and a river runs through it, making it a great place to grow Christmas trees. (Right?) Honestly, Google Earth showed three things in, near, or around Lickskillet: the Jennings' mansion, the Jennings' Christmas tree farms, and the Jennings' small private landing strip and huge airplane hangar. You can barely see any of it through the forest terrain. The Jennings' lived way, way off the beaten path. And their son Quinn was on the other side of the door smoking a bowl with Little Sanders and between them, what looked to be a hooker.

If I lost my job over this, and I very well may, Baylor was going down with me.

I'm not so shocked that the boys were smoking pot, even at Thomas Sanders's tender age, I was more shocked about the girl, and I was horrified they were in our offices. Under no circumstances should Little Sanders have the codes to get in and out of our offices. When I left him safe and secure on the sofa two Pop Tarts ago, I left him in a fortress he couldn't exit. I know I certainly didn't give him the code to get out, or back in, for that matter, or for elevator access, also supposedly secure, and I know neither No Hair nor Fantasy had passed out passcodes either. That only left Baylor. Then I remembered what a sneaky little shit Little Sanders is. Maybe I'd let Baylor have three seconds to defend himself before I killed him. Just in case.

Our offices had never been breached, until now.

Did the Jennings kid get a good look at me when I threw open the door? Did the hooker? If they did, did it matter, since Quinn wouldn't recognize me in the casino, because he wouldn't *be* in the casino? And the hooker wasn't in much of a position to point fingers. Where and how did they get weed? How much dirt were Little Sanders and I going to have on each other before this was over? How long was I going to stay locked up in here contemplating my disastrous future? Wasn't it about time for these two boys to go back to school?

#Furious

* * *

@STRIKE_TEAM Countdown till GO—3 days. #StrikeItRich

* * *

"So you're in her good graces."

"I think."

It was two in the morning. Fantasy and I were parked across the street from Elspeth Raiffe's apartment on Cedar Lane Road. Watching. Waiting. On, so far, nothing.

"Honestly, Fantasy," I said, "it's simple. Take good pictures, write clever little captions, make slide shows, put it to music, find a kid who can put it all together, then blast it out to everyone." I trained my thermal-imaging monocular on Elspie's bedroom again, and again, she was still passed out in the bed. Sawing logs. (#Jealous) She hadn't moved a muscle since we'd arrived at midnight. "Every time I did it today, she texted me little cartoons of fireworks, party hats, and smiley faces wearing sunglasses. So I think I'm good."

"It's the new way to communicate," Fantasy said. "We're going to have to get onboard."

"I'm already overboard."

"It is irritating," she said. "The phone dinging every three minutes."

"Tomorrow, she wants me to stop bothering Strike employees and start bothering Strike players."

"I don't want to be you tomorrow." She stretched her long legs. "I want to be me tomorrow." Fantasy had to show up for Bellissimo Barre in just a few short hours, but after that, she got to go home and sleep all day. Her reward for accompanying me tonight. I didn't get a reward for accompanying her.

"It's all set up on something called sweet hoot," I said. "All the little movies of Strike hors d'oeuvres, those chairs, and Baylor's boots? All done."

"Brilliant." Fantasy's head popped up. "Yo. Car."

A dirty white Ford Fusion pulled in and parked in front of Hashtag's ground-level apartment.

"Why would someone drive that car if they didn't have to?"

"Go get yourself a new car, girl," I said to the shadowy figure. "You look like you work for the government."

The woman climbed out and slung a large bag over her shoulder. She paused to beep the car door locks, then walked at a pace and posture suggesting she'd been on a road crew for three shifts.

"They're roommates." Fantasy said as the girl worked the lock on the door to Elspie's apartment.

"Maybe."

We jumped a little when Elspie's bedside lamp lit. Her fuzzy red image crossed the room to meet the other fuzzy red image in the front room.

"Should we be watching this?"

"If you can't handle it," I said, "don't look. And don't discriminate."

"Are you really talking to a black woman about discrimination, Davis?"

It never crossed my mind that anyone would discriminate against Fantasy. Ever.

"If you want to talk to someone about discrimination, Davis, you go talk to Elspie."

Fantasy's right. I should be ashamed. No telling what Elspie dealt with.

One thermal image sat on one side of the room. The other blurry orange blob sat on the other.

"Did we bring the bionic ear?"

"No," I said. "That thing doesn't work anyway. It's just a bunch of murmuring and static."

"We need to learn how to read lips."

I pulled my monocular down and turned to her. "How would we read their lips? Press our noses up against the window?"

"I guess you're right," Fantasy said. "I'm going to press my eyelids up against my eyeballs and rest for a minute. You watch them."

The two women sat across from each other, talking, I presume, for twenty minutes. I'd never seen Hashtag Elspie sit still for that long. Finally, the lights were out, including Fantasy's. "Hey." I gave her a gentle prod. "Wake up and take me home."

"Who's sick?" Fantasy's head spun around and around.

"Reggie?" Reggie is Fantasy's husband. Reginald. Reginald Erb. He's a freelance sports writer. He covers a lot of New Orleans Saints stuff.

I patted her arm. "You're gonna be okay. Start the car. Drive."

I would run the blonde girl's plates after I got some sleep to see if she could shed any light on who gun-toting Elspeth Raiffe might be. So far, it looked like Elspie was simply one of those people who carried a gun. There were no records of her being the victim of a crime, no affiliation with anything radical, and she wasn't from Tennessee. (Always packing, those Tennessee people.) There's a slice of society that carries guns simply because they can. For no apparent or discernible reason. (I do. I carry a gun. But I have a discernable reason—work. Social Media Directors, on the other hand, aren't on any discernible-reason gun list.) The first layer of Elspeth's background check came up clean. The second layer, again, nothing popped. It was the third round of Who's Elspeth that raised all the flags, because there was no third layer, and that's why we were parked outside her apartment in the middle of the night instead of at our respective homes in our nice warm beds.

The Social Security number Elspie was using had only been hers for four years. It had been in the system for sixteen years, used by three different individuals during that time. Digging deeper, I learned that her beaming parents, the same ones photographed with young Elspie at the Grand Canyon and teenage Elspie at Six Flags Over Texas, didn't exist. Nor did the University of Kentucky have anything at all on Hashtag Elspeth but a bachelor's degree in communication. Apparently, she'd walked into the Chancellor's office, gotten her degree, and walked right back out. There wasn't an ounce of proof she'd lived in Lexington, taken a class, attended a basketball game, or eaten even one package of ramen noodles. Which warranted a stakeout.

Fantasy was driving two miles an hour. At this rate, I'd get to bed as the sun was rising.

"How'd we get so busy all of a sudden?" she asked. "What if it had worked out and you had gotten married and you were off on your honeymoon?"

"Well, it didn't, we can't, and I'm not."

"When are you planning on taking care of that?"

"What's today?" I asked. "Tuesday?"

"No, that was yesterday."

"I'm going tomorrow," I said. "First thing."

"Wednesday?"

"No." I looked at her. "Are you awake? If this isn't Tuesday, then it's Wednesday. That makes tomorrow Thursday."

"And what's next?"

Now she was scaring me. "Friday?"

"Strike it Rich!"

I dragged into my condo as if I'd worked four straight shifts on a road crew. It had been a gruelingly long day. I dealt with the pot-smoking teenagers and a high-as-a-kite hooker, then attacked Baylor, who, as it turned out, was off the hook for this one. It was Bianca who'd given Quinn Jennings access to our Super Secret office, and according to Baylor, Missy and Red Jennings (hang onto your hat) *hired* the hooker to babysit their son. But it was Bianca who'd allowed our Super Secret offices to be violated. "It's your fault, David, because *you* didn't answer the phone." Blame David. All the time, blame David. "What was I supposed to do? I'm homeless! I can't entertain *children*."

What. A. Day. I woke up with the dark cloud of my PRIOR EXISTING MARRIAGE looming over me, which I'd worried about all the way through Bellissimo Ballet (#Overslept! #Sorry @ElspieBabie) Then I'd met with and still didn't confess to my boss about the alleged shooting in the lobby. Next it was Bianca, who demanded I sufficiently scare the living daylights out of the incompetent home furnishings people or find myself a new job.

On to her pot-smoking teenage son letting strangers and hookers in our offices, which interrupted me trying to get divorced, then the next eight hours devoted to gun-slinging Hashtag Elspie. At the end of the day, which was well into the beginning of the next day, when I finally walked in my own door, I undressed in a trail down the hall. I climbed into the bed beside sleepy Bradley and vowed to never get out of the bed again.

I got out of the bed.

I ran the Ford Fusion plates. The blonde's name was Brianna Strother. She drove a government-issue looking car for a very good reason, a reason that might shed some light on why her roommate packed a pistol. Brianna was FATF. She worked for the Federal Action Task Force.

*   *   *

@LuckyStrikePlayers #WelcomeToTheBellissimo #WhereDreams #ComeTrue #StrikeItRich Let the winning begin in 2 days!

*   *   *

No Hair and I had coffee at his place Thursday morning before the chickens were up and before I took off for enemy territory. His office was an extension of his physical person—large, threatening, and neat as a pin. He had a circular electric tie rack beside his desk, and everything smelled like his car, leather and spice. I've never been a guest in No Hair's home, but I'd venture a guess that the Man Cave Business stops right here. No Hair's wife, Grace, is porcelain-doll feminine, and I bet somebody has to leave his big shoes at the door and use little doily coasters under his drinks.

I didn't frequent No Hair's office. Maybe once, twice a month. Fantasy and I were careful not to be seen in the same disguise in the same place twice, and it was easier for No Hair to come to us downstairs in our basement offices, where we didn't have to hide and had more room, or for all of us to meet in Mr. Sanders's office when he was out of town. Mr. Sanders had been way *in* town for several weeks in a row, which was nice. Things ran smoothly with him at the helm.

He and Bianca were leaving the property soon to take Little Sanders to Million Air, the private airport in Gulfport, and see him off for his return to school. Thank the Lord. Bianca had come *this* close to asking me to dress up as her and say goodbye to her son at the airport. *This* close.

No, I didn't rat on Little Sanders. To Mr. Sanders, anyway. I'm still avoiding Mr. Sanders lest I get roped into another conversation about the shootout in the lobby business. I ripped Little Sanders a new one, started ten sentences with, "If I *ever...*", then tossed it to No Hair. Let No Hair throw his little butt under the bus, because to my knowledge, Little Sanders didn't have any dirt on No Hair. Thomas didn't rat me out on the small gun incident, or for slamming his head into a car hood, or for making him piggyback me up twenty flights of stairs, so I didn't go straight to his dad with his juvenile delinquency.

Now we were even, and all bets were off. I don't know if No Hair turned him in or not. I do know if No Hair threatened him with his eyeballs, the Laser Lock, Little Sanders won't even unclench for five years, much less burn a fat one with a prostitute.

After sleeping until noon on Wednesday, then spending the rest of the day in control central hacking through NSA-worthy firewalls to put these suspicious players we were suddenly surrounded by in their respective places, I was going over everything with No Hair before I ducked out for a divorce.

"There are two things I'm concerned with, No Hair." Actually, at the moment there were three, but we'd had all the conversation about my marital status I wanted to. I was dressed in Social Media Assistant wear, so I could go straight to my Strike job when I returned. My hair was Chocolate Covered Bing Cherry and my eyes were, unfortunately, purple. I was going back to my old boring green and blue camouflage contacts as soon as this deal was over. Boring was easier than all the stares I was receiving. Lip-curled backing-up staring. My appearance was supposed to deflect attention, not invite it.

"Let's hear it." No Hair's tie was a Sudoku puzzle.

I flipped through my notes and passed him one of the photographs Fantasy had taken several days ago during orientation. "These women are sisters, No Hair, Missy Jennings and Cassidy Banking Williams."

"Not good."

A casino employee and their immediate family are never good.

"I picked up Cassidy's trail ten years ago. She's thirty-two years old and lived in Vegas for ten years before moving to Biloxi with the Strike team a few months ago. She's from northeast Alabama, born and bred. It looks like she took a weekend trip to Vegas when she graduated from college and never came home. She got a job at the Montecito as a cashier, and worked her way up to cage manager. A few years later she was promoted to in-house accounts, which is when the Jennings began visiting her in Vegas."

No Hair's chair squealed. "So far, I'm not overly impressed."

"Maybe this will help."

I passed him a mini spreadsheet. "Look at the Jennings's reported income before they started going to Vegas. Then after." Jennings Tree Farms, on paper, hadn't made a dime. Ever. The first few years, startup, were understandable.

What defied reasonable explanation was that from the moment Cassidy Banking began handling her sister's casino accounting, the Jennings got a big bump in lifestyle, and all in the form of casino winnings. Lots and lots of casino winnings.

No Hair studied it, then looked up.

"Okay," he said, "they're bad at farming and good at gambling. The only thing I see is the sister shouldn't be handling the account."

"That's just for starters," I said. "There are several other things off, No Hair. For one, the Christmas tree farm takes up half a mountain. Red Jennings pays more in property taxes than he reports in income from the farm. No one keeps an unprofitable business around this many years. For two, these millions and millions they've won at the Montecito?"

"Yeah?"

"One trip a year." I held up a single finger.

No Hair looked up. "One six-month long trip a year?"

"No," I said. "One weekend a year."

"No way," No Hair said. "The odds of winning this much," he shook the sheet of paper, "in a single weekend are astronomical. And to do it this many years in a row would be like winning the lottery every year, buying only one ticket."

"Exactly."

"So what kind of casino favors is Cassidy Banking doing for her sister and brother-in-law?"

"I guess we need to find out, No Hair."

"Red flag."

"Bright red," I agreed. "That's our first deal, and I'm concerned. I think we need to watch all three of them, starting yesterday, and I think there needs to be a ton of distance between Little Sanders and the Jennings kid before Thomas gets caught up in something we can't get him out of. But in a way," I said, "I'm more worried about Elspeth and her government-issue roommate than I am this whole Jennings business."

"Don't get ahead of yourself, Davis," No Hair said. "We don't know the relationship between these two women. It might not have a thing to do with us. The Federal Action Task Force is an international organization. Elzbath's roommate is probably tracking down money launderers, most likely under the umbrella of terrorist financing, and it doesn't look like she's doing it here." He pointed at the top of his desk. "Last I checked, terrorists don't take blackjack breaks."

We had plenty of terrorists here. Not *that* kind of terrorist, but you show me an old lady being separated from her slot machine and I'll show you a violent fanatical extremist. I ran Brianna Strother through our facial-recognition software all afternoon yesterday and didn't get a hit. I even did weird searches, like iris pattern, nose slope, jaw curvature, and in the end, Brianna Strother simply wasn't in our system. No one with her faceprint had *ever* walked through the doors of the Bellissimo.

"We could put a tail on her," No Hair said, "and most likely, find her working at one of the ports. Ninety-million tons of cargo come in and out of these ports."

True. Last year, the Port of Gulfport alone received a million tons of bananas. Chiquita trucks ruled the roads around here. That number didn't even include the bananas coming into Mobile, New Orleans, and points between. "How could bananas finance terrorism?"

He looked confused, then said, "Let's not get off track, here, Davis."

It happens.

"They could be," he said, "just friends. Or roommates. Or whatevers."

"I'd go with that, No Hair, if Elspeth alarms weren't going off all over the place."

"Such as?"

"Such as," I passed him a copy of Elspie's employment application, "I didn't know until I finally found her employee file that she wasn't a part of the Vegas Montecito team."

"Sure she is."

"No, No Hair. She's not. She went to work the day they did, but she's out of New Orleans. Not Vegas."

"What are you thinking?"

"I'm thinking Elspeth's federal, too."

We sat silently while that sank all the way in.

"Well, Levi Newman hired her himself." No Hair pointed to the signature on the application he was holding. I passed him a second employee application, exact same information, but this one signed by Richard Sanders himself.

"I'll be damned."

"She snuck in the backdoor, No Hair."

"I knew something was up with that girl."

"You were right."

"And if you're right," No Hair said, "and she's federal, she sure has a good cover."

"Doesn't she?" #PurpleEyedWithEnvy

"If Elzbath's federal, and the roommate is FATF, and they're working together" he said, "then we have someone coming in on a big-time watch list."

"Exactly."

"Did you run these Jennings people through Homeland Security?"

"And the Terrorists Watch List," I said. "They're not on either."

"Are there any international players coming in for Strike?"

"No," I said, "as far as I know, there aren't. But I'm looking harder and I've set up alerts."

We quietly contemplated scary stuff.

No Hair pushed away from his desk. (Meeting almost over.) "Let's not jump the gun here, Davis. It could be exactly what it looks like. Which right now isn't much."

I agreed. The Jennings may be cheats, and we took down cheats every day of the week. I could catch and apprehend Cassidy Banking in my sleep. And I totally bought into the reasonable explanation as to why Brianna Strother would be in our neck of the woods. (Bananas.)

More curious, and a larger problem, is if Elspeth actually is a federal employee. In what capacity? Why is she here?

I have a funny feeling. Which could be the low-grade nausea I've been dragging around since I found out I've been married to Eddie Crawford the Rat Bastard all these years. But something going down at the Bellissimo was definitely adding to it. A life rule of mine: Never ignore a funny feeling. Another life rule of mine: Don't tell No Hair my suspicions are based on funny feelings. Historically, he wasn't impressed.

"Let me ask you something, No Hair."

We paused at the door.

"Why'd you put me on Elspeth to begin with?"

His hand dropped from the doorknob.

"You suspected something was going on with her, right?"

He rubbed his whiskery jaw. A No Hair move that meant he was choosing his words carefully, knowing if he misled me or withheld information and it came to light later, I'd feed them to him. He said, "I had a funny feeling."

*   *   *

I had a James Bond pen.

It looked like a normal Bic, something you'd accidentally swipe from a cashier, but this abnormal Bic had a GPS tracking device in it that fed straight to my cell phone. Time was a wastin', and I didn't have time to go through hours and hours of surveillance feed tracking Hashtag Elspie's every move, nor did I have time to traipse through the employee parking garage three miles away and tag her car.

I love my job. I love the people, the casino, the clothes, the work, and I love the cool spy toys.

Elspie would be supervising plié pulses about now. I made my way to the rehearsal room behind the theater to (drop a cool spy toy in her big black bag) make up a reason why I'd be off property for the next five hours. No, I did not plan on telling her the truth.

I pushed through the swinging door to see everyone in workout clothes, but no one working out. The ballet music was on. Fantasy was stretched across the slick wood floor sleeping. Two or three waitresses were huddled in a corner drinking coffee and gossiping. Several more were scattered around the room poking on their phones. Baylor was in the middle of the dance floor on his knees straddling a blonde waitress splayed out beneath him, either giving her a back rub or counting her freckles. I couldn't tell.

"Where's Elspeth?" I asked.

"She didn't show." Fantasy only moved her lips. The rest of her stayed asleep.

"You," I pointed. "Gold cowboy boots. Get off that girl. You're coming with me."

Baylor looked at me as if I were interrupting brain surgery. "I'm not done here."

"Oh, yes you are."

* * *

@LuckyStrikePlayers Are you ready to #StrikeItRich? Everyone ready for the VIP #StrikeParty tomorrow night?

TEN

Smerle T. Webb got his law degree off the back of a box of Froot Loops. There's no other reasonable explanation, because there's no way an institute of higher learning would have agreed to him practicing law if they'd actually met him. Or maybe Smerle T. had it together way back when, and it was a Teflon, or an oxygen-deprivation situation, that happened *after* he got his law degree, rendering him barely able to sit up and feed himself, much less practice law. Thankfully, the good people of Pine Apple, Alabama didn't need that much legal advice, because the only trick we had up our sleeve was Smerle T., and he couldn't cross the street without instigating a four-car pileup and three fistfights. He certainly couldn't mediate any manner of dispute or adequately represent anyone in a court of law. Smerle T. was a constant *source* of conflict all over Wilcox County, and his courtroom deficiencies were forever landing his clients in more trouble once they got in front of the judge than they ever were to begin with. Smerle T. had a lucrative real estate side business going on, too, constantly stirring it up between neighbors, then raking in all the closing costs when he talked everyone into playing musical chairs with their mobile homes. He would wait awhile, then stoke the fires again, and talk everyone back where they were to begin with. Smerle T. stayed busy. If you think that's something and your life insurance is paid up, you ought to make an appointment with Pine Apple's only physician, Dr. Cliff Kizzy. I went to him once for a quick tetanus shot after I had an unfortunate collision with a possum trap and almost lost my arm. To the tetanus shot. Not the possum trap.

His secretary answered. "JoElla, it's Davis Way. I need to talk to Smerle T."

"He says he's not in."

"Tell him I need to sue someone."

"Holt on."

Only in Pine Apple do you holt on to sue someone.

I heard him suck in a huge breath. "Smerle T. Webb, the law is on my side."

"Smerle, it's Davis Way."

"Well, if this isn't my lucky day. Davis Way! How in the wide world are you, young lady?"

"I want to talk to you about my grandmother's divorce."

"Hold your horses, there, Davis. You know I can't discuss ongoing litigation with you. I don't care if it is your grandmother."

I heard clicks and a ding. Smerle T. was winding up the avocado green kitchen timer he kept on his desk for billing purposes. "Smerle," I said, "I am not your client. Do not charge me for this phone call."

"Time is money, young lady. And you are my client. I've got a file on you right here."

"Yeah, Smerle? Well, you're fired. I'm on my way to get my file."

"Now, you holt on there one minute, sassy pants."

"Don't you sassy pants me, Smerle. I've had it with you."

"I am an innocent party here! All I did was answer the phone, and I'm getting fired?"

"Get my paperwork together, Smerle. I'll be there in an hour."

My driver didn't look overly enthusiastic about stopping by my attorney's office. "It's on the way," I told him. "Ten minutes, tops."

"Yippee," Baylor deadpanned. He added one drop of enthusiasm and asked, "What was the point of that exercise?"

I yawned. "I need that file without him going around town telling everyone I asked for it." I yawned again. "Baylor? I'm going to rest my eyes for ten minutes, okay?"

When I woke up, we were in Birmingham.

* * *

I bolted upright, searched for landmarks, then screamed. "You missed the exit!" Baylor was drumming on the steering wheel with Beats earbuds plugged into his brains. I yanked out the one I could reach and the air was flooded with rap music. "You missed the exit, Baylor! By about a hundred miles!"

He pulled the other earbud out. "My bad."

"You think?" This is the guy who No Hair assures me has my back.

I looked at my watch. Noon. I looked at my phone. Fourteen text messages, seven missed calls, and one voicemail. "Pull over, Baylor. Let me figure out where we are." Thirty seconds later, on a sigh, "I didn't mean pull over on the shoulder, Baylor. I meant pull over at the next exit."

I swear.

The next exit was Trussville. We were on the *other* side of Birmingham.

Baylor spotted, pulled into, parked, and made a run for the border. Every single day of his life, the boy eats a #3 Special from Taco Bell: three Taco Supremes.

I speed dialed No Hair. "You're not going to believe this."

"I'm sitting at my computer watching the dot that is you, Davis, and I will believe it, but let me guess. You decided to drive to the place where the Christmas tree people live and check it out since it was right up the road."

I watched Baylor in the rear-view mirror crossing the parking lot with a drink the size of an Igloo cooler dispenser. "You guessed it." It wasn't a bad idea. We were only an hour away from Fort Payne, thank you very much, Baylor. And it was a better idea than telling No Hair I'd been sleeping on the job while Baylor drove the brand-new Bellissimo-issue Town Car, which I'd signed out as Amy Medina without putting Baylor on the driver list.

I drove, because I knew where we were going, because of insurance and liability, and because Baylor was busy squirting Fire

Sauce on his tacos. I lectured while he ate: responsibility, sexually transmitted diseases, following directions, punctuality, respect, reliability, flossing daily for gum health. "I worry, Baylor, that one of these days, we're going to get in a really tight spot, and I'm going to need you, and you'll be off in La La Land. You've got to be more *alert*. You're missing the forest for the trees. I have to be able to count on you."

His only response: "I heard you were getting married."

I was exhausted from trying to talk him into growing up.

One right off the main drag in Fort Payne onto North Valley Avenue, then one left in the direction of Lickskillet, and we were at the base of the Cumberland Plateau.

"Someone lives up there?" Baylor asked.

"We'll see."

The road was steep with hairpin turns and one wide gravel lane. I couldn't see past the first curve, and the tree cover was so dense I had to take off my sunglasses.

"What's that ladder?" Baylor asked.

"Did you grow up in downtown Philly, Baylor? That's a tree stand. Deer hunters get in it and shoot Bambi's mother."

"That's so not cool for the deer."

"And that's a hunting blind," I pointed, "same purpose. The hunter can see the deer, the deer can't see the hunter. And that's," I craned to get a better look, "I'm not sure what that is." It looked like a park ranger watchtower. After the tenth steep curve, elevation Mt. Everest, we finally saw the edges of the tree farm.

"What the hell is this place?"

"It's a Christmas tree farm, Baylor. Can't you smell the Christmas trees?"

He lowered his window. "Uh, Davis. I need to smell one up close and personal."

"Are you kidding me? Could you not have said something back in civilization? Are you *twelve*?"

He ran over the river and through the woods in the direction of yet another elaborate tree stand. This one, a cabin on stilts in the middle of a Christmas forest. The deer around here didn't stand a chance.

The trees formed thick lines on both sides of the road. They were planted in a modified zigzag line to accommodate the terrain, and they digressed in size. The trees closest to the road looked ready to decorate. The trees behind were progressively smaller; they stair stepped down in size for as far as I could see. The only thing that struck me as odd was the one-lane gravel road leading to all this Christmas cheer. Transport had to be an absolute nightmare. And what happened when one truck was going to the farm and another was coming from? There was no way two flatbed trucks could share this road.

I rolled down my window, and a cross-breeze of Christmas Day filled the car. Then I heard, "DRIVE! DRIVE! DRIVE!" and Baylor filled the car. All of Baylor. He dove headlong through the passenger window with such momentum, that he'd have flown straight out my window and landed in the gravel on the other side of the car had my body and the steering wheel not stopped him.

"GET OUT OF HERE!" he screamed into my lap.

My hands were in the air and I was screaming bloody murder. He had me pinned down and he broke at least twenty five of my ribs as he tried to right himself and get to the gun at his hip.

"What the holy hell, Baylor!"

Just then, a loud spray of gravel caught the passenger side of the car. Baylor was halfway out the window returning gravel.

We were taking fire.

I made a dangerously fast three-point turn that stirred up enough dust for cover, but the shooter knew exactly where we were. I tore down that mountain in a hail of bullets. I was as low in the seat as I could go; I could taste metal; I had it on the floorboard; I straight-lined it through the curves. Baylor grabbed for and dumped my purse, then two seconds later, he was out the window again emptying my gun.

I covered the seven miles of vertical mountain pass in six minutes. We'd lost the rear window, the back bumper, and the car's electrical system.

On cue, the sky opened up, and a monsoon rain descended out of nowhere.

I backed into a self-serve carwash on the edge of town for shelter, threw it in park, hid behind one hand, and batted for Baylor with the other. "Are you okay? Are you hit?"

"I've never. Seen. So much pot. In my life."

"What?" I was panting. It might be tomorrow before I caught my breath.

"They're growing, Davis. Right past the trees. It's not a Christmas farm, it's a pot farm. There's a shit-ton of pot in those woods. Pot plants as big as the Christmas trees. There's a million dollars of pot in those Christmas trees."

*   *   *

A sad truth about Alabama: A car on the interstate with a bright blue duct-taped tarp for a back window, missing its bumper, license plate, three hubcaps and both side mirrors, riddled with bullet holes, side panels crushed, driven in the pouring down rain with the windows wide open by two people wearing Roll Tide rain ponchos, didn't attract attention. Sad, sad.

"I'm never coming back here," Baylor said.

We finally drove out of the weather after the first of our three-hour trek to Pine Apple. Baylor held it in the road while I climbed out of the poncho.

"Uh, Davis," he said. "You might want to check out your hair."

We had no mirrors whatsoever. I don't know what happened to the rear-view mirror. I pulled a handful of my hair in front of my face to watch the Chocolate Covered Bing Cherry temporary color drip into my lap. This couldn't be pretty. Note to self: Don't get spray color wet, then cook it under a plastic poncho hood for an hour.

"Check me over there, Baylor."

Baylor hung out the passenger window. "You're good."

When we took exit 128 to Pine Apple, I said, "Listen, Baylor. It'd probably be best if I don't run into anyone I know. Considering."

He surveyed me and nodded agreement. "So you don't want to try to ditch this car?"

"I didn't say that."

Smerle T.'s office was above the hardware store on Main Street. We took the back roads, which weren't really roads at all. We took the back paths, and got rid of what was left of the paint on the Town Car. I rolled it to a stop behind the hardware store, then pulled the wet glob of Roll Tide poncho back on. So no one would recognize me. "See that car?" I pointed to a red Dodge Dart a hundred yards away. "There's no doubt the keys are in it. Get all our stuff, get it running, aim it at Main Street," I pointed, "and I'll be back in three minutes."

I climbed the back steps and quietly entered through the law office's kitchenette. Smerle T.'s part-time secretary and full-time mistress JoElla was in the front room watching "The Young and The Beautiful" on an old portable television that looked like it weighed forty pounds. It had long silver antennas.

"JoElla? It's Davis Way. Where's Smerle T.?"

She didn't tear her eyes away from the grainy daytime drama. "He's at your daddy's office," she said, "complaining about you."

"Did he leave anything for me?"

"He said," and here she finally turned, got one look at me, and said, "holy crap Jesus, Davis. What happened to you?"

"Where's that file?"

Her mouth hung wide open as she admired my new fugitive look.

There was a single stapled stack of papers on the desk between JoElla and the television. I took a giant leap, snatched it, then bolted for the back door. "Good to see you, JoElla!"

"He said you couldn't take it, Davis!" She was on my heels. "Gimme that back here before I call the police!"

I turned at the kitchenette door and let her think about how stupid that was. Her brow furrowed as she considered calling my father to have him arrest me for taking my own divorce file from my lawyer's office. I held it out. "Here, JoElla. Take it. But I'm calling Dusty." Everyone in Wilcox County knew JoElla was doing everything but secretarial work for Smerle T. Except Jo Ella's husband Dusty.

She looked like she'd seen a ghost. She reached for my arm instead of the file. "One of your eyes is purple, Davis," she whispered.

Baylor revved the engine. I bolted down the rickety steps, poncho flying. JoElla shouted after me, "Smerle T. said if you showed up you couldn't take that!"

Did he say anything about his car?

*   *   *

We parked the Dodge Dart at a meter on the street in Camden, a block past the courthouse.

The same court clerk was behind the desk who'd been there when Bradley and I were here Monday. She took note of our disheveled appearances, stretched her arms wide, then flipped them in a way that hyperextended her elbows. The noise was excruciating. "Rough day?" She rolled her arms back into their sockets.

I passed her the Eddie the Ass paperwork I'd cooked up, plus the divorce decree I'd swiped from Smerle T.'s office, and she studied it all way too long. So long, that I thought I'd lived through being gunned down in Lickskillet only to be locked up in Camden. I really should consider staying out of Alabama altogether and let things cool off. My phone buzzed. I gave it a glance. "Excuse me," I said. "I need to step out in the hall and take this." I gave Baylor a stay-put-and-watch-her look.

"Daddy."

"Honey." Daddy sounded tired. "Are you alive?"

"Yes."

"Long story?"

"Yes."

"When are you going to bring Smerle T.'s car back, and do you want me to send this one you left to Montgomery for processing?"

"I'll get Smerle's car back to him as soon as I can," I said. "Tell him I said sorry, and don't send the whole Town Car to the crime lab. If you could, Daddy, pull a slug out of it and have them run it." It's a miracle upon a miracle that I wasn't able to reach up and pull a slug out of the back of my head for processing.

"Where *were* you, Sweet Pea?" Daddy asked. "What in the world happened?"

I glanced up and down the hall for nosy people, then through the doorway where the clerk was still studying the paperwork with a stern look on her face. "I was in DeKalb County, Daddy, and those people are crazy as all get-out."

"Davis, stay out of DeKalb County starting right now."

(No shit.)

"There's a DEA task force sting going down there, right outside of Fort Payne, and you don't want mixed up in that."

No, I did not.

Wait a minute.

Had a division of the United States Federal Government just about killed me and Baylor?

"Good to know, Daddy. I love you." I hung up my phone because the clerk had picked up hers. I rushed back in. "Do you have me ready?"

She dropped the phone and gave me the evil eye. "Here's the problem." She craned her neck until it clicked. Then the other way. Click, click. "This isn't the address we sent the notification to. See here?" She flipped two pieces of paper and pushed them to me. "This here says Shady Acres, slip eighteen? But we sent the notice to Shady Acres slip thirty-two. These two should match." She bounced a finger between the two sheets of paper. "I wonder why they don't."

"I have no idea," I said. "Not a clue."

"Something tells me you do." She picked up the forged notice and held it up to the fluorescent lights. My life flashed before my eyes. As it had been doing. All. Day. Long.

"Do you know who lives in slip thirty-two?" she asked.

I do. I certainly do. "No. Not a clue."

"That's who got this notice." She pushed up her sweater sleeves. One at a time. She bent over the counter and got in my face. "And that's who I need to be talking to. You have whoever lives at this address here give me a ringy-dingy, let that person tell me your husband lived in Alabama at the time of the divorce, and then I'll try to help you." She shook the forged document in the forger's face. "It doesn't make any sense that the one you're bringing in here isn't the one we sent. Where'd you get this?"

I snatched it out of her hands, scooped up my unfinished divorce, and ran before she could study it, or me, one more second.

"What just happened there?" Baylor was on my heels. We were ten feet from the Dodge Dart. "Who lives at the other address?"

"My ex-ex-mother-in-law," I panted. "Bea."

*   *   *

Baylor and I took the back roads from Camden to Biloxi at a clip, tearing through LeMoyne, Saraland, and Pritchard, but backing off when we crossed into Mississippi, because I'd have to jump through too many hoops to get out of a reckless-endangerment-while-driving-a-stolen-car-citation in a state where my daddy wasn't on the payroll. We made it in the doors of 3B as Fantasy was leaving.

"Oh, holy mother." Fantasy dropped everything she was holding. "What happened to you two? Baylor, did you beat Davis up?"

"No."

"Davis, did you beat Baylor up?"

"No."

"You lost one of your purple contacts."

"I know."

Baylor dropped into one of the bean bag chairs. "Those Jennings people are pot farmers, Fantasy. They have a whole mountain of pot. A whole mountain."

Her eyes popped open in shock, then narrowed in concentration as she thought about it, then the pieces fell into place. "That explains why they'd hire a hooker to babysit their kid."

Baylor couldn't make the connection. "How?"

"That stuff kills brain cells, Baylor."

He tried to look up at his own head.

"Is he lying?" she asked me. "Is there really that much pot?"

"Yes," I said, "there is." And Baylor was all but tipped over backwards, still trying to look up at his own head.

"I thought you two went to Pine Apple to get a divorce."

"We did," I said.

"How'd that turn out?"

"We're still married."

ELEVEN

@LuckyStrikePlayers #StrikePeek @9tonight #You'reGonnaLoveIt!
#WaitTillYouSeeTHIS!

* * *

Friday morning all drug farmers, dingbat country lawyers, social
media assistants, artillery support, car thieves, and federal agents
chasing bananas had to take a breather, because Bianca Sanders
was moving out of Jay Leno's place. Three construction crews
working three shifts alongside seven decorators, two project
coordinators, four home stagers, and a representative from
Sotheby's in Santa Fe had, in just minutes outside of a week, put
the Sanders home back together again.

It's truly amazing what money can buy.

Physically, Bianca didn't move a thing but her lazy butt to a
limo, which took her to New Orleans for the day, away from the
stress of the move, while Fantasy and I were "entrusted with her
beloved possessions" and charged with "everything in its place by
three chop chop", and we were babysitting the dogs, because their
trainers, handlers, and groomers were upstairs installing their new
rooms. I ordered them each a T-bone steak, then lured them into a
closet. For their own safety. Lest they get accidentally packed.

"Shouldn't we cut them up?" Fantasy asked.

"The steaks?"

"Yes, Davis. The steaks."

"That's half the fun for dogs, isn't it?"

"I don't know," she said. "Those steaks are bigger than those dogs."

"It'll be fine." I told them to take naps after lunch, they growled at me, I closed the door.

We wandered around packing everything that wasn't nailed down.

"Let me ask you something, Davis. Shouldn't this be Jimmy Fallon's place now?"

We had a canvas laundry cart the size of a refrigerator in the middle of the room and we were lobbing things into it willy-nilly. "Yes." I sailed a hardback Mommy Porn how-to reference manual of Bianca's through the air and got two points. "To hell with Jay Leno."

"Davis!"

"He's moving on to another stage in his life, Fantasy. And in doing so, he has to give up everything? Even this place?"

"First of all," she stretched her back, "this suite will forever be known as Jay Leno's place, okay? Are you happy now? And second of all, are you still singing that song? No one is discriminating against you and I wasn't discriminating against Jay Leno."

I had a Louis Vuitton tote in my hand, probably worth a million dollars, stuffed with two million dollars' worth of dog clothes that had just been returned from the cleaners laundered, ironed, folded, and labeled in teeny boxes. "I honestly think the minute I get married my job is going to get to this right here." I shook the Louis Vuitton. "I will be in charge of the dog clothes. I'll be put out to pasture just like Jay Leno. I'll be nothing but Bianca's slave and you'll be mine."

"I'm already yours," she said. "Watch this." Fantasy walked to a house phone and ordered us a pitcher of mimosas and several trays of food. "Whatever looks good. We're in the mood for brunch. And chocolate," she said. "Chocolate brunch."

She dialed housekeeping next. She had them pick up the laundry bin stuffed full of Bianca's trinkets and sex manuals and deliver it all upstairs to the newly remodeled Sanders residence with a note to the Sotheby's person: *Bianca said put all this up where it goes.*

We spent the next several hours at Jay Leno's indoor pool.

"These mimosas are all orange juice." Fantasy polished off another one.

"We'd better order more." I did the honors.

"We need our vitamin C."

Two pitchers of mimosas later, the subject rolled back around to my irrational wedding anxiety.

"You promise me, Davith?" Fantasy was propped on an elbow, stretched out on one of Jay Leno's oversized pool loungers, when her chin fell off her fist. She stayed there, horizontal, and asked, "This has nothing to do with Bwadly? Nothing'sh happened?"

"Crush my eyes." I was deep in another one of Jay's oversized loungers. "Poke my heart out."

"Then whass the problem?"

The problem was nothing and the problem was everything.

We may have accidentally dozed off when our phones woke us almost two hours later, dinging with regularly scheduled Strike It Rich propaganda, this time a mini movie, made up entirely of photobombs of almost-naked waitresses, courtesy of Little Sanders.

"Are those my boobs?" Fantasy was still on her back holding the phone above her head. "This is a good movie, Davis. X-rated, but good."

"Thank you." I eyed the three empty mimosa pitchers. "Did we drink all that?"

Fantasy was gently prodding about her head. "My face is numb."

"What time is it?"

"Two o'clock."

We both bolted up and said it together. "The dogs!"

I peeked in the closet, then slammed the door closed.

"Davis. Are those dogs dead?"

I couldn't blink. Or breathe. "Not too much."

She pushed me aside, cracked the door, and peeked for herself.

She closed it as quickly as I had, then turned to me. "You're bathing them."

When Bianca found us at Jay's indoor pool, she clapped gloved hands to her face. "My babies! Swimmy-swimmy! Puppy stroke!"

We called housekeeping about the closet.

*   *   *

Then I went swimmy-swimmy.

My hair caught fire. I jumped into the Bellissimo swimming pool to put it out in front of five hundred people, several dozen of them representing news outlets, so Bianca Sanders's humiliation was well documented. GulfCoastNews(dot)com was first, posting the video of me tearing into the night with a foot of flames trailing from my head, arcing through the air in a cocktail dress and a perfect cannonball, then landing in the deep end of the Bellissimo swimming pool with a great big splash. It got seven thousand views on YouTube before we could get it down. I missed it at the time, because I was in the pool putting my hair out, but my Amy Medina phone had received instructions from Hashtag Elspie, somewhere close enough to know what was going on but not at the party, to Snapchat a photo only, because we wanted to be part of the solution, not part of the problem. (#Snapchat?)

The first problem was the dress Bianca had me in. She's so cutting edge, she has to have it right off the runway, and I pray the day doesn't come when naked is the new black, because she'll have me going out in public naked. When I asked her to reconsider the dress, which was hideous and surely already a fashion don't, she said, "No. YOLO, David."

(It's Davis. And what she constantly missed was that she wasn't taking fashion risks based on the fact that she only lived once, when she was, in fact, living a double wardrobe life—her own, which was almost solid black, and through me, which was almost solid ridiculous.)

The dress was a peacock blue number. The fabric was a

metallic Jacquard, and very little of it. It had peek-a-boo cutouts everywhere, so the only parts of my body that were covered were the ones required by law. The dress had no sides. Or front. Or back. And I had no leverage with her at the time, because she was aggravated with me already for being late. Any other time, I could go downstairs and change into something fit for public consumption from the stash of Bianca clothes I kept in the office, but there wasn't a stash. She'd confiscated it days ago.

"If you'd been here on time, David, I might have considered it. Now it's too late for me to choose something else; I'm no longer in the mood. Wear the Giambattista, and right this minute, before I'm so late Richard gets upset with me."

Bianca Casimiro Sanders believed in arriving fashionably late or not at all, so her giving me a lecture on tardiness when I'd run in panting and apologizing was absurd. I sat through the sermon—she paced back and forth in front of me in a silk lounging getup covered in black feathers—wondering where the logic was in wasting what little time I didn't have to get ready screaming at me.

"Are you even listening to me, David?"

"It's Davis."

"An hour of my life is lost waiting on you."

I was twenty minutes late. Some days, like today, when I have three pitchers of mimosas for breakfast, I lose track of time.

She made several other moot points, and I wondered, for the millionth time, how Mr. Sanders stayed married to her. Her father owned this casino, and that had to be a big part of it, and then there was Little Sanders, the teenage terror tie that binds. From the outside looking in, though, it appeared that Mr. Sanders genuinely loved Bianca. He'd certainly put up with enough of her loose interpretation of their marital vows through the years. And they touched each other often, subtle stuff. He was often amused by her behavior. The rest of us weren't.

"My time gone." Her hand fluttered through the air. "Never to be retrieved."

I took my lumps.

"If I start smoking again and it's your fault," she threatened, "*you* will be the one going under the knife. Not me."

See? Not only is it not funny, it makes no sense, but Mr. Sanders would turn his head and smile at that.

"I've had a terrible afternoon." She peered into her gigantic martini glass. "Gianna and Ghita don't feel well."

Too much swimmy-swimmy.

A feather escaped Bianca's robe, and she batted through the air trying to catch it, sloshing martini everywhere. "Angela is ready for you. Angela has *been* ready for you for hours, David. You've totally wasted her life, too. Now, shoo." Bianca waved me into her recently restored dressing room. Our hair and makeup woman Angela was, as Bianca promised, waiting. We exchanged a "she's-so-batshit-crazy" look, and I plopped into the director's chair.

"Have I wasted your life, Angela?"

Our eyes met in the mirror. "Totally, David. My whole life."

I found Angela several months ago, because I got tired of Bianca complaining that I was misrepresenting her. (Well, Bianca, stop sitting around here all day chasing feathers and go represent yourself.) She wanted me to have better hair, better makeup, and looser morals. I began sneaking Angela, who I knew from the salon on the mezzanine level, into our inner-sanctum to doll me up when I did my Bianca duties and was immediately caught. "David, I know you're not responsible for your hair tonight, because when left to your own devices, it looks as if a feral cat has attacked your head. Who did my hair for you?"

I was forced to produce Angela.

Bianca claimed her as her own. She took total credit for Angela's genius with makeup brushes and total control of her life. I warned Angela to keep a nice distance between herself and Bianca, but by that time, Bianca had already given Angela a CEO salary, a baby Mercedes, a set of Bottega Veneta luggage to roll the makeup around in, and unlimited shopping passes at Sephora and Neimans. So now poor Angela was Bianca's bitch.

Tonight was the VIP soft opening of the Strike It Rich casino.

It would be attended by local dignitaries, media, and Alabama marijuana farmers. No gaming until the official opening tomorrow. Tonight was gawking at the gold waitstaff and test driving the incredible chairs. We'd be showing off *future*Gaming to the media, city dignitaries, and to the other dozen Biloxi casinos which had been issued five passes each so they could wonder how we did it. From the Grand Palace Casino, we were welcoming the president, the casino manager, and the heads of customer relations, marketing, and legal counsel—Bradley Cole.

The star of the show, the biggest showoff of them all, Bianca Casimiro Sanders, was running late. And it was all my fault.

Angela waved all her magic wands, sprayed me blonde, then pulled my hair half up with the rest in loopy gold curls down my back, loaded my face with makeup, then, ta-da! I stepped past the mirrors to slip into something appropriate, took one look at the extreme inappropriateness dangling off a silk padded hanger, and almost passed out. Surely not. The first hour of this shindig was on a piazza between the Bellissimo pool and the ocean. Closer to the ocean, but down a twenty-foot seawall to get there. People were married on the piazza all the time, in the *summer*. I would literally freeze to death in the two ounces of blue fabric Bianca had chosen for the evening's festivities. Had the woman stepped outside lately? The temperature had dropped twenty degrees since noon and the wind whipping off the Gulf was enough to knock down small homes. Which is when I asked Bianca if I might wear Plan B and she told me she only lived once.

"Where's the jacket?" I asked Angela. "And tell me its floor-length."

"There is no jacket."

"Angela." My hands were in perpetual motion trying to cover up various things. "There has to be a jacket."

"She said for you to wear the..." Angela reached into the pocket of her jeans and pulled out a slip of paper. "It's a white mink hooded fur with ermine tips. The one you wore the other night."

The fur coat that had taken a chocolate milk bath. It was

"Let's get you to the fireplace."

I backed up to it to the point of roasting my rear end, which brought about the evening's final problem. A spark rose, floated through the air, and landed on the two cans of Honey Kiss Gold Colour Couture on my head. It was a flash fire. Poof.

* * *

The Sanders' recently remodeled living quarters on the thirtieth floor went black. Fantasy cut the Wi-Fi and cable, and Bianca's phone was disabled. Mr. Sanders's jet was fueled up to take Bianca somewhere far, far away, and keep her there, until the chances of her seeing herself soaring through the air with her hair on fire were minimized. It was all very Olivia Pope—organized, detailed, and not everyone would make it out of this mess alive.

I cried while Fantasy cut the wet blue dress off me in the deserted Bellissimo spa locker room. Much of the length of my hair was still there, but I could only feel fuzz and rawness around my face. Fantasy helped me into warm dry workout clothes she'd snagged from the Bellissimo spa shop on our way in, the whole time saying soothing things.

"It'll be okay, Davis. Stop howling, Davis." She was still in her gold waitress bikini with the cape tied around her waist like a gold skirt, and she was biting the tag off a Bellissimo sweatshirt.

She tilted my chin left and right. "It's not that bad!" But when I turned to look in the mirror, she spun me like a top and landed a purple Bellissimo ball cap on my head. "No, no! Not now! Everyone's waiting on us." We convened in Mr. Sanders's office—me, Fantasy, Baylor, No Hair, Mr. Sanders, and Bradley Cole. Also in attendance, a dermatologist, a medic, and Hair and Makeup Angela had been called back in. Liquor was poured and passed.

It had been a very drinky day.

Bradley Cole held my hand while everyone else stared. Angela let what was left of my hair fall out of the hat, I heard lots of sharp inhales, a few muffled gasps, and Baylor snorting.

The dermatologist dabbed something soothing, butter, maybe, along my hairline and down my neck, then presented his findings. "You have spots of first-degree burns," he said. "Think bad sunburn. They'll heal quickly. The product," he shook the empty can of Honey Kiss Blonde Angela had produced, "contains cyclopentasiloxane and dimethiconol, which, as you can see, are highly flammable."

I couldn't see a thing. Everyone else was circled around me staring at my head, and I had yet to look in a mirror.

"How tender is your head, Davis?" Angela asked. "Can I go ahead and work on it, or would you like to wait?"

"Now's good," Bradley Cole said. "Please."

I began hyperventilating.

The only sounds in the room for the next twenty minutes were the snip of Angela's scissors and my scorched vanity hitting the floor. Finally, she held up a mirror. I had a sleek layered bob that tapered to my chin.

"It looks good, Davis. You look real nice. Very sophisticated."

"Thank you, Jeremy."

I will never call him No Hair again. Ever.

* * *

I sat up most of the night watching Bradley sleep. If I had been able to lie down maybe I could have slept, but the pillow hurt my head. A crescent moon kept me company. Every once in a while I reached over and touched Bradley's hair—all on his head, none singed, no burned bald spots.

I couldn't keep my brain on one channel. Probably because it had been lit on fire. My angst went from personal (still married to Eddie the Ass) to public (humiliation) to panic, about (my hair) the Strike It Rich kickoff. We'd dropped the ball somewhere. I didn't know if our biggest problem was internal or external, but I knew where it started: people dump.

As a rule, we don't hire a new catering manager without

shining a flashlight into the corners of his closets and under his bed, then running a quick trace on the woman he lived with the whole time Bill Clinton was in office, just to see what popped. If he said he graduated from California Culinary School but I discovered he'd actually dropped out of California Welding School, no way he's coming in our door. Or it could be the old girlfriend was our wedding coordinator, who had fifteen years of running restraining orders against the guy applying for the catering job, and the only reason he was applying for the job was so he could stalk her harder. If so, there's no way we'd hire him.

This is how we do it.

If Jeremy and I don't vet these people, we don't know who's in our house. We can't protect our house if we don't know who's in it. The Strike It Rich team, forty strong, had blasted in as a unit. We barely took a peek. I ran quickie background checks and criminal records, and the only thing that popped was a computer guy, one of the five on the Information Technology team, with a DUI in 1994. A sprinkling of ugly divorces and two bankruptcies, and that was it. Elspeth Raiffe had passed only because nothing on the surface was out of place. I cleared her myself, along with Cassidy Banking, because I was vetting forty people in a day instead of one in a week. We felt like we were covered because they came with casino credibility via the Montecito. If they were good enough for the Montecito, surely they were good enough for us. Had Cassidy Banking Williams been the only file at my elbow, I still might have dug deep enough to know she was from Alabama. Or that Elspeth Raiffe was an add-on, not part of the core Montecito unit, which would have raised a flag. As it was, we needed it done. I did it, then I dumped it all on No Hair's—sorry, Jeremy's—desk, and he gave everyone the green light too.

I should have checked their dental records, Starbucks reward card, and frequent flyer miles like I always do. Every single one of them.

The Strike employees were only half of what we'd missed. By giving them a pass, we'd given the Strike players a pass too. They snuck in through Facebook.

I had nothing against social media. I hadn't jumped on the bandwagon and I probably never would. It's my law enforcement background: The risks associated with putting that much personal information out there greatly outweighed the cute puppy pictures. Even if I wanted to or had the time, who would I be cyber friends with? Meredith? Smerle T. Webb?

Major players have always come to the Bellissimo through the front door, and for the most part, single file, not in a posse. Most have gambling histories, if not local, then certainly in Atlantic City or Vegas, two clicks and a player-account hack away.

Anyone bringing a sizeable amount of money into the Bellissimo is always introduced by a casino host, who knows their shoe size before they put a foot in the door. Marketing knows who they are, because ninety-percent of the time they're the ones who sniffed them out and tossed them to a casino host. We have their background, banking, and brokerage information. We know the make and model of their European cars. We know where their yacht is docked. We know Lydia is the wife and Carmen is the girlfriend.

We knew none of this about the Strike players. The Strike team knew more about the Strike players than their own mothers knew, but it wasn't shared information, and now we had felons as honored guests. Strike had snuck them in the cyber backdoor, electronically, and so many at once, it didn't occur to Mr. Sanders, to... Jeremy, or to me to see if they might be pot farmers.

We'd dropped the ball. We'd dropped several balls.

"Davis?" He was a dream. "You need to sleep."

"I can't," I whispered.

"Your hair hurts?"

I would have laughed at that, but I didn't want to interrupt the moonlight. "Do you still love me, Bradley?"

"Of course I do. I'd love you if you were bald." He propped up on an elbow. "Do you still love me, Davis?"

"I will love you forever, Bradley."

He took my hand in his. My left hand. The one that never wore the engagement ring he gave me.

I cried a little bit, then I slept.

* * *

@LuckyStrikePlayers #StrikeItRich winners! It's here! Casino doors open at 3. #BringItOn #Where'sMyChair?

* * *

Jeremy and I started Strike It Rich Opening Day behind the closed door of the 3B with a gallon of coffee and four computers up and running. I'd gotten in late, because I had two hours of sleep and because I had to do my hair three times to get it decent. Shopping list: huge round brush with the softest bristles on Earth. #Ouch

On a brighter note, when the smoke cleared, I still had eyebrows and eyelashes.

I had twenty aerial shots up of the Jennings Tree Farm properties in DeKalb County, Alabama, a locale that would haunt my nights for years to come.

"Where'd you get these?" Dire government warning in a halo font marched across every shot. "Did you hack all this?"

"No," I said. "My dad."

"It looks like a maze." Jeremy studied. "A labyrinth of Christmas trees."

"But they're not all Christmas trees. See the slight color differentiation when you get past the first three rows?" I traced a line across the screen with my finger.

"Yep."

"Marijuana puts out some crazy chloroform that makes it an odd color, easy to spot from above, which is how so many growers get caught," I said. "The DEA does constant satellite surveillance, and picks up on the *color* of weed. But in this case, the color of the pot is barely distinguishable from the color of the blue spruce trees. They're growing Christmas trees to camouflage the pot." I directed his attention to the next screen. "But watch this." I started a timeline slide show.

When it ended, Jeremy—I'm not sure how long I can keep up this Jeremy business—started it again. After he viewed it for the third time, he said, "They're never harvesting the trees, but harvesting the pot twice a year."

"Right," I said. "The Christmas trees are there for show. And this airplane hangar?"

No Hair squinted. (See? I don't know if I can do it.)

"They have one little plane. This hangar would hold fifty little planes. It isn't an airplane hangar at all," I said. "It's a marijuana processing plant."

"Since when does it take a satellite dish that big to process pot?"

I took a closer look at the NASA-worthy parabolic dish on the west corner of the hangar, the same color as the roof, barely distinguishable. Maybe the hangar was more than a pot plant.

No Hair—sorry, I just can't do it—leaned back in his chair. "So why all the gunfire, and who did the shooting? Do we think this farm is protected by a Mexican cartel?"

"I don't know who did the shooting," I said, "not yet, anyway. But they weren't shooting to kill."

"How do you know?" No Hair asked.

(Not one hair on my head had even thought about growing back yet and I'd already given up on calling No Hair by his name. I am so weak.)

"Because Baylor and I are still alive."

He sat very still for several minutes.

"Why are these people here, Davis?"

"I don't know. But I have a feeling we're about to find out."

"I have the same feeling."

The air was thick with regret, apprehension, and hair product.

"Two questions." He stood.

"Shoot." I began shutting down computers.

"Did you get any sleep last night?"

"Very little," I said.

"Are you divorced?"

"Not at all."

TWELVE

Bea Crawford, my ex-ex-mother-in-law, was born somewhere on the back end of eleven children to Homer and Ida May Arnold of Minter, Alabama, seventeen miles north of Pine Apple. She met my ex-ex-father-in-law, Melvin, when they were both fifteen at Camp Salvation, a church camp off Butter Springs Road where Wilcox County residents could ship their kids for a month of every summer. On the last Friday of that month, they burned a straw man in effigy to demonstrate the wages of sin. The next day, they'd baptize the terrorized campers in a bacteria-riddled pond, participation 100%, then send them home to their parents walking the straight and narrow. The story goes that once they had the bonfire up and running, and they'd already scared the living daylights out of the campers circled around the fire, a counselor would tear out of the woods brandishing a straw man dressed in Liberty overalls screaming, "Repent! Repent! Repent!" Then toss him on the fire. The preacher, using a stream of butane as a directional aid for emphasis, condensed the finer points of the month's devotional messages into broken sentences, squirting gas at the blazing straw sinner with each inspirational word. "This. Is. What. Will. Happen. If. You. Backtalk. Your. Mama." And more. "This. Is. What. Will. Happen. If. You. Dance." And on.

Water activities in the toxic-waste-runoff lake a half-day's hike away were used to weed out unrepentant sinners, beginning with water moccasin snake-bite first-aid pep talks. "If a snake tries to bite the sin out of one of your friends, God commands you to help that friend out of the water and get them to the snake bite station."

A teenage counselor with a supply of dishrag-strip tourniquets and rusty straight razors manned the snake station.

Camp Salvation touted horseback riding as another one of their major amenities, and the stories told about the old swayback one-eyed horse can still be heard around Pine Apple today. Apparently, the horse was hung like a... horse, afflicted with oddly placed tumors the size of soccer balls, and every year, some poor kid's summer camp vacation was cut short because the horse, Glory, either bit them in the face or kicked the holy shit out of them. They say the ghost of Glory still stampedes through the backwoods of Wilcox County and if you sin in some major way, he'll appear in your bedroom, bite you in the face, then stomp you to death with one of his tumor feet. (True story: The Legend of Glory was actually used as a defense in a spousal-abuse trial when I was in high school. A truck driver named Red Eggleston claimed he didn't beat his wife, Sue-Sue, half near to death, no, it was old Glory who did it. Locked jury, mistrial, and three years later when Glory showed up and beat Sue-Sue to within an inch of her life again, she got after the old ghost horse with her shotgun, but accidentally shot and killed Red. Buckshot everywhere. No criminal charges were brought against her.)

It was the Health Department who shut down Camp Salvation a few years before I was born, and not because of the annual head lice infestation. Someone did the math and traced the spike in babies born to unwed teen mothers during the month of March back to Camp Salvation. I guess by their teenage years, Camp Salvation either scared the pants off the teenagers, or they'd been hit over the head with the Bible enough.

And so began the epic romance of Mel and Bea Crawford, the result of a meet-cute at Camp Salvation. They married, then several years later, the Crawfords abducted a baby from somewhere, and he grew up to be the man I married twice, and, apparently, I'm still married to.

Bea is made up of fat rolls, roll after roll, like a tower of blow-up donuts on feet, and she's flushed all the time, so make them blow-up strawberry donuts, and Mel would be a very tall thin man, if he didn't suffer from textbook early-onset osteoporosis. They owned Pine Apple's only three-square's restaurant, Mel's Diner, a regional health hazard, and Mel had spent so many years bent over the fryer (casing the fryer basket for the errant rodent, I'm sure), he could no longer stand up anywhere near straight. Their son, however, looked like Alabama George Clooney, which is why it's so hard to believe he's their *real* son.

I did not marry Eddie Crawford the Ass for his looks. Or his brains, which wasn't even an option, given that he didn't have any. The first time I married him was by total accident, and the second time was one of those "If you were on a desert island, would you take one man and ten sandwiches or ten men and one sandwich?" I was on Pine Apple Island where there were exactly zero sandwiches and even less men. There was Eddie, and I married him, a mistake I've paid for in every way imaginable. To this very day.

His mother, a lifelong friend of my mother's, didn't like me a bit as a child, liked me considerably less as a teenager, and has made hating me as an adult a part of her daily routine, because her son and I had gone through a mud-slinging, name-calling, hair-pulling, eye-gouging divorce, and she, naturally, sided with him. Eddie the Rotten Rotten Rotten Human and I managed to split the whole county in half. #TeamDavis. #TeamEddie.

It is what it is, it's years behind me, and Bea and I had recently found some common ground. I actually enlisted her aid on a Bellissimo sting last year that had changed her life for the better. And by changed her life for the better, I mean she stopped coloring her hair fireball orange, had a luxury casino vacation, and came out of it with a little cash.

Since then, I'd run into Bea once or twice when I'd been in town, and she'd actually said hello instead of sticking her fat donut foot out and tripping me on the sidewalk.

I picked up the phone to call Bea on Saturday morning, knowing the war was about to begin again. I felt sure it was Bea who had signed for the notification that the divorce needed a little

It's not like I didn't know what I was in for when I dialed her number, which she still told people was W-I-9, 3229.

"That's not it," I said. "I'm healthy." With a hairline recently receded by a half-inch all around. "It was rejected because"— #Help—"you're going to think this is funny, Bea. I think it's hilarious." (Like root canals are hilarious.) "Alabama thinks Eddie and I are still married. Can you even believe that?" I batted down the sudden urge to (throw up) run screaming into the Gulf of Mexico and keep going. #Backstroke "It's a simple paperwork error, Bea, but I need you to make a phone call to the Camden courthouse and help me clear it up."

No. Squirrels. Left.

"Well, well, well," she said. "Davis Way needs my help. Again."

"Bea." I could hear the edge of a plea in my voice. "You know Eddie and I aren't married."

"No, Davis, I don't know anything of the kind. In fact," she said, "it sounds to me like you are."

#SquirrelSpeciesExtinct

"Bea?"

I looked at my phone.

It said call ended.

* * *

@LuckyStrikePlayers Welcome! See you in T-Minus 3 Hours!

* * *

The camera Hashtag Elspie gave me was a Canon PowerShot Elph 330 HS and I'd finally made friends with it. It was so small I could tuck it away in a pocket or my bra, and it had a 10X zoom lens. The best? Built-in Wi-Fi, so only one step between taking pictures and the various cyberspace destinations Hashtag wants them distributed to. I'd had a nice break from all things social media, but now that the games were going live, Hashtag Elspie expected the Strike Klout score to take a leap. Whatever in the hell that was. Baylor had given me the best advice: "Since you don't know what you're doing, Davis, take a million pictures. You'll accidentally get good ones." Which, incidentally, was an extension of his general life philosophy, especially with women—hit on everything and you'll accidentally score some wins. And it was good advice.

I walked away from each and every Bellissimo assignment with another little life lesson—never pass just the salt when someone asks, pass both the salt *and* pepper, think of the corners of fitted sheets as pockets to slide your hands into, then clap your hands together and, wa-la, it's folded neatly, and never use flour for sauces or gravies, use cornstarch, then you'll never have lumps—so if nothing else, my takeaway from the Strike assignment would be this: Don't record your life in photographs taken on your phone when there are itty bitty cameras that are easy to use and take much better pictures.

My objective was to show the world what they were missing at the Strike It Rich Sweepstakes, but not live gaming or players. I couldn't release photographs of anything on the play screens or identifiable player faces. I snapped lots of *future*Gaming chairs in motion, food, drink, the glittering icicle light fixture, and more of Baylor's boots. The Strike staff had all signed waivers; I could shoot them at will. (Ha ha.)

Angela Hair and Makeup Woman painted my hair Chocolate Covered Bing Cherry with a whisper-soft paint brush, then spiked it up a little. I wore the cutest Milly suit I've ever seen. #GoingHomeWithMe The jacket had multi-directional gray and vanilla stripes, bracelet sleeves, and striped flap pockets. The bottoms were striped shorts. Not linen, but looked like linen. Ivory silk shell, ivory heels.   #Fab   #TweetedNeckDownSelfie #LetTheGamesBegin

* * *

If the thought of leaving the casino business had ever passed through my brain, which I doubt it had, because I stayed too busy to live anywhere but in the moment, or the past as it were—it never would again. If this is the future of gaming, I'm in.

When Strike gaming went live, it took all of two minutes for me to see why fifteen thousand people had Instagramed so hard to earn a spot. *future*Gaming was social integrated wagering, starring the player, from the comfort of individual entertainment centers. Starting with the eight-million pixel sleek screens, displaying theatre quality high-definition graphics and 3-D imagery in front of them, to the Dolby surround sound enveloping them, and the heated, massaging, chocolate chip subwoofer they were sitting on, these people were making casino history. It was high-tech entertainment at a level I'd never dreamed of, and I only had one question: Who wrote this programming?

The players only looked isolated in the individual gaming stations. They were actually competing against one another for several levels of community jackpots and they were in competition with each other to earn overall points. At any time, they could pull up live feed of any other gaming station to see, talk directly to, or combine efforts with any other Strike player. From the same left screen, they ordered truffle this or caviar that. Of these players, the ten with the lowest overall points twelve hours from now would be eliminated. To earn points, they won rounds, beating the game, and in doing so, unlocked bigger and better and bonus games, and with each advance, they also unlocked richer media content.

It was hard to imagine, given where it started, where it might end.

I could see how the players could stay in the chairs for twelve-hour shifts, especially since the chair let them pause the game, shut out the world, and nap. And I could definitely see where the ten who were eliminated in this round would be back in the chairs for the next round, on their own dime. ("Their! Own! Dime!")

I was glued to a black granite wall taking it all in through the LCD screen of the camera, when I zoomed out to see Hashtag Elspie had stopped cartwheeling around the room ponytail flying. I peeked over the camera to see her holding up the granite wall directly opposite me, staring me down. I hopped to and began snapping *future*Gaming images for the insatiable Twittersphere, and, before too long, evidence. Because a good accountant can take a stack of W-2Gs, win-loss statements, and IRS 5754s, and turn you into a professional gambler. But there isn't an accountant out there who can keep you out of federal prison if you're caught spending your marijuana money.

* * *

I sat on the edge of the bed and put a hand on his shoulder. He woke slowly, stretched, and reached for me in the moonlight. "Come to bed, Davis." He looked at the clock on the nightstand. "It's two in the morning. Come to bed."

"Bradley," I whispered. "We have two players laundering drug money through the Strike casino."

You could have heard a mosquito blink.

He threw back the covers and sat up. "I'll make coffee."

At a quarter till ten, the Strike casino rocking, the crowd well past its legal limit, Red Jennings quietly made his way to the cashier's cage, where he signed a slip of paper Cassidy Banking had waiting, then she passed him two banded stacks of cash. He slipped them inside his jacket and continued playing. Forty-five minutes later, he did it again. When his pockets were stuffed, it was Missy's turn. She shouldered her big bag, made her way to Cassidy Banking's window, where she signed for and received inch-thick stacks of hundred-dollar bills. By my count, the Jennings withdrew $140,000 from their player account on the first night of Strike. Cash. Bellissimo cash. Drawn off a player account they wired money into before the tournament began. Drug money. The Jennings were laundering drug money through the Strike casino.

brain down enough to sleep, he reached for me. "Has it occurred to you, Davis, that if and when we ever do manage to get married, and if and when we even think about having a family, you can't do this job?"

THIRTEEN

To: dway@bellissimo.com

From: bsanders@biancacasimirosanders.com

David. Pack your bags immediately. I need you to complete my spa retreat in Versailles. If one more person touches my body I will lose my mind and the exfoliant products here smell as if they were extracted from camels. In addition, I find the palace to be drafty, too crowded, the therapists undertrained, and the accommodations borderline pedestrian. I intend to discuss the matter with Forbes Travel because this location is, at most, four and a half stars. Certainly not five. In fact, you call Forbes. Immediately. Express my concerns. I'd call them myself, but like a prisoner, I do not have access to life's necessities within these castle walls. No telephone, no news of the outside world, and I'm only able to send you this correspondence after paying one of the maids, a heavy girl named Griet, who has fingers so thick I insist she keep her hands in the pockets of her apron, two hundred American to smuggle in this ancient laptop computer, which is no doubt leaking high-frequency electrons and initiating some manner of malignancy within me as I type.

So I'll make it brief: <u>S.O.S. Come immediately.</u> I will do you the favor of making your travel arrangements. I'm sure you will love it here. Think of it as a vacation, compliments of me. There's much to do in the area—explore the Normandy Region, visit Mont Saint Michel, tour through the Castle of Vaux le Vicomte—all within a day's walk, which is if you're able to escape the tendrils of the overbearing staff. I know Richard meant well when he booked this, and I don't want to upset him by shunning his kindness. So get here quickly, David. Right away.

B.

To: bsanders@biancacasimirosanders.com
From: dway@bellissimo.com
Mrs. Sanders,
I received an email from you with no content. Whatever you intended to say was blocked by the spyware on our system. I hope you're having a lovely time and will see you in two weeks.
Davi<u>s</u>

What a great idea, I thought, the spa. I logged in and found the only open appointment on the books at 11:00, an organic bull sperm hair mask. Dis. Gus. Ting. (Under what circumstances would bull sperm be inorganic?) The blurb on the spa menu said it would promote vitality and growth, both of which my hair could use.

*　*　*

@StrikeItRichers 10 eliminated from competition on opening day of play. Don't be next! Get in there! #futureGaming #PlayersPlayOn! #GimmeMyChair

*　*　*

Flight Aware, and other Internet sites like it, have made it impossible for men to lie to their wives about where they are. If you know the tail numbers of a private plane, you can track it all over the map. "You said you were going to Boston." "I am in Boston." "You are not, you pathological liar. I'm looking at your flight. You just landed in Palm Springs."

The most popular private plane tracked used to be John Travolta's. Tail numbers N707JT. Until a year or so ago, you could go to flightaware.com, plug in the tail numbers, and track his Boeing 707. Someone spread the word, and Edna Turnblad fans began storming private airports banging on the gates with their We Love You, John! signs, which became somewhat of a security issue. If you plug in his tail numbers now, you get a message informing you that the owner/operator's flight information is set to private.

As is Red Jennings's. He doesn't want anyone knowing his comings and goings, either.

It's a safe bet that JT's privacy requirements have nothing to do with hauling pot around for distribution, including to a richie-rich private boy's school in New Hampshire. The boarder who was caught smoking a bowl behind laundry services squealed like a little girl, and after much interrogation of a parade of higher-than-kites boarding students, the evidence suggested the free-for-all weed party began exactly a week ago, ten minutes after Red Jennings's Pilatus PC-24 landed bringing Quinn Jennings and Thomas Sanders back to school. Both boys denied knowing anything about any illegal drugs on the plane. So while the school tried to (stay out of the news) sort it out, both students, Quinn Jennings and Thomas Sanders, were to be in their parents' custody on the weekends. No lazing around the dorms possibly selling and definitely smoking pot. The Jennings, having made the Bellissimo their home away from home while they (laundered drug money) played in Strike It Rich, sent the Pilatus to pick up the boys.

I tapped a knuckle on the back door of Mr. Sanders's office at ten on Saturday morning, and walked in to help put a plan together that might keep us all out of jail. No Hair was staring out the window, Mr. Sanders was fuming at his desk, and Thomas Sanders was slumped in a chair in the corner. He looked up. "Dude. Your hair."

Mr. Sanders was furious. On several levels. I walked in on one of the higher ones.

I'd missed the "Just Say No" part of the Little Sanders interrogation, arriving for the tail-end of Mr. Sanders's extreme dissatisfaction with the school's lax policies allowing fifteen-year-olds to hop on a private plane and jet across the country without parental permission.

"Mom said I could."

"Your mother is out of the country, Thomas."

"Dad." (Just a hair off from "Dude.") "I emailed her."

"She doesn't have access to a computer, Thomas. And I'd appreciate it if you'd stop lying to me."

"She found a computer." They all looked at me. "She did have computer access sometime during the night. I got an email from her."

Mr. Sanders threw his hands in the air.

A funny thing about Richard Sanders: He ruled the kingdom that was the Bellissimo machine. We'd been named one of the top 100 hotels in the continental US and Canada by *Travel + Leisure* for seventeen years running, with gross gaming revenues of $690 million last year, $110 million of that net casino profit, and the property was valued at more than $890 million. Every one of those bucks stopped here, at Richard Sanders's desk. But his wife and his son? The two of them were forever bringing this man to his knees. This captain-of-industry leader-of-thousands powerhouse was all but helpless when it came to Bianca and Thomas Sanders.

"Thomas. Go upstairs and don't move. Do. Not. Move."

"When's Mom coming home?" Little Sanders whipped his head up and back, his hair grooming routine.

"Go, Thomas."

No Hair and I took seats in front of Mr. Sanders's desk while he regained his authority. Mrs. Pader, a librarian-type who kept up with Mr. Sanders's dry cleaning and daily calendar, brought in a tray of donuts and coffee none of us made a move for.

"Tell me everything you know, Davis." Mr. Sanders settled in. "Everything."

I cleared my throat. "When the Strike contestants were chosen and registered for the tournament six weeks ago, Mr. Sanders, they were given the options of applying for casino markers or depositing into a player account. Missy and Red Jennings opened an in-house account and wired what looks to be a substantial amount of money into it."

"Do we know how much?"

What I said: "No. The banking software, like the rest of the Strike, is proprietary, and while I can guess, based on the daily numbers Strike reported to the Bellissimo system, I can't get in and look at individual transactions." What I didn't say: I warned you six months ago they shouldn't be allowed their own operating system. #FortKnox

"And the deposit wasn't flagged?"

"There were multiple deposits, and none of them were flagged. There's no record of a Suspicious Transaction Report filed on the Jennings, ever."

"Do we know *why* they wired so much money into the account?"

"The Jennings are drug manufacturers and distributors, Mr. Sanders."

His gaze shifted to the chair recently vacated by his only son. Who'd just flown on the drug manufacturer and distributor's airplane.

"And I believe they deposited such a large amount of money into a Strike account for the sole purpose of withdrawing it, using the accompanying documentation to establish themselves as professional gamblers for tax purposes."

"And we know—" he snapped his fingers, trying to come up with the name.

"Cassidy Banking," I said.

"Cassidy Williams," No Hair said.

"Cassidy." Mr. Sanders decided for us. "The head of banking for the Strike casino is an accomplice."

"Yes, sir," I said. "She's Missy Jennings's sister. She accepted the unusually large deposits and she's personally processing the withdrawals."

Mr. Sanders clasped his hands together and leaned in. "Who else? Who else in Strike is part of this? Levi Newman? Have we seen anything that would lead us to believe he suspects? Or anything to indicate my new casino manager is in on this?"

"That's what we don't know yet, Richard."

"We may not know about Levi Newman," I said, "but I believe Elspeth Raiffe is playing a major role."

"Why does this woman's name keep coming up?" Mr. Sanders asked. "She's the one hired out of the New Orleans PR firm?"

I nodded.

No Hair helped himself to a glazed donut.

"Do we think she's an accessory?" Mr. Sanders asked.

"Quite the opposite. I think she's here to take them down," I said, "but I don't know who she's working for. She could be federal; she could work for a Mexican cartel; it might be personal."

"Pull something out of your bag of tricks, Davis." No Hair brushed donut crumbs off his Daffy Duck tie. "Figure it out."

"What do you have on her so far?" Mr. Sanders pushed away from his desk.

"The Jennings are in a Strike suite on the twenty-fifth floor," I said. "Room twenty-five seventeen and I just found this." I placed my phone on the desk between us displaying a screen shot showing Elspeth keying herself into a Bellissimo guest room. The ponytail was stuffed in a ball cap, her wardrobe bland and unremarkable, head down. But it was definitely Elspeth. The teeny diamond Monroe piercing gave her away. "She's in the hotel. She's booked in a guest room under an alias, room twenty-five nineteen, which makes her the Jennings's next-door neighbor. She checked into the room ten minutes after the Jennings checked in."

"She was waiting on them," Mr. Sanders said.

"Yes sir."

"And you're tracking her? You have her under surveillance?"

I nodded. Actually, Baylor was tracking her. "Drop this in Hashtag's bag at ballet, Baylor." I passed him the James Bond Bic pen. He played with it for a while, then asked if he could have one. I told him if he'd be a good boy, we'd see. (He is so not ready for my job.)

"Where is she now?" No Hair adjusted the knot of his tie.

"I lost the signal on her an hour ago." I looked at my watch. "Which means she's at least ten miles away. Making this a good time to get in the room and nose around."

"Don't go up there and swipe yourself in wearing street clothes, Davis," No Hair said. "She may be spying on us while we're spying on her. Go under some kind of cover."

"I'm going the spa route."

"Is there anything else?" Mr. Sanders asked.

"One more thing," I said. "Missy Jennings won a substantial amount of money last night, and she's at the top of the leader board after the first night of tournament play."

"You say that as if you don't think it's a lucky streak."

"No, Mr. Sanders, I don't."

"What *do* you think?"

"I think the problems within Strike go further than banking. I think it's possible the gaming might be tipped in the Jennings's favor as well."

Mr. Sanders closed his eyes and tapped three fingers against his forehead. "How?" He looked up. "How?"

"It all goes back to the programming, Mr. Sanders. Someone, somewhere, is pulling the strings for the Strike system. The Jennings marijuana business is at the heart of it."

Something on Mr. Sanders's phone beeped. "And you're going to Paris in the middle of all this?"

"Excuse me?"

"Flight Aware says you have a Bellissimo jet scheduled to take you to Paris this afternoon, Davis."

* * *

Baylor was on the sofa scratching. He looked up as I keyed myself in the basement bullpen. "Gold skin itches, Davis. You got the very good end of this deal. When can we play those Strike games?"

I pushed my hair back and showed him the line of burned skin and baby fuzz framing my face. "This itches, too, thank you. We have way bigger problems, go play your Xbox."

Fantasy stood at the doorway to the office. "Stop. You two are making me itch." She scratched her neck. "Davis? Let's get in there and play those games."

"Whose side are you on, Fantasy? We have work to do."

"Oh, hell yes, let me play, Davis." Baylor stopped scratching. "How cool is it they order drinks from the television? I waited on one guy last night whose whole game is Formula One. Every level he went up, the course got harder. He was throwing money at it to get to the bonus round. Coolest thing I've ever seen in my life. Another guy was playing World War Two, shooting a submachine gun. Every time he gave the game more money, he got a bigger gun. Coolest thing I've ever seen in my life."

"Where did these games come from?" Fantasy asked.

"That's a very good question." I found a seat. "Every single one of them is an individual microprocessor," I said, "and the games are skill-based and personalized. I can't imagine what kind of genius is behind this."

"There's a lady in there playing the piano," Fantasy said. "Every level she advances, she plays a harder song. She started with Chopsticks and she's advanced to Chopin. It's crazy. Is anybody thinking what I'm thinking?"

"That Davis should let us play?" Scratch, scratch, scratch.

"No, Baylor. That we should've paid a little more attention to this before it got here."

One of us was thinking that. Exactly that.

"What's up with Little Sanders, Davis?"

Baylor slowed the scratching. "I didn't do it," he said. "Whatever that kid did, I had nothing to do with it."

"Little Sanders is here because there's been a pot party at his school, and the school suspects it has something to do with him and the Jennings kid."

"Surely those people don't have their kid dealing for them," Fantasy said.

"They hired him a hooker," Baylor said it like *best parents ever.*

"Let's hope whatever that kid's doing Little Sanders isn't involved."

"When can I play that game, Davis?" He said it like *when can I have another cookie?*

"Baylor. Sit there and scratch. I have to go to the spa. I'll see about sneaking us in before it opens tomorrow." I'd like to take a crack at breaking into the Strike banking system. And I wanted to play the game too.

* * *

Vanity Fair gave the Bellissimo Spa and Salon a five-star rating on the same day three lawsuits were filed against it—a slip-and-fall in the men's steam room, a sexual misconduct charge against a masseur, and a pain-and-suffering complaint from a laser hair removal. The last one was tossed out of court, because the Sasquatch man bringing the charges had wall-to-wall shag carpet on his back, and obviously, the judge ruled, there'd be some pain and suffering involved in frying it off. The masseur under fire was accused of giving his client a full-on breast exam, not a service she'd asked for, but once in court, giggling, she got in the box and couldn't remember exactly what had happened. She didn't recall. Two weeks after the charges were dismissed, the defendant and the plaintiff opened a spa of their own. Happy Endings.

All this came down on the seventh day of operations at the Bellissimo. On the eighth day, Mr. Sanders, a younger and edgier CEO with a newborn casino-resort to tend to, sold it before anything else could hit his desk. He had enough to deal with.

The spa was now a leased venue, much like McDonald's would be if we had one, which we didn't. The Bellissimo Day Spa is owned, staffed, and run by an LLC, StatCo Enterprises out of Cincinnati, which somehow climbs up a long corporate ladder to the Nestle Corporation. As in teeny division of. It's 30,000 square feet of

Swedish massages, lime and ginger salt-glow body scrubs, congested skin facials, and I needed one of their uniforms. I had one of their old uniforms, but they'd recently redecorated and I didn't have a spa suit in the new chocolate brown pink trim flavor. Since the Bellissimo didn't own the spa, I couldn't send Baylor to fetch one from uniform distribution, so a swiping was in order.

I walked in dressed in workout clothes, a Saints ball cap, and sunglasses.

The receptionist checking me in, Margarite, looked up from the desk. "Really?" she whispered. "The bull sperm? You're brave." She tapped on her keyboard. "Let us know how you like it."

The spa smelled like essential oils, chlorine, and rich people. The piped-in music was crickets and pianos, the lighting low and subsidized with red candles in globes on every flat surface.

A girl at the next desk, Caty, passed me a robe, fuzzy flip-flops, and a locker key. "Enjoy your services." She whispered too. I whispered back a thank you. I walked through a room full of naked women ignoring one another, found my locker, and stepped behind a curtain (thank you) to change into the robe, which was more like a down-filled comforter with a belt. I was stepping into the fuzzy flip-flops when I heard someone loud-whispering my name-of-the-day. "Justy? Justy Tanner?"

I pulled the dressing room curtain back. "I'm Justy."

He was short, built like a tank, and had a Marine buzz cut. He was Popeye. "Semen mask?" A dozen naked women's heads snapped up. I smiled.

"Let's go, doll."

(Why did Nestle allow men in the women's changing room?)

We passed a lady with a tattoo of Tinker Bell on her butt.

"I'm Ricky," he said over his shoulder, "I'll be doing your semen mask today. This way." He pushed open the door of a treatment room as I scanned for an employees-only door along the dimly lit hallway, spotting one all the way down on the left. He told me to take off the robe and get under the covers. "You don't want to wear this stuff," he advised. "It's fragrant."

And why wouldn't it be?

The bed was heated, contoured, the blankets soft, and I was instantly ready for a nap. Ricky stepped back in.

"Girlfriend." Hands on hips. "I can't give you a hair mask with that hat on." I felt him sit down and roll up behind me. He pulled the Saints cap off my head and we both yelped. "Oh shit, sweetheart! What happened?" He gingerly combed through what hair I had, examining the inch of fuzz at my hairline. "Your color is to die for." My shoulder-length hair slipped through his fingers. "Who mixes it?"

"It's mine." I talked in my sleep.

"Lucky duck."

He placed a warm, eucalyptus scented weighted mask over my eyes. "You're going to love the bull sperm mask, except it's cold. And smelly." I could feel him rolling around in a chair behind me. "After I put it on, I have to ice it down with cold towels."

"Why?"

"Because it's a big ol' mess if I don't keep it near frozen. The good news for you is it will make this hair grow back in no time." He began painting an ice cold paste along my hairline.

"Ricky?"

"Hmmm?"

"How do they get the bull sperm?" I was imagining bulls behind closed doors with cow magazines. *Have a Cow. Cows Come Home. Holy Cow.*

"They cut the testes off and boil them down." Ricky painted. "Then the broth is infused with Katera root and whipped into a paste." He'd painted almost all the way around. "They call it Viagra for the hair." He used his hands to glob it onto, then pull it through the rest of my head. Which is about when the smell hit me. I bolted off that bed, wearing the warm blanket, and made a run for it.

"Every time," I heard Ricky say.

* * *

I needed to be dressed as a virtual assistant and in the Strike It Rich casino in less than an hour, so I didn't have time to wash the bullshit out of my hair. I ran screaming into the employees-only room, scattered it of three therapists emptying a pizza box, dressed in a spa uniform, and buttoned my semened head into a spa turban towel I grabbed from a laundered stack. My only shoe option was the standard-issue spa flip-flop. I loaded a small cart with a dozen random bottles of spa stuff and a stack of towels, then pushed out a door at the back of the room into a back hallway. I dabbed at the bull semen dripping down my face with one of the towels. As the elevator climbed, my scalp began itching like it had a poison ivy chickenpox. I drummed my fingers all around the turban until I grabbed a big bottle of glycolic resurfacing lotion and began hitting myself in the itchy head with it. Which is what I was doing when the elevator stopped, the doors opened, and Hashtag Elspie dressed again in her unremarkable, don't-take-a-second-look-at-me camo, open-mouth stared at me. I ducked my turbaned head, shoved the cart out, and flew past her before she could get a better look. I cleared a corner, froze until she was gone, then flip-flopped down the hall, bull goo running down my back.

Why hadn't James Bond let me know she was back at the Bellissimo?

Room twenty-five nineteen had a Do Not Disturb placard on the doorknob.

I looked both ways as I snapped on gloves, swiped, pushed the spa cart through, then threw the bolt and locked myself in. I paused a second to catch my breath, got a whiff of bull, but geared up again. Speedy was the way to go. That way, the smell trailed me.

Nothing in the foyer but a mini Farmer's Market all over the bar—squash, kale, bananas, Hostess Twinkies (kidding), Taco Seasoning (not kidding), raspberries—and a Vitamix blender. This would be where Elspeth prepares her liquid meals. I stepped through to the sitting room to see that she'd redecorated it into a surveillance suite, complete with a two-way mirror looking into the Jennings sitting room. (How'd Hashtag get in here and knock out a square foot of wall? Then get into the Jennings suite next door and hang a mirror?) All was quiet at the Jenningses, but Elspie had done a *Beautiful Mind* number on hers. Dozens of aerial shots of the Lickskillet property were double-stick taped to the walls, along with head shots of the Jennings and Cassidy Banking, copies of financial transactions going all the way back to the Montecito, photographs of Missy Jennings's dance studio (Strike Up the Band), photographs of the Pilatus airplane, and in the middle of it all with a wide blank border, a photograph of Hashtag Elspie and Brianna Strother cheek to cheek, laughing and clinking fruity drinks, with sunburned noses and hers-and-hers signature-Elspie ponytails. They were on the deck of a cruise ship with a sparkling teal-blue ocean behind, white-hot sun directly above, and flower leis around their necks.

I took a wide shot photo of the wall.

I poked my head in the door of the bedroom, expecting nothing, because Elspie was coming and going from the Bellissimo, not sleeping here, and this room didn't have any access to the Jennings's suite, so I doubt she'd have knocked out any walls. In the middle of the king-sized bed was my James Bond Super Spy pen. In forty pieces.

FOURTEEN

"Your hair is growing back," Angela said.

"I know." I was in the makeup chair. "It itches."

"No." She met my eyes in the mirror. "I mean it's *really* growing. You have a half inch of growth since yesterday." She put her nose to my head and sniffed. "What have you done?"

It was four o'clock. I was already late for my virtual assistant job at Strike. Time heals all nightmares, and I had very little time, so I'd agreed to make friends with Colour Couture aerosol again. I looked at it from a math perspective: my hair had been sprayed hundreds of times without catching fire and only the once going up in flames, so the odds were in my favor.

"I went to the spa today and had a bull semen hair mask."

"That's the smell."

"That's the smell. I washed it twice."

Angela held up a handful and let it drop. "You need to get a hold of more of that bull mask and not wash it out. Sleep in it. At the rate it's growing, you could have your length back in a month."

"I wouldn't want to put my pillow through it." Not to mention Bradley Cole. I put him through enough as it was.

"I swear I can almost see your hair pushing out of your scalp. It's a miracle drug." She finished spray painting me. "Maybe you should rent a bull."

"And what, exactly, Angela, would I do with it?"

She chewed on that.

(Don't go there. Just don't.)

(Can you even rent a bull?)

Angela reached for a blazing hot flat iron. "Let's vogue you up."

Twenty minutes later, I presented my credentials and vogued through the Strike It Rich doors. I asked the beefy bouncer what I'd missed, dropped my camera at his feet, let him be a gentleman, and in a very ladylike way, picked his pockets as he picked up the camera.

"A lady playing the dancing game hit a big one." He tugged at the lapels of his jacket. "Two hundred thousand."

That put her tournament take, on Day Two, at half a million dollars. Missy Jennings couldn't stop cracking the code and advancing. Could we stop her before she bankrupted the Bellissimo?

I went about my social media business as instructed, letting the tech-savvy gaming-hungry world know what they were missing and what they had to look forward to. I kept the little camera going, and when I could stop taking evidence shots of Missy Jennings miraculously winning, and Cassidy Banking laundering money for her brother-in-law, I tweeted a community jackpot win. Or a picture of the gold icicle chandelier. Or Fantasy's butt.

The phone in my pocket buzzed. *We need to talk.*

I scanned the room for my boss, Hashtag Elspie, who was holding up the same granite wall she'd been observing from yesterday. It would seem that tonight she'd been observing me, and I'd been too busy trying to nail the Jennings and Cassidy Banking to notice.

Our eyes locked, then Elspeth and I shared a long look. I took a deep breath and returned her text with a picture of the Beautiful Mind wall in guest room twenty-five nineteen. *Yes, Elspeth. Let's talk.*

✳ ✳ ✳

"Cool hair."

"Thank you."

We met in a liquor storage closet behind Strike. Metal shelving held row after row of premium liquor. I stood, tapping a foot, while Elspeth rested on the metal rim of a keg of beer. Hipster supercharged "On! Their! Dime!" cheerleader was gone and in her place, a dead-serious federal agent. With a mile-high ponytail and glitter on her face.

"Who do you work for?"

"I work for the casino. Who do *you* work for, Elspeth?"

"I work for the federal government and I need to know who is working with the Jennings. Is it you, Amy, or whatever your name is?"

She was probably packing. I had a camera.

"No, Elspeth. I work undercover for the Bellissimo. I want to know who's working with them too, which puts us on the same team."

Of course, she didn't believe me, and I could see now that the only way out of this was to bring her into our circle, combine our resources, and probably in the next two minutes. Before she shot me.

"I won't let you compromise my case."

"What case?" I asked. "Are you drug enforcement?"

She didn't trust me enough to answer, and had she, both our covers would have been blown. One of the three bartenders, the bald one, the mean bald one, the quiet mean bald one, opened the door so quietly neither of us even heard him approach.

Elspeth was off that keg and on me in a millisecond. The bartender looked from my face to hers, then back, trying to decide what he'd interrupted.

"Excuse me, ladies." He smiled, a wicked, twisted grin, grabbed a bottle of liquor, then backed out. "Carry on." He closed the door.

*   *   *

My hair grew another half inch during the night, so I had to touch up my red roots with squirts of Colour Couture before I left for work the next morning. Five short hours after I'd come home from work the night before. Bradley snuck up behind me.

"It's dark out, Davis."

"I know." I dropped a short Alice + Olivia black and white A-line dress over my Chocolate Covered Cherry hair, then climbed into big black suede boots. Bradley smiled his I-like-it smile. I smiled back my I'm-all-yours. "I'm going to sneak into Strike early, while it's closed, and see if I can hack into the system to take a look at the Jennings in-house account."

"You need to let the feds worry about hacking into the system, Davis."

"Oh, right."

"You did bring the feds in yesterday, didn't you?"

"Absolutely." Hashtag Elspie's in. She's federal.

Bradley raised one eyebrow. I got busy looking for my mascara.

"Actually," (and this is the whole truth) "I'm sneaking in to take a peek at the game. I need to see how Missy Jennings is winning so much. No Hair, Fantasy, and Baylor are coming too, but later, daylight or so, because we're meeting with Elspeth."

"Why would the four of you meet with Elspeth?"

"We're meeting with her," I finally found my Dior Show, "because she nailed me last night."

"Your cover's blown?"

Coat two, Dior Show. "Uh-huh." I barely swiped my bottom lashes. "She made me." Lip liner. "After that, if she doesn't shoot us, we want to play the game while the casino's closed."

"You should work on this aspect of your job, Davis."

"Which one is that?"

"The gambling addict one."

"Just wait till you see what that game does, Bradley. You'll want to play it too."

"How are you going to get in this early?" He wrapped me up in his arms from behind and we talked to each other in the mirror.

"I swiped a bouncer's keys last night."

"No!"

"Yes!"

"Davis!"

"Bradley!"

"I'm having an affair, living with, engaged to, a woman who breaks into casinos and is *married*."

I pushed free of his arms.

"I was kidding."

"It's not funny."

We observed a moment of silence. (#Squirrel)

"Want me to go with you?"

It was my turn to raise an eyebrow. There were times I felt as if Bradley were more concerned with what happened at the Bellissimo than what happened at his own casino.

"Sure," I said. "Come with me."

"Want another shower?"

A tempting offer. "Rain check," I said. "I'll make us to-go coffees."

Thirty minutes later, which would have been four hours later had we not let a Bellissimo valet park Bradley's BMW, we were at the front doors.

"You go right, I'll go left, and we'll meet at Strike." Everyone watching, all the time.

Seven-thirty Sunday morning was a quiet time in gambling land; Saturday night drunks clear out around six, and even the diehard poker players sleep in. I passed a couple staring at the floor, dragging their feet and rolling suitcases, counted four blackjack tables with a little business each, and there might have been fifty slot players on my side of the building. Bradley beat me to the Strike It Rich doors.

I raised my arm and made a semi-circle swipe through the air with my Strike It Rich badge for the cameras on the off chance someone in surveillance was awake. We got one foot each in the door when I fell against Bradley.

Elspeth Raiffe was spread out on the mahogany bar, one arm

dangling off. She stared at us. Seven inches of a gold glass icicle protruded from the middle of her chest where it had been driven in like a stake. Drops of dried blood were suspended and frozen on the tips of her dead fingers.

* * *

"For now," No Hair pocketed his phone, "we clean."

Fantasy and I had already snapped on gloves, jumpsuits, and goggles. No Hair removed his Swiss cheese tie, rolled it, and placed it on a table across the room. Near Bradley. Who was fifty shades of green and ticking off a list of how many laws we were breaking. He used the words tampering, hindering, abuse, aiding, abetting, destruction, corpse, and breakfast, which he said he no longer wanted and might never want again. I told him he was free to go. He said he would stay with me.

No Hair gloved up. He peeled back the edge of one to look at his watch. "We have thirty minutes max. Baylor, go get some wheels."

"How big?"

"Enough for Elzbath." No Hair pointed.

"Luggage cart?"

"That'll do."

We went to work. Dusting the granite bar for prints was pointless, because it had eight gazillion, so we removed trace. We videoed, bagged, tagged, bleached, then restored the crime scene, clearly primary, enough blood pooled around her to see she'd not been moved. We used bar towels to absorb all we could from the black carpet, then bagged the towels, until there was nothing left but her cold body. Still on the bar. Baylor, bless his heart, extracted the gold glass icicle, which hopefully would have prints. She'd already bled out, so it was only horrifying. We all looked up at the blown glass light fixture murder weapon above our heads.

And then there was her.

Elspeth's right hand was pierced cleanly through the middle, like Jesus, as she'd tried to defend herself. She'd seen it coming. There was no other evidence of a struggle on Elspeth's part, so she'd known her killer. There was nothing in her pockets and no weapon on her. We rolled her in a tarp, sealed it, arranged her on the luggage cart, and covered her with a tablecloth Fantasy found in a storage closet. Baylor pushed her out the back way and transported her to our 3B offices. Fantasy and I cleaned the bar where her body had been. No Hair paced, and alternated between holding his breath and letting it out in whooshes. I tore out of my CSI clothes, rolled them, and added them to the evidence bag. I crossed the room slowly, fell into Bradley, and sobbed.

* * *

@StrikeWaiters #Congratulations @ElspieBabie Good luck at your new job!

@StrikeWaiters #Promoted #NewBoss @Tra_Raines a.k.a Gold Cowboy Boots!

@StrikeWaiters #BellissimoBarre cancelled until further notice.

@StrikeWaiters #GoldTan cancelled forever. #Itchy

* * *

I drove a Strike Town Car to The Pointe apartments on Cedar Lane Road. I parked in Elspeth's space. I sat there five minutes staring at my lap and listening to myself breathe. I knocked on the door, Brianna Strother answered in a bathrobe, I introduced myself. Real name. Real job. Chocolate Covered Cherry hair. I asked if I might come in.

She collapsed at my boots.

* * *

The women met at the Criminal Investigators Training Program in Glynco, Georgia, nine years ago. Half of the class, like Elspeth, was ATF. The other half of the forty-eight CITP students were, like Brianna, from other federal agencies. They were randomly chosen as partners in a federal court mock trial and that led to the women deliberately choosing each other for better or for worse. They were married on the Fourth of July, 2007, in Montpelier, Vermont. Their jobs kept them geographically separated, most recently for eight months, together on scattered weekends and occasional holidays, and stolen months between assignments. Then Elspeth was placed on the DeKalb County, Alabama drug task force. Target: Jennings Christmas Tree Farms. At the time, Brianna was working out of the New Orleans Office of Homeland Security & Emergency Preparedness on Perdido Street—as we guessed, working a cargo drug smuggling ring—and it took the women less than two weeks to determine they were working the same case. At which point, they were able to share a rare roof.

This was to have been Elspeth's last assignment. Having completed the six-year waiting period and an additional year of paperwork, then two bank-breaking trips to Kajaani, Finland, the last strip of red tape had been torn and the ink was drying on the adoption papers for their nine-month-old daughter. They'd already booked business class seats on Air France for December 28th.

My heart broke, and broke, and broke, and broke. Then broke.

* * *

By early evening, Strike in full swing, the last of the proper authorities had arrived, and our 3B offices were invaded. Crawling all over the three large rooms that made up our work space were representatives of the Department of Justice and an even larger crew from the Federal Action Task Force. A forensic chemist team from the Bureau of Alcohol, Tobacco, Firearms, and Explosives took gentle care of their fallen comrade Elspeth. They praised our preservation and documentation.

I called catering. "Sandwiches, salads, cookies, coffee," I said. "I don't think it matters. Just lots of food." Someone behind me in a blue jacket—they were all wearing blue jackets—asked for shrimp.

"And you really want all this delivered to Gamer, Mrs. Sanders?"

Gamer is a kiddie casino around the corner from the darkened doorway, which gets you to the Super Secret elevator, the one that leads to our offices. "Is there a problem?"

"No, ma'am."

Fifteen minutes later, Elspeth's bagged body rolled out the door on a gurney and five minutes after that, a gurney full of food and drink rolled in. The blue-jackets swarmed. A man, who'd been sitting quietly in a corner, rose from his seat. He was pale, with thick white hair, steel-gray eyes behind Drew Carey eyeglasses, and a neck like a tree trunk. When he stood, the blue-jacket people stopped chewing. When he opened his mouth to speak, the blue-jacket people stopped breathing.

"You have forty-eight hours."

"We need more time." The way No Hair said it caused a semi-circle of open air around him as everyone and their sandwiches took a giant step back.

The white-haired DOJ man sniffed. "Bring me the killer by Wednesday."

"I need ten days." No Hair took a deliberate step in his direction. The DOJ man raised him, taking two steps toward No Hair. Any second now I expected to hear zippers and there'd be pants on the ground, then the rest of us would be asked to vote on whose was bigger.

"You have until Saturday, then I'm taking over this investigation."

"Midnight," No Hair said.

"Deal."

* * *

"I'm ready to deal. Deal or no deal. Let's make a deal. Deal me in."

"Bea."

Strike Casino was blowing up, every *future*Gaming station occupied; I was watching from a safe corner. I'd been wearing black suede boots for eighteen hours. I was half asleep; Elspeth was dead. Fantasy had been bringing me coffee since midnight, and before she sat it down on the table in front of me, she took a slug of it. Then stood there waiting on her tip. For drinking my coffee.

"Have you been drinking, Bea?" I switched ears. "Can't we talk about this tomorrow?"

"Hey," my ex-ex-mother-in-law said. "I'm not the one in a pickle. That'd be *you*, Davis. And I thought you might want fair warning."

I'm up. "Fair warning? Fair warning about what?"

"Eddie might have accidently found out what was going on."

"What? Bea? Accidentally?"

Now I was wide awake. I was in the quietest corner Strike offered, but I still had trouble hearing her over the gaming. I switched ears again. "It's the simplest thing in the world, Bea. Call the courthouse, verify the paperwork, and the whole thing will be over. And you *told* Eddie?"

"I did not tell Eddie," she said, "and you can stop with your smart mouth right now or I'll hang up. It was Smerle T. who told him."

Next up on my to-do list, take Smerle T. Webb down.

"You can't expect to steal somebody's car and there not be... be..."

In a million years, Bea Crawford wouldn't come up with the word, so I handed it to her. "Repercussions."

"Damn straight, Davis. You play, you pay. Smerle T. told Eddie what was going on, then talked him into filing for a divorce, and I'm being *nice* to you. Calling and telling you up front."

"Who told Smerle T., Bea?"

We observed a moment of silence as an innocent squirrel detonated.

"Well," Bea said, "I can't reveal my sources."

"You mean you can't incriminate yourself."

"Don't start talking shit to me, Davis."

Never. "When did all this happen?"

"Just a while ago. I missed Conan." She pronounced it as two names: Co Nan. "I'm wondering if you might want me to step in for you. And then maybe you'll do me a little favor."

Here it comes. She started the fire, now she's volunteering to put it out for a price. "What, Bea?"

"I need a little help with Melvin."

"What's wrong with him?" Other than he has Bombay gin for breakfast, lunch, and dinner, and Eddie the Ass Crawford for a son.

"The bank's gonna take the diner from us. You breathe a word of this to your family and I'll wring your neck. You hear me, Davis? I need you to float me a loan so we can keep the diner and for payback I'll get Eddie off your back and I'll call the courthouse in Camden."

My temples throbbed.

"I'm offering to sell you part of the diner under the tables. This is a good deal for you, Davis. You get your divorce and you get to secretly own part of Mel's Diner."

The flat screens around the room running Strike commercials on a long loop lit up with a win video: Missy Jennings hit a $70,000 jackpot and advanced to the next level.

#SurpriseSurprise

"Sliding me a little is going to be a whole lot cheaper than Eddie taking you to the cleaners in another divorce, Davis. And you just ask yourself this," she said, "is your lawyer still going to want you after you and Eddie go at it again like junkyard dogs in court?"

A very good question. One I reluctantly pondered after I told Bea I'd see her in hell before I'd give her a penny. (No, I didn't.) (I told her I'd call her back after I'd had some sleep, then against all that is good and right in the world, I told her to have a number ready for me.) (She asked why I wanted a number when it was money that she needed.) (I hung up.)

I love Bradley Cole. He loves me. We'd been through so much in our three years—too much—and we both believed one day we'd live a life that didn't involve holding our breaths until we worked through the latest fiasco, courtesy of me. We wanted a family. We wanted to grow old together. These facts played on a loop in my brain when I was in the shower or at a red light.

However.

There were times when it hit me like a freight train—now was one of them—when I knew it could fall apart in a heartbeat. Of course it could. Arnold and Maria. Brad and Jen. Scarlett and Rhett. I couldn't stay in the giddy place about my relationship one hundred percent of the time. (Who could?) He said the right things, he made the right moves, and the engagement ring I wore at home and on my off days was perfection. We laughed, we cried. We knew how to connect on a level that far surpassed anything I'd even known existed. But how much of our relationship could be attributed to me having a different color of hair several days a week? (It's there. I just don't think about it.) And me being in the thick of all things Richard Sanders, Bellissimo, I-can-get-front-row-Maroon 5-tickets? How much of how Bradley loves me is about the me with an exciting job that keeps me busy ninety hours a week? He never complained. What man would? My obligations meant he could work late, sleep late, be alone, play golf, have the whole bed/pizza/remote, be *this* close to single, and never hear a peep out of me. The biggest question of all: isn't it somewhat suspicious Bradley Cole has the stamina to go through it and through it and through it with me and my ex-ex-husband?

The dress up routine? Would end. Along with my round-the-clock schedule. If all goes as planned, and in a year or two (tick tock tick tock) I will give up my job, and there's a chance in letting it go, I'll be giving up my relationship as I know it. I'll be waiting at the door for him forty pounds heavier wearing yoga pants and stringy hair, with a teething baby on my hip demanding to know where he's been. Will he still love me? Will he love me like he does today? Let's say yes. Let's say he'll still love me the same in spite of the yoga pants. Maybe he loves me even more. (!) Invariably, though, without a doubt, there's no way around it, *this* will happen: my ex-ex-husband will pop up and bring yet another nightmare into our lives, and when everything is different—stay-at-home-mommy-yoga-pants-Davis—will Bradley still be willing to deal with my ex-ex-husband?

I'm going to have to kill Eddie Crawford.

It's the only way to protect what I have with Bradley.

The Jennings, one at a time, on their way to the bar or from the lounges, cashed another combined $120,000 from their Strike account while I was busy channeling my mother—the sky is falling.

Two in the morning. One more hour of Strike. One more hour to pick a killer out of this crowd. The doors burst wide open and a killer waltzed in. Bianca Casimiro Sanders, backlit from the big casino, stood in the open doorway looking, for all practical purposes, like Lady Macbeth Miranda Priestly Cinderella's Stepmother, the blonde in *Fatal Attraction*. She'd found her way home from Paris, she'd found her ruined fur, and she'd found me. She did her runway walk and dropped the totally trashed $38,000 white mink fur with ermine tips at my boots, then told me I'd better have a wig on, because if I'd cut my hair without her permission, I could find myself another job.

FIFTEEN

Before Brianna Strother caught a federal flight to Florida, the last trip she'd take with Elspeth, where she'd join her wife's family in Cocoa Beach and say goodbye, she gathered everything they had on the Jennings and left it on her dining room table for us. She was having no trouble making the big decisions, but the smaller ones were knocking her down. "I don't know where Elspeth's keys are! She puts them everywhere! Anywhere! They could be in the *freezer* for all I know!" There was a sharp edge of hysteria that wasn't there three minutes ago when we were talking about Brianna's single-parent options. "I don't understand why she can't just put them in her *pocket* or her *purse!*" I told her we'd work it out. Fantasy was working the front door lock. I was standing guard. "We should have brought a dog."

Fantasy stopped with the tension wrench. "Why?"

"So I could look like I'm walking a dog."

"You look," she stood and popped the door open, "like a nut job already, Davis. A dog would just make matters worse. And if I failed to mention it, you smell just horrific."

She'd mentioned it. She made me hang my head out the window on the ride over. Hair and Makeup Angela had somehow gotten her hands on a gallon jug of bull goo (I did not ask) and I was treating myself to a Viagra mask before this Monday got into full swing. Angela taped a note to the bucket: *Get it on for an hour in the mornings, let it sink into your scalp, and even after you shampoo it out it will work its magic all day.* A good plan. I had a shower cap over the bull mask and a cashmere sweater tied around something equally prohibited, going on within the banking division of Strike. (Smurf·ing, [noun] to break up large sums of money into smaller sums so as to stay off the bank's/casino's/IRS's radar.) (So he was paying attention.)

I'd worked with Mr. Sanders and No Hair long enough to know that these two tidbits hadn't been Levi Newman's ticket into the Loyal Order of Bellissimo. It was only when he slapped down ten photographs of me in ten different hair colors/compromising positions, they had no choice but to induct him. "This woman is behind it all," he'd said. "Is this woman your *wife*, Richard? *What* is going on here? *Where* is the social media girl?" One thing led to another. Most of it led to me. Soon I'd be wearing a gold engraved Bellissimo name tag like everyone else.

Davis Way

Pine Apple, Alabama

Super Secret Spy/Bianca Sanders Body Double

"Sit down, Davis," Mr. Sanders said. "Bring Levi up to speed."

I didn't tell all. (I rarely do.) (Especially to fifty-year-old men who get in tanning beds.)

"So Cassidy is in on this?" Rather than angry, or panicked, the casino manager acted personally offended. "Cassidy has been with me for years. Someone is forcing her to do this. She knows exactly what will happen if she's caught laundering money."

"It happens, Mr. Hasselhoff."

Uh-oh.

"Mr. *Newman*! Mr. *Newman*!" I rushed his name out ten more times. He finally let me stop by waving his pinkie ring. No Hair growled, and Mr. Sanders hid behind his wedding band. I wish I didn't *think* nicknames, then I could stop saying them out loud and humiliating myself. Mr. Sanders came out from behind his hand and rolled it. Keep going, Davis, I'll kill you later.

"The Jennings opened an in-house account and deposited an unusually large amount of money into it before the tournament started. Now they're systematically withdrawing it."

"Why?" Levi Hasselhoff asked.

"Because they report and pay taxes on casino transactions. They're using the Strike casino to give themselves a legitimate source of income."

"I take it their primary source of income isn't legitimate," Levi Newman said.

"You're right."

"I thought he was a farmer."

No Hair and Mr. Sanders were watching it like Wimbledon.

"He is. He grows pot. Tons of it. He has twenty-five thousand marijuana plants hidden between rows of Christmas trees in the hills of northeast Alabama."

One of Levi Newmanhoff's eyebrows tried to move. (Levi Botoxhoff.) He seemed a little stunned, paling under his fake tan, twitching. "What will that net? What's the street value?"

"At the end of the day, fifty million."

"What else?" His posture and speech became a tad manic. "What other leads are you following? Who else from my team is in on this? What other evidence do you have?"

I waved a one-finger signal to No Hair to let me take this. If we were going to talk about Missy Jennings making it rain, well on her way to winning the tournament, I wanted him to bring it up. "That's it, Mr. Newman."

"What are we going to do?" Beads of sweat marched across the Botox.

"We'll wait for the Strike competition to end," I said, "then we'll have them arrested."

No way I was telling this man anything else.

We sat quietly in his wake. I was panting.

"Davis, he's our casino manager."

"I know, Mr. Sanders, but he wasn't here because he's the casino manager. He was here to find out how much we know."

* * *

At the end of the day, it would cost me twelve thousand dollars to buy a divorce from Eddie the Ass Crawford by cutting a deal with my ex-ex-mother-in-law. A big court brawl with her son would be decidedly more expensive. Not that I was the least bit happy about the arrangement; it was the principle of the matter. No part of me wanted to give money to Bea Crawford. No part of me wanted to be a silent partner in Mel's Diner. And no part of me wanted her to have a secret to hang over my head for the rest of my life.

However, all of me wanted to be divorced, and this looked to be the most expedient and least painful path. I didn't have time to explore any other divorce avenue short of throwing myself at Eddie the Snake Snake Snake's feet, and I didn't have time for that. (Not that I would if I did.) If we didn't find Elspeth Raiffe's killer and hand he/she/it over to the feds, this whole place would shut down. So twelve thousand dollars to Bea Crawford it is.

"You won't regret this, Davis."

"I already do, Bea."

"This'll take some of the sting out," she said. "From now on, you can eat at Mel's free."

My next call was to Bradley Cole, who I'd slept in the same bed with last night, but hadn't had a conversation with other than a quick text message exchange since Sunday night. Bradley, whose only brush with dead bodies had been of the funeral-home-visitation variety, was still shaken up about Elspeth. Actually, he was shaken up about me.

"How," he'd asked, "can you *do* that? I couldn't even *look* at her, Davis, and there you were on *top* of her."

It's just this: When a life is violently cut short, then that life's body falls in your lap, the gore of it all is replaced by a fervent desire for justice for the person who lived in the body. That's in your lap. It's disgusting. It's heart-stopping. It's the stuff of nightmares. But if everyone ran from dead bodies, there'd be no one to right the wrongs.

The thought of eating at Mel's Diner made me sick. Processing a murder scene didn't.

I can't explain it.

"Bea's agreed to do it."

"How much?" Bradley asked.

"Peanuts." Lie number one.

"The feds are taking over the Elspeth case today, right?"

"Right." Lie number two.

"So you'll be home at a decent hour? Tell me you'll be home at a decent hour."

"I'll be home at a decent hour." Lie number three.

* * *

Now that I was out of the closet with Levi Newman and didn't have an immediate supervisor at Strike (may she rest in peace), I didn't have it hanging over my head that the Strike casino was open, busy, and I needed to be there. I still Instagramed and Tumblded, but (a) I had a stash of great stuff on the camera, and (b) it was a little after the fact, with the competition nearing the halfway point, and (c) Fantasy texted me hourly as Missy Jennings won, and I let the ravenous cyber public know. (*These gold shoes SUCK and Dance Mama Dance just won another 125K.*) (#WinnerWinnerChickenDinner @DanceMamaMissy #She'sStrikingItRich!) It was two in the afternoon on Monday, and I needed some electronic time of my own. In my own office on my own mainframe talking to my own father.

First, we caught up. Pine Apple's dodo bird excuse for a medical practitioner, Dr. Cliff Kizzy, was out fishing on Mountain Laurel Lake a week ago and hooked himself an ear. He panicked, I'm skipping the next part, and now he was convalescing at home after plastic surgery at Baptist Medical Center South in Montgomery. Filling in for him was Dr. Corey McKinney, MD, Family Medicine, on loan from Stabler Memorial in Greenville. It just so happened that my niece Riley woke up with an earache and middle-of-the-night phone call about our son, and I don't appreciate it."

Her dogs sat in her lap and glared at me. One curled a lip. The other rumbled, deep in its throat. How quickly they forget T-bone steaks.

"What do you have to say for yourself?"

One of these days.

One of these days.

"I'm sorry you have to deal with this, Mrs. Sanders." They call it parenthood, Bianca. "And it's circumstantial. Thomas is most likely innocent." (Honestly, using the words "Thomas" and "innocent" in the same sentence almost choked me.) "It's more likely that the Jennings boy is the one involved in drugs, and Thomas is only guilty of being on the same airplane with him."

"He's been *suspended* from school, David."

It's Davis. And his suspension is over tomorrow. Thank goodness.

"You'll need to meet with the parents again and report directly back to me."

Yes, I do need to meet with the parents again.

"Arrange something."

Done. Quick drinks at Strike at six this evening. They wouldn't commit to dinner with Bianca because it would cut too far into their legitimate livelihood.

"I expect you to get to the bottom of this quickly."

#CanIGo?

"Now." She crossed her legs the other way and leaned in. "I have a few more items to discuss with you."

The redecorate after the remodel after the lightning strike was called Blizzard. What wasn't blindingly white in the new and improved corner of the Sanders' residence was mirrored. Everything hard goods was distressed mirrored. Everything soft goods was white—floors, walls, upholstery, window treatments, accessories. Bianca, no surprise, was dressed head-to-toe in black. For an hour after she finished lecturing and threatening me, I had a dark ghost image slicing through the middle of my field of vision. She went on for a while telling me I looked like a birth defect duckling with the new growth of hair framing my face—it had grown more than an inch after just four days and three bull treatments, it was fuzzy, and it did stick straight up. I could see her tiring on the subject of my hair, and knowing where we were headed, I tightened my grip on the arms of the snow-white chair. Her. Fur. Had I reacted in a timely manner, the fur could have been saved. It was—did I realize?—a limited production Valentino, no longer available in the United States, she wasn't up to any additional cross-continental travel at the moment, she certainly couldn't trust *me* to pick it up for her, and my days of wearing her furs were *over*. Got that, David? Over.

✳ ✳ ✳

@StrikePlayers Day 4 done, 20 lucky players left standing. #WhoWillWin? #StrikeItRich

SIXTEEN

It's a strange phenomenon when the qualities and attributes you're initially attracted to in a person end up being the very issues that split you apart. I've seen it many times. A girl I went to high school with, Candy Mobry Reese, used to stand in the middle of Banana Street on Thursday afternoons to flag down Roll Me One Rufus, a lunch wagon specializing in burritos, on its weekly Greenville-to-Selma run, so she could get a chili potato burrito. One Thursday when we were in 11th grade, she climbed in the food truck, married the owner/operator (Rufus, who was seventeen years older than Candy Mobry), and from that moment on, did nothing but complain about burritos—the smell, the heat, the thirty pounds she gained, life on the road chopping onions ain't easy. The innocent burrito, the very thing that brought them together, was the very thing that ripped them apart. Candy Mobry divorced Rufus five years later. By then she'd suffered irreversible loss of tooth structure as a result of chemical dissolution from living on a steady diet of chips and salsa. The acid erosion took fifteen of her twenty-eight teeth, and it wasn't too long before Candy had to have the other thirteen yanked out. At age twenty-two, Candy woke up in a dentist's chair with a set of ComfyLites stuffed in her mouth she owed $23.99 a month on for the next eleven years. To this day, if you use the words "refried" or "bean" in her company, she will pop out her lower acrylic plate and nail you between the eyes with it.

Fantasy dealt with it too. Her husband was hysterical. The way Reggie sat in a chair was funny. He ate breakfast (burritos) funny. The man just thought funny. Spending time with Fantasy and

Reggie could be a painful experience, because when Reggie's there, everyone's doubled-over. Ask Fantasy the how-did-you-know question, and she'll tell you she'd never laughed so hard in her life. As it turns out, though, constant laughter and family life don't always mix. When their second son, K2 was born (the boys' names all start with K; I call them K1, K2, and K3), Reggie had the delivery room so in stitches with a story about a four-foot-long corn snake he'd rescued along the side of the road, locked in the trunk of his car, then forgot about until the next day when it crawled through the backseat ski slot and wrapped itself all over an Assistant Special Teams Coach for the New Orleans Saints Reggie was taking to lunch, that halfway through the story, Fantasy delivered K2 on the floor. She tried to get someone's, anyone's, attention, but her cries were drowned out by the hilarity. The obstetrician, wiping corn-snake tears from his eyes, literally dropped their newborn son on the delivery room floor. And the laughs just wouldn't stop. Last year, Reggie took his three sons through an eye-hand coordination exercise involving a basket of clean matched sports socks and a domed ceiling light fixture. The story was side-splitting. The fire was four-alarm. The very thing that brought Fantasy and Reggie together was the very thing that repeatedly threatened to put them asunder.

So, when I tiptoed through my front door at two in the morning, having not gotten in at a decent hour, Bradley was waiting up for me. I stood face to face with the increasingly sticky situation that threatened our happiness—my job. The very thing that brought us together. My picture-perfect husband-to-be was the perfect picture of anger and frustration. He said two words. "Dammit, Davis." He turned, marched down the hall, then slammed the bedroom door.

Our first six months together, Bradley couldn't get enough of my job. He was fascinated by it. He wanted details. He strategized with me. He understood. He helped, tossing out legal opinions. His appreciation of my work peaked around our one-year anniversary, and since then, it's been on a slow downward spiral. Last year, my near-miss, bullet-whizzing, and computer wizardry stories went from the "You're amazing, Davis!" column to "You could be arrested for that, Davis." This year? On our bumpy way down the aisle? Bradley was sick of my job—the hours, the danger, the circumvention of traditional (and by traditional I mean rational) methods of discovery and apprehension. Elspeth's death sent him over the edge.

If Bradley presented me with an ultimatum, it would break my heart. I'd never choose the Bellissimo over Bradley, but those wouldn't be the stakes: he'd be asking me to agree to a relationship in which he was the lead. And what would that make me?

#TheBehind

Maybe it's my short hair causing all the problems around here.

* * *

I gave him his space and I took mine.

The to-do laundry was at Code Red.

#Guilty

Actually, everything under this roof was in a neglected mood. I hiked around the clothes mountains in the laundry room. Note to self: Raise hell with Erika Cleaning Woman. I found a comfy enough pajama combo in the dryer, both items Bradley's, and left Bianca's Rebecca Minkoff pink zip-crepe dress in a puddle on a basket full of damp towels. I was too wired to sleep after a long night at Strike, and too tired to resist biting if I got in bed and Bradley dangled any bait, so I fired up my laptop.

The laptop I drag from work to home and home to work is a thirty-two gigabyte with a one terabyte hard drive, plus turbo boost, so it operates at speeds up to three-point-four gigahertz. It had 10/100/1000 gigabit Ethernet LAN, so it will work fast and anywhere—Narnia, Hogwarts, Middle Earth, the Regent Beachfront Luxury Condos in Biloxi, Mississippi. The operating system is your standard Microsoft issue, but I had it loaded with all sorts of goodies. Like ShareWork. In simple terms, ShareWork makes comparisons. Type in apples and ask the software to compare it to oranges, then the program comes back with attributes they have in common. (Trees.) I hacked it years ago. I went to the source code, found the compiler, and broadened the fields. Next, I programmed it with a Magic 8 Ball feature that merged the data, then took a lucky guess at what it all meant. Bottom line, I super-sized ShareWork. So when you enter apples in one field and oranges in the other, then shook the Magic 8 Ball, the program returns thousands of Sangria, smoothie, and fruit salad recipes. With the upgrade, I could enter huge amounts of data for detailed comparisons. I could upload lists, embedded tables, kitchen sinks, images, PDFs, then ask ShareWork to compare it to a different set of statistics/files/data, and if the two sets of information had any commonalities, if they crisscrossed anywhere, the software would find it.

I uploaded the memory card from Brianna Strother's computer. Then I uploaded the memory stick from Elspeth Raiffe's computer. I asked ShareWork to compare everything from the two sets of data and find anything that was remotely related. Like *Match Game*. A show Granny Dee loved when I was little. (#GeneRayburn) After ten minutes, ShareWork popped up a clock. Based on the uploads, give it four hours for results. Which I didn't mind. Four ShareWork hours were the equivalent of four hundred manual hours. Which I didn't have.

I turned out lights until the only hint was the glow of my hard-at-work laptop on the dining room table. It was new moon. It was pitch black. I made my way down the long dark hall to fix things with Bradley and ran smack dab into him as he was on his way to fix things with me.

"I don't know what you're afraid of, Davis."

(This was hours after we went bump in the night.) (In the hall.)

We were nose-to-nose and whispering. "I'm not, Bradley. I'm not afraid."

"You are. You know I would never ask you to quit your job.

Never. If and when we have a family, if you want to work, and that's your decision, I think you should have a more supervisory position like Jeremy's than the in-the-trenches job you have now, because it'd be safer. Or you might want to think about cutting back to just the Bianca end of your job. But again, Davis, that would be up to you."

I could do a job more like No Hair's. All day long. Full-time Bianca? No way.

"I think something's bothering you," Bradley said, "and whatever it is, you're avoiding it by throwing yourself into Elspeth's murder like you're the only one who can get to the bottom of it. And you're doing it, I think, to keep from dealing with whatever's bothering you."

"Why are you saying all this, Bradley?"

"Because while you're intent on clearing up the divorce, you've said nothing about getting married."

(Really? I hadn't?)

"And I'm not the only one working the Elspeth case."

"You've gone total Lone Ranger on this one," he said. "When's the last time you talked to Fantasy? Gotten her take? Delegated anything? What about Baylor? He always has a fresh perspective, yet you're intent on doing everything yourself."

Oh, dear.

"So," I could barely hear him, "I don't think it's because you want to be the hero, Davis. I think it's so you can avoid dealing with whatever it is you don't want to deal with."

"Where's this coming from, Bradley?"

"My heart, Davis." He ran a finger along my baby-fuzz hairline. "It's coming from my heart."

* * *

Happy! Happy! Happy! Happy Wednesday Morning @StrikePlayers! 10 more out, semi-finals tomorrow. #StrikingItRich

* * *

"Richard and Thomas left for New Hampshire at seven this morning. He's meeting with Thomas's advisors and such."

No Hair's Tie of the Day featured the Superman shield. It was nine in the morning, and we were in his mancave of an office, each with a cup of Coffee of the Day from Beans, the coffeehouse in the lobby. After one sip, I wanted to pull my gun out and shoot it. Baked Alaska. (#Ridiculous) (#Nasty)

"Did Bianca go with them?"

"She thinks she did." No Hair polished off his coffee and looked at mine inquiringly. I pushed it over. Be my guest. "So lay low until mid-afternoon," he said. "If she sees you, she'll know she didn't bother to attend her only child's disciplinary hearing."

"I'm a terrible mother."

"That you are, Bianca," No Hair said, "but you're good with a computer. What'd you come up with?" He peeked at his watch. "We have sixty hours before the feds take over and this place closes."

"So far, a bunch of nothing, but maybe a little something."

We locked brains.

"You think you have something?"

"Maybe."

"Who?"

"It's not a who," I said. "It's a what."

"Okay, Davis. What?"

"Chairs."

No Hair looked to the heavens and shook why-oh-why hands.

"What do you need?" he asked.

"Time at my desk."

"Okay," he said. "One more thing before you go."

"What's that?" I began collecting my things.

"You knew when we hired Levi we'd be working with him."

"I didn't think it was a good idea then, No Hair, and I don't think it's a good idea now."

"Get used to it."

* * *

My casino career, to date, had me answering to two men. Two men I trusted, respected, and, at the end of the day, cared about. Throw Bianca into the mix, who, at the end of the day, I'm not so sure I care all that much about, and I had one too many bosses. We worked around the former casino manager, Ty Thiboduex, not for him, and in my opinion, that's the way it should be. Internal Affairs doesn't brief the Chief of Police every morning, because invariably, the Chief's going to hear something that hits too close to home—his training officer's name, who would never take a bribe, or his buddy's son's name, who would never steal from the evidence lockers—and the next thing you know, the whole system is compromised. The checks and balances are gone. I say keep Special Forces special.

Mr. Sanders was the one who suggested, with Mr. Thiboduex retiring and Levi Newman coming in, we should make our team available to him. I didn't like the idea at all. I presented my argument, was voted down, but a compromise was reached: We wouldn't have to report to Levi Newman until after the Strike It Rich sweepstakes. Which, at the time, meant I could get good and married before I became the casino manager's whipping girl, and we all know how that turned out.

I didn't like the casino manager position in the first place. I think it's structured for failure. One man responsible for how profitable the casino is, every employee on the casino floor, and every casino patron. There are several conflicts there. Have one person responsible for the employees, another for the patrons, and charge them both with profitability. As it is, I can't see how a casino manager wouldn't lean one way or the other: he's either going to lean in the direction of the player, slighting the employees, or the other way around. Give a casino manager an investigative team, and his ultimate responsibility for how his casino performed would go away—he'd have someone to blame.

Me.

I can't understand why anyone would want the job in the first place. Christmas off? Forget it. A home with a yard? No. A family? Vacations? Never. If you are the only thing between a casino owner and profit margins three hundred and sixty-five days a year, you live on site, you're on call, you're in the fire all day every day, and you're lucky to get to the casino manager's residence for even a few hours of sleep at a time. (Down the hall from Jay Leno's place.) Casino managers had an attitude too: I make a million dollars a year, therefore I am gold. You, spy girl, wouldn't have a job if it weren't for me. Which brings us to the upside of being the casino manager at the Bellissimo: the million. What kind of person trades their life and everyone in it for a big title and money they don't have time to spend? The kind of person I don't care to work for.

I didn't like anything about it.

I guess I'd better get used to it.

* * *

I had the office to myself. Fantasy, having passed out liquor until closing time again last night, would check in around two for her gold spray tan (back by popular demand) before another shift in a bikini and gold heels. Baylor, who'd been working during the day keeping Little Sanders busy, then working the Strike shift at night, probably hadn't even rolled over yet, but would be in around the same time. I probably should sit down and talk to them both.

And I probably should grow my hair back.

Every day, I get better results from bending over double with a hair dryer and a round brush so when I stand up and shake my head, what's left of my long hair points to my nose and chin—think Victoria Beckham—covering the new growth, but I want to be able to pull it back, out of my face. I miss my ponytail. So before I hit the computers, I loaded my head up with noxious bull goo. I dug through the accessory drawer in our dressing room and came up with a knit snow hat. It never snows in Biloxi. I don't know why we even have this hat. It was powder blue with a pompom on top, ear flaps, and long knit ties tipped with tassels. The hat contained the smell and was absorbent, so it kept the rest of me bull-free. Not to mention I looked perfectly gorgeous.

I went from the dressing room to the bullpen, where I gathered pizza boxes and fake beer bottles—the décor of Little Sanders. I bagged it all and tossed it out the door. I disconnected all things Xbox, and tossed it all in Baylor's little closet. I went back and got the stupid bean bags we'd all tripped over a hundred times and stuffed them in there too. I brewed a pot of non-Alaskan coffee. Having taken care of things in two of our three rooms, I opened the office door and woke up the computers. Now. I rubbed my hands together, mad-scientist style. To work.

*   *   *

ShareWork matched a shipping manifest filed with Gulf Container Cargo submitted by one Melanie Turner York on Brianna's computer with a UPS delivery confirmation signed by the same Melanie Turner York on behalf of a Fort Payne, Alabama, chair manufacturer, Have A Seat, which it found on Elspeth's hard drive. It ran Melanie York back through Brianna's data and found her name listed on an APIS (Advanced Passenger Information System) manifest filed with the FAA as a passenger on 0821MS, a Pilatus PC-24, the same private plane listed in an incident report filed by the DEA office in Bedford, New Hampshire, naming the Brewster-Exeter Academy for Boys in Haverhill, New Hampshire, as the location of the incident. Included in the report, a (non-minor) student's name, Quinn Jennings, which pulled a match with Jennings Tree Farms in Lickskillet, Alabama, which sent the software flying to TuscaloosaNews.com's photo attributes under a Roll Tide Crazy feature naming Melanie Turner York and Missy Jennings Roll Tide Crazy Fans of the Day. The matches zigzagged for seventeen computer screens and somewhere in the middle, ShareWork pulled a link to a DVD collection that guaranteed I'd never miss another putt or my money back. On sale for $49.99.

Nothing's perfect.

I wiggled my fingers in the air, squeezed my eyes closed, then clicked the Magic 8 Ball icon. I watched data fly until ShareWork came back with a flashing name. The name popped up sixteen times in Brianna's evidence and twenty-three times in Elspeth's, and neither had flagged it, acted on it, or for all I could see, even noticed it.

I sat perfectly still until I reached for the phone. I dialed.

"Have A Seat. This is Melanie."

"Hi, Melanie. I need to speak to Walter Shaefer."

"Mr. Shaefer's not in."

#GotHim

"Can I take a message?"

"No," I said, "but maybe you can help me. I bought a chair from you and it's broken. How do I get a refund?"

The line went dead.

#Bingo

I spun my chair around in surprise when the office door banged against the wall. Fantasy was wearing an open trench coat, a gold bikini, fuzzy pink slippers, and she had my ex-ex-husband Eddie the Ass Crawford by the ear. "Look what I found."

"God almighty. Is there a skunk in here?"

"Shut up, Eddie. What are you doing here?" Then I asked Fantasy, "Have you ever seen this man?" I held up Walter Shaefer's picture.

Eddie made a very derogatory comment about my headgear. Fantasy kicked him out the door and into the bullpen with a fuzzy slipper to his rear end. "No," she said. "Wait. Maybe. He looks familiar."

* * *

"Your sister is dating a doctor."

"So I heard." I was on one sofa; Eddie sat as far away from (the scent of) me as possible on the other sofa. His stupid legs were slung over the arm. He was stretched out and propped on an elbow.

"Is that why you're here, Eddie? To fill me in on Meredith?"

"I'm here to talk about us." Eddie Crawford sucked his teeth.

"There is no us to discuss."

Chairs. The chairs were somehow connected to the pot farm and the pot farm was connected to the Strike casino. How? The chocolate-chip-cookie chairs in the Strike Casino? Could Have A Seat be the supplier?

"Don't you move a muscle, Eddie."

"I'll be right here for as long as you want me, Davis."

Eddie Crawford delivers all his lines as if his life were one big porn-movie audition. He says these bedroom things to everyone: me, my mother, his first cousins, the teenager in the speaker at Sonic, and graveside, to the widow.

I ran back to the computers, logged into the Bellissimo system, dug through, and found the bill of lading from the Strike furniture delivery. The Wonder Chairs were manufactured and shipped directly from Imminent Furniture, Inc. in Indianapolis. Strike One.

"I'm very busy, Eddie." I took my seat again, peeked at the time, scratched at my snow hat. "You have five minutes."

Eddie was wearing tight stonewashed jeans (he's such a girl), black square-toed boots, a black silk shirt only half buttoned (at three o'clock in the afternoon), and his hair was graying at his temples (ha ha).

"I'm here to do you a favor, Davis, so you can maybe not bitch at me before I change my mind."

"Alright, Eddie." My eyes were beginning to sting and my scalp was on fire. "Go ahead. Do me a favor."

Wait. Gulf Container Cargo had popped up too. Have A Seat was shipping chairs overseas. Maybe office chairs? The only office chairs in Strike were in the computer room. With the IT crew. Who controlled the gaming.

"Stay right there." You ass.

I ran back to the computers. The Strike IT office chairs, six of them, had been requisitioned internally. They were Tempur-Pedic

TP8000 Ergonomic Mesh Mid-Back Task Chairs, and they'd come straight from Staples on Denny Street in Pascagoula. Strike Two.

"Okay, Eddie." I plopped. "What's this favor?"

"I'm going to sue you, Davis." He said it like *I'm going to have the mahi-mahi.*

"How is that you doing me a favor?"

"My favor is telling you up front."

"You're too late. I've already heard."

He was irritated at being scooped. I knew this because he was grunting.

"What is it, exactly, you're suing me for?"

"Abandoning me." His humor returned. He cat smiled. His eyebrows danced. "It's a law. Call Smerle T. and ask him. You ran off and deserted your husband."

"Eddie." You are so sad. "You are absolutely out of your mind. I didn't abandon you, you idiot. We divorced fair and square. You can't take me back to court and divorce me again for a different reason. What happened, and obviously that brilliant legal mind you have working for you didn't bother to mention it, was a simple paperwork error. That has since"—now it was my turn to cat smile—"been taken care of."

"Oh, bull*shit*." He bolted upright, his boots hit the floor, and a stowaway Xbox controller popped out of a sofa cushion.

My head whipped around so fast the tassels from the pompom hat hit me in the nose. I ran back to the computers, yelling a string of things at Eddie on the way—talk to your mother, it's done, we're *very* divorced, go play in traffic.

Had Have A Seat ever shipped anything to Brewster-Exeter Academy for Boys? My shoulders drooped with the answer before my fingers could start the search. No. Anything the Jennings sent to the school would have been transported on their private plane. I had no way of knowing what was on that airplane. Strike Three.

"If you get up and run out of here one more time while I'm talking to you," Eddie poked a finger, "I'm leaving."

(Promise?)

beneath the whisper-thin veneer of civilized society lurks a fat, broke, opinionated beast, who doesn't see the glass half full, and expects, maybe even eagerly anticipates, the worst. More than half of Alabama residents have registered firearms. The other half, and I know this for a fact, have unregistered firearms, mostly of the sawed-off variety. Alabama is locked and loaded. "It's on!" says Alabama. About everything.

None of this applies to football. Alabama football fans are an extremist group all their own, the most vocal and violent of all the extremist groups in the state, and that's a whole different story.

So when I found Walter Shaefer, only to lose Walter Shaefer, then I found him again, then I lost him for good, being from Alabama, knowing how Alabamians operate, I had a pretty good idea where to start looking.

*　*　*

Wednesday afternoon turned blur.

Eddie the Stupid Crawford was heavily escorted off the property. He was eighty-sixed two years ago when it was discovered he'd been (a) aiding and abetting a slot-machine heist and (b) sleeping with Bianca Sanders.

I know. It makes me seasick too.

She'd since repented, reformed, and recommitted. He was then, and is now, beyond help. Eddie hadn't even tried to move on. I'm not sure he'll ever get over having punched so high above his pay grade. He lived for the day Bianca remembered him, said his name, or even acknowledged his existence. I believe his Bianca fixation was a large part of the reason I couldn't get him off my back. To see me is to dream of her. To show up and bother me is to be in the same zip code as her. To sneak into the Bellissimo and screw up my life is to possibly run into her.

I can't say I wasn't a little shaken by his parting sentiment, which had nothing to do with Bianca and everything to do with me, and I secretly planned to run it through my psyche later and check it for viability. I did, after Stupid's speech, stop breathing, and had to be led to the sofa and served two fingers of Maker's Mark. Could it be I didn't have it in me to be the wife Bradley Cole deserved, and that sorry dog Eddie went and said it out loud? If I had any anxiety about being married to Bradley—and I'm not saying I do—but if I did, it was nothing but perfectly normal pre-wedding jitters. In spite of even Bradley suggesting otherwise. Unless not having his mother's blessing was really doing a number on me. I couldn't do Bea Crawford again. I barely lived through it the first time. Not to mention the second go-around. No way I'd sign up for that kind of grief a third time. It could be I'm just too spooky, and somewhere deep down, I thought these roadblocks—lightning striking the Bellissimo, Little Sanders showing up, Elspeth dying, me still being married to Stupid—were the universe trying to tell me something: wait. Or what Stupid said.

Fantasy stood behind me and patted my shoulder. Pat pat, there there. No Hair sat down with me. He reached out and took one of my hands in his big paw and gave it a shake. "Do you want me to kill him, Davis? Because I will. Say the word." I opened my mouth to say the word, but before I could take him up on his kind and generous offer he added, "Please get whatever that is off your head or I will have to kill you before I kill him."

I hit the showers.

*　*　*

Have A Seat and Walter Shaefer dropped off the map five years ago, which was, probably not a coincidence, when Cassidy Banking was promoted at the Montecito in Las Vegas. And within months of when the Jennings bought an airplane, built a runway and a hangar for it, and shipped their son off to boarding school. Have A Seat was still in business, but for whatever reasons, they'd gone dark. Walter, I don't know about. Yet.

It's hard for me to believe, in this day and age, Have A Seat did everything manually. The only recorded documentation of any manner of business transaction I could find wasn't generated by Have A Seat. The only traces were produced on the other ends—Fed Ex, Moffett International Transport, Onweave Incorporated, Soon Fatt Buffet, Southern Textiles—by tangent businesses associated with Have A Seat, either shipping materials in, receiving product from, or delivering Szechuan Shrimp to. But there wasn't corresponding documentation from Have A Seat that they'd ordered anything. Or received anything. Or shipped anything. There wasn't a trace of anything Have A Seat in the marketplace, in the media, or in their own backyard. Google Earth couldn't even find them. The IRS knew nothing of them.

The only way to be as anonymous as they are in today's free market is to meticulously clean up after yourself. Wipe your cyber slate clean each and every day with each and every transaction. Which I'd bet Walter Shaefer was perfectly capable of—9th grade State Science Fair winner for crypto-system software development (sold to Alabama Technical Enterprises), perfect SAT score at age fifteen, Fort Payne High School valedictorian (duh) at age sixteen, honors B.S.-M.S. degree in computer sciences from Rutgers at age twenty-two—which meant he was perfectly capable of manipulating the protocol software running Strike too. Walter Shaefer probably *wrote* the Strike software. At a red light. Or during a television commercial. Or between salad and entrée.

Walter Shaefer made me look like a toddler with a VTech.

And I couldn't find him.

I couldn't find him, I couldn't find anything on Have A Seat, and I had no idea what they were manufacturing—boat seats, church pews, bus-stop benches—but one thing I felt certain of: Whatever it was going out the back door of Have A Seat was stuffed plumb full of pot. And both Have A Seat and Jennings Tree Farms were turning it all into legitimate income at Strike Casino. As a team.

These people had grown up together, they'd gone into business together, and they'd formed a Northeast Alabama drug cartel together. A drug cartel cleaning their houses in our house. Walter

Shaefer, computer geek extraordinaire, was probably the brains behind it all. And he was lost in space.

Walter Shaefer was the key. He had the answers. But, where was he?

#FindWalter

I loaded the most recent photograph of him I had into the Bellissimo's facial-recognition software. It was five years old, and it was a newspaper article announcing the retirement of Archie M. Shaefer, of Lickskillet, Alabama, and the passing of the Have A Seat torch to his sons Walter and Wesley. It was the last solid documentation of Walter's existence.

It was six o'clock. I needed to scoot, so I didn't take the time to crop Wesley the brother out before I ran the photograph through the age-progression app of our facial-recognition software. I zipped it to Fantasy, Miss Gold Shoes Bikini, who was passing out drinks.

Here's what this Walter guy might look like today. Have we seen him? (The one on the left.)

She texted right back. *No. But make the one on the right bald.*

Fantasy, I don't have time for this.

Do it.

I did it.

That's our bartender. I'm standing right in front of him.

Which meant Fantasy and Wesley Shaefer were standing directly under the gold icicle glass sculpture. The same one Elspeth took her last breath under. And bald, mean, creepy Wesley Shaefer was the same man who'd busted in on me and Elspeth in the liquor closet. Chances were he knew where his brother was.

*　*　*

I stood in the middle of our dressing room. Of the three rooms that make up our 3B offices, this was my favorite. A safe haven. A place to breathe. A great place to think.

One wall is solid Beauty Station, split into hers and hers vanities complete with Hollywood spotlights. The countertop is an

"Let's say I don't find anything," he said. "What would my next step be?"

"Thermal imaging."

"That might be hard to come by, Sweetie."

I bit my lip. I didn't want to go back to Lickskillet.

"I'll find a way." He didn't want me to go back to Lickskillet. "I'll be in touch."

I texted No Hair and asked him to make ten minutes for me and tell Levi Hasselhoff I was on my way to the casino. He texted back. *Who?*

Levi Newman, No Hair. Tell him Bianca wants to play the Strike game and she wants total privacy.

I called Bradley.

"Another late night?"

"The latest ever, Bradley. I don't know if I'll make it home tonight at all. I'll be in Strike. Do you want me to get you a pass?"

"It depends. Are you going as Bianca or the social media girl?"

"Bradley!"

"I'm kidding," he said. "And I'm *never* setting foot in Strike again, I wish *you* weren't, and Friday can't get here soon enough."

"Bradley. Do you want to get married this weekend?"

The world stood still. Even the squirrels.

"Let me think about it, Davis."

"Let me know."

"I've thought about it," he said. "I do."

*   *   *

"I'm not coming in there."

"I'm not coming out there." I was still glued to my spot in the middle of the dressing room. I was clutching my phone to my heart. "I won't be able to say it."

"Dammit, Davis." There was nowhere for No Hair to sit. He would flatten our stools to pancakes. The upholstered bench was a foot thick with clothes needing a car wash, a seamstress, a Goodwill drop off, or, mostly, a hanger, not that he wouldn't crush all that to smithereens too. He stood in the doorway.

"See this guy?" I held up Walter Shaefer's picture. "He's been missing for almost five years."

"Who is he?"

I rattled off a mini This Is Your Life Walter.

"There's no way that man's alive. That man is dead, Davis. He's been missing for almost five years because that's how long ago they got rid of him."

"No Hair," I said, "this man," shake, shake, shake, "is running the Strike casino from a remote mainframe and he's probably doing it with a gun to his head. He's buried all right, I'll give you that, but he's not dead."

"Buried where?"

"In one of those crazy underground bunkers crazy Alabama people build."

* * *

@StrikePlayers #DownToTheWire Who will walk away with the million? #StrikeItRich

EIGHTEEN

InVade is the Oxycodone of malware—the Kobe beef, the blue diamond, the hen's teeth.

Malware is a nickname; it means malicious software. It's used to disrupt computer operations and/or gather information (and for this intent, it makes the news) or infiltrate a system. There are cheap, barely viable malwares all over the Internet. It doesn't take much to download and run one, wreaking havoc along the way, but it doesn't take much to detect and shut them down either. Not that they don't leave their mark. Street malware is used for financial gain, exploitation, and cyber espionage. Malwares are written and implemented by three groups of people: White Hat Hackers, who mean no harm, mostly testing the security of their own systems, Black Hat Hackers, who definitely mean harm, and Elite Hackers, the most skilled, the most concealed, and usually members of secret organizations like Masters of Deception. Elite Hackers never see the light of day, as they take every breath from the pit of a hardware amphitheater and live on a steady diet of Totino's Frozen Pizza and Orange Crush, from deep in their grandmother's basements. InVade is a malware maintained and circulated among the Elite, and the vetting for procurement of it makes getting a seat on the Supreme Court Justice Bench look like getting a seat on the front pew at Early Service.

I knew one person who might be able to hook me up with InVade. I made the call.

"Yes, I remember you, Davis! Of course! How'd you find me?"

"Oh, you know."

"You hacked me!" (True.)

"No! I found you through the Alumni Affairs Office." (Not true.)

His name was Evan Allison, and yes, I slept with him in college. We met in Data Structures (Java) class, were partnered on a final-exam code-writing assignment, and wound up naked in the back of a Dodge Durango parked behind the Blue Monkey Lounge. Turns out, it wasn't his car. All very humiliating. Especially since the screaming car owners—"Hey! What the hell?"—were carting little kids on their hips, one each. Haven't spoken to Evan Allison one time since. Until today.

I knew he was a six-figure software development engineer for the Marshall Space Flight Center in Huntsville, Alabama, and I'd read he'd sold proprietary software to Pixar, so I felt confident, as close to the frontlines as he was, he'd be able to point me in the direction of InVade. I also hacked his Facebook page. He'd grown a thick and unruly beard, wore thick and unruly eyeglasses, had three hairs on his head—I could trade him bull goo for InVade—and was divorced.

For recreation, it looked like he built and raced soapbox derby cars. He also collected cats and named them after reality television celebrities: Honey Boo Boo, Bruce Jenner, Ivanka. (Trump.) He was very happy to be thrown back in time to the backseat of that Durango, and not without hesitation (me begging), did he agree to set me up with a flash version of InVade.

He would only send it to a dedicated and secure line, and I had to wait until he could get to a workstation at Best Buy on Memorial Drive, one of those geeky drop-off pick-up points the Huntsville cyber underground used, and the only place he was willing to do the deed. He would be attaching a twenty-four-hour shelf life accessory with an anti-piracy bonus feature he assured me would be harder to penetrate than Fort Knox.

(Did the guy not trust me?)

"I would love to see you too, Evan."

"Anytime. Anytime you're within a hundred miles. Or two

hundred. Have Durango will travel, Davis. Just call me."

Walter Shaefer was going to owe me big time.

* * *

What to wear to catch a den of thieves.

I was going Bianca, because no one else could walk into Strike and demand a seat at the table. Or in one of those chairs, as it were. Maybe her husband could, but he was busy with her son. She was upstairs busy doing who-knows-what. Hiding from the blindingly white décor. Staring in the mirror. Plotting my demise.

"What is it, David? I'm busy."

(Plotting my demise.)

"Mrs. Sanders, I wanted to let you know I'll be in the Strike Casino tonight, and I'll be attending as you."

"You know I no longer have an interest in gambling, David. It's crude."

"It's Davis."

"What?"

"I need to speak to Missy Jennings."

"Who?"

"The mother of Quinn Jennings, Thomas's classmate."

"Yes. Straighten that situation out, David. You made that mess. Fix it."

She hung up. She would be mad about her fur for a long, long time.

I stared at the clothes in the dressing room. I had two choices: Santa's Helper (last year's Have-Your-Picture-Made-With-Santa's jolly old elf took terrible liberties with good little gamblers in his lap and was behind bars on multiple indecent exposure convictions) or Carolina Herrera. I went Carolina, in a silk cocktail dress, black with a white crossover bodice, notched V-neck, princess seams, and on my feet, Louboutin python T-strap skinny heels, and in my bag (matching Louboutin python wristlet), my phone, a Burt's Bees Lip Shimmer in Watermelon (my dinner, probably), a flash drive, and a

Ruger LC9. Point. Shoot. Bang. I guess I got a little carried away (I love guns), because I never heard Hair and Makeup Angela coming. She appeared out of nowhere, found me in stop-right-there mode, screamed bloody murder, and hit the deck. "Oh my God, Davis!"

"Oh my God, Davis? How about oh, my God, Angela! You scared me to death! Don't sneak up on me!"

She rolled over onto her back, hand to heart. "Don't shoot me!"

I reached out a hand to help her up. She crawled away backwards on all fours, petrified. Her boots were red leather with little black buttons.

"I would never shoot you on purpose, Angela." She stood—her eyes were Frisbees—and was trying to make a run for it, but she bumped into the vanity, which scared her to death all over again. Movie screaming. "Angela!" She took off scooting down the length of the vanity, clearing a path through the bronzers and blushers. Which is when it occurred to me to stop waving the gun around. "When you pick up a gun, one of the first things you do is make sure the front and back sights are lined up! That's all I was doing! Settle down!"

Angela flipped and bent over the vanity, gripping it with both hands, head flopping, tongue lolling. "This. Job."

I pushed her down onto a stool because her knees were Jello.

"Between her and you, I swear, Davis, I'm going to go work a makeup counter at the mall."

It's not like I didn't warn her.

It took a shot of bourbon to steady her hands. Geesh. One little gun non-incident. She eventually (second shot of bourbon) calmed down, sprayed me Honey Kiss blonde, and finally able to speak, gave me the details of the brutal tongue lashing she'd taken from Bianca earlier about "the state of David's hair." My new hair was at an impressive, and challenging, length. Long enough to cover my scalp, but too short to lie down without being asked repeatedly.

"I had to hold the phone away from my head," Angela said. "She was having a fit. Look down." We were at the eyeliner part.

"Tell me about all the chairs you have in your house, Angela. Every one."

"Look up." Mascara. "Okay. I'll start in my kitchen and work my way to the play room. We have lots of bar stools. Do they count? Then we have to decide how we're going to get out of the casino business, repackage this bull stuff, and get rich quick." She tugged on a strand of my baby hair. "The new hair is twice as thick as your old hair, Davis. This stuff is miracle hair grow tonic. Although, we're going to have to put some strong scent in it. Maybe strawberry. We'll make a fortune off bald guys if you don't accidentally shoot them first."

I was headed downstairs to order a drink from a bald guy. And I may very well have to shoot him first.

* * *

"Welcome to Strike, Mrs. Sanders."

I threw my Rachel Zoe cashmere wrap at the big burly bouncer and kept going. (Bianca is such a raging bitch.)

Day by day, as players have been eliminated from the competition, then gone as far into debt as they possibly could, the gaming stations had, one by one, closed. I had my choice of four empty gaming stations. I went left, because there was less attention, noise, and crowd, all of which was radiating from the right side of the room, where Missy Jennings's winning streak had set up camp. I avoided the little cafés and the cashier cage, and made my way to a corner, the most obscure of the four empty *future*Gaming Wonderchairs. Fantasy and No Hair were between me and everything else. I sat down and was welcomed by a waft of Chocolate Chip Cookies. The chair discreetly adjusted to my height and weight, and a small panel on the right armrest blinked and asked for my thumbprint.

Not yet.

I pushed the button and the three play screens lowered from the ceiling. I pulled a flash drive full of venom from my python clutch, then tilted the middle screen enough to get to the console behind it. There wasn't a visible port. If I couldn't get into the system, we were toast.

I used the flashlight app on my phone and still couldn't find a port. If I tore the thing up, someone from IT would be out here in a heartbeat. I closed my eyes and used my fingertips (when one of your five senses stops working try a different one), finally feeling a small flat panel with a pinhole. Except I didn't have a pin.

"No Hair. Psssst."

"What?"

"I can't get this thing open. I need something small and pokey. Like a straight pin or an earring."

"I don't wear earrings, Davis, but *you* do."

Right. I get nervous.

Bianca's jewelry was all booby-trapped. Hard to get off and on because of security clasps, complicated fasteners, and burglar alarms. For the most part, I went fake. Tonight, I was faking Chanel black enamel Camellias with the little CC logo on one petal. I pried one out and stabbed the pinhole with the silver stud. A black panel the size of a postage stamp popped off. I let out the breath I'd been holding and took another deep one. The armrest panel blinked for my thumbprint. Give me your tired, your poor, your thumbprint. In a minute, Walter. In a minute.

Here goes nothing. I plugged the flash drive into the USB port. Bikini Fantasy Mind Reader passed me a glass of something, and asked how it was going. I gave her a quick nod. The download was almost complete; the drink was a smoky Chardonnay.

One, two, three.

I used the touchscreen on the left screen to get to the gaming menu, system, help, located a keyboard, then tapped out a message: *Hi Walter. My name is Davis. I'm here to help you.*

Three, two, one.

The Strike gaming system went black.

Cries went up through the room as the gambling came to an abrupt halt.

I counted to ten. The armrest panel began blinking again. I squeezed my eyes closed, then pressed my right thumb to it. Walter Shaefer would know everything about me there was to know in three minutes, and we could both be dead in five. There was a chance I'd set wheels in motion that would result in a bullet to Walter's head and his bald bartender brother hopping the bar and coming at me with a gold icicle of death.

He'd have to get through No Hair to get to me. And Walter was already as good as dead; this was his only chance.

When the monitor began swarming with floaties, it occurred to me to blink, to breathe.

A lifetime/two minutes later, the game reset and I collapsed in the chair. It coughed up a cloud of Chocolate Chips. It was chaos on the small casino floor; I could hear Levi Hasselhoff flipping his wig saying, "power surge power surge power surge."

Walter Shaefer was still alive. My gaming monitor flashed *HELP*, and beneath it, 34.34 -85.696. My hands shook as I shot a message back: 2014:ja7:a:4x70:C:777:8:1.

* * *

@StrikePlayers   #Hiccup   #All'sWell   #PointsRecorded
#PlayersPlayOn

* * *

No Hair and I rushed down the dark hall to 3B doing some heel clacking (me) and heavy breathing (him).

"What were all those numbers?" He left all things electronic to me.

"I sent him an IP address to contact us." I had a terminal up in Control Central in a flash. "He sent geographic coordinates." I plugged them in. The red dot radiated from Lickskillet, Alabama. We watched it like a heart monitor.

"Talk to him again, Davis. Find out exactly where he is and how we can get to him."

"No way, No Hair. I've taken the game down once. Five IT guys behind Strike are trying to figure out what just happened, and if all five of them aren't working this heist, at least one of them is and right now he's telling himself it was a fluke. If I break into the system again, he'll know it wasn't an accident and they'll kill Walter before we can get to him. If anyone realizes their system is compromised, they won't need Walter." I grabbed the clean laptop I'd used earlier to receive InVade from Durango Lover Boy. I clicked open the Microsoft Messenger and read the only message:

.-.. . ...- .. / -. . . .-- -- .- -.

We stared at it. After a few seconds, the message began to fade, then the laptop glowed with the blue screen of death.

"What happened?"

"He InVaded me." I slapped the laptop closed. I rubbed my forehead. "He wiped this computer." I knew going in that if I managed to make contact with Walter, and if he managed to respond, he would destroy the evidence to protect us both, which is why I didn't give him an IP address to anything Bellissimo. (Boy, would I catch hell if the Bellissimo system was wiped.) (We have Pentagon-worthy backup.) (Still.)

I fell against the back of the chair. "I knew Morse Code back in the day, but I never knew how to *read* it."

No Hair was in a chair beside me. Elbows to knees. Staring at the floor. "I caught it." He looked like he'd caught Flesh Eating Bird Flu Rabies.

"What did it say?"

"It said Levi Newman."

*   *   *

We needed the dog off the scent, so No Hair got Levi Newman on the phone. "We've looked into this, Levi, and we've got nothing." He told him we had carefully examined every aspect of Strike operations and we couldn't find a single thing wrong with the exception of a little loosey goosey banking, and we felt sure the girl who'd been missing since Sunday afternoon, the social media girl, Elspeth (he said, "Elzbath") took off for parts unknown for personal reasons unrelated to any Bellissimo business. He went on to remind Levi that Strike was his domain, and we needed to get back to the business of monitoring our domain, everything else, before Richard got back in town and fired us all. "We're security, Levi," No Hair said, "and Davis is all I have. She's more Inspector Lucille Ball Clouseau than anything else."

I had nothing to throw at him.

NINETEEN

The Regent, where Bradley and I live, has twenty-six units, each with its own private elevator. We're the only ones with access, and believe it or not, there are times when it becomes another room to clean—umbrellas, Bradley's golf clubs, the chair with the broken leg. There are times when I hop in the elevator, then step out on the parking level having forgotten something crucial. Like my car keys or my Starbucks travel mug full of perfect coffee. If Bradley's still upstairs, I call him and he sends whatever down, once my whole suitcase, when Fantasy had been waiting for me at the little airport in Gulfport for an hour. She kept texting. *Come on already, Davis.* We were on our way to the World Game Protection Conference in Las Vegas, and Fantasy doesn't get out of town all that often without husbands, kids, and dogs. (The conference was so boring. We ditched it immediately and for the rest of the week we gambled all night, slept all day, saw a car disappear, Donny and Marie, Carrot Top, and Britney Spears.)

Bradley and I leave each other notes in the elevator and he's never left me one that wasn't a treasure. When there's been something he's wanted to say to me before I even stepped in the door, it's been a keeper, and they're all tucked away at the bottom of my jewelry box.

When I finally left the Bellissimo on Wednesday night, drove home, and put a python shoe into the elevator, I looked up to see something taped to the elevator wall. It was the paperwork from the Camden County Courthouse.

I was finally free of Eddie the Ass Crawford.

We celebrated.

*   *   *

Richard Sanders was stuck in New Hampshire.

The DEA office in Bedford sent a drug task force crew in to turn the Brewster-Exeter Academy for Boys upside down. Six boys, including Little Sanders, were called on the carpet for having off-the-chart levels of THCA in their rooms. The presence of THCA, tetrahydrocannabinolic acid, means there is or there was a substantial amount of marijuana in the immediate vicinity. Nice, fresh marijuana, not already-been-smoked marijuana, which would put out THCA's byproduct, TCA. The task force couldn't find the pot, even after tearing through the mattresses and walls, but they knew it had been there, and told the school their rich white-kid Republican students were masters at hiding evidence and most certainly underage dealers. They didn't have enough evidence to bring charges against the boys, but it was plenty enough for Brewster-Exeter to expel them. Mr. Sanders was throwing his substantial-donor weight around trying to reverse their decision. I got this news on Thursday morning over coffee in 3B.

No Hair's tie said No Parking.

"Did you tell Mr. Sanders about last night? About Walter? About Levi Hasselhoff?"

"No." He scratched the back of his bald head. "I couldn't do it to him. This is on us, Davis."

*   *   *

@StrikePlayers And then there were 5. #Finals begin @ 5:00 #StrikeItRich #TheWholeEnchilada #GoodLuck

*   *   *

"I like your headband? Very tres chic?"

She pronounced it "tress chick."

I'd managed to avoid Missy Jennings all week. It hadn't been hard; she's been gambling twelve hours out of every twenty-four since the Strike doors opened and I'd been busy. Too busy to do anything with the one-plus inch halo of hair standing straight up around my face, so I wore a wide black silk headband to flatten the newest of my Bianca Honey Kiss hair.

"And what about these kids these days? Can they just wear you out or what?"

Casino gaming can be intense without being a major player drug manufacturer in a grand larceny ring at the end of a pressure-cooker tournament; I got itchy and squirmy after just a few hours of solitary no-risk gambling and I didn't grow pot. I would think at this point, with such high stakes, Missy Jennings's head would be about to blow off, but she didn't look a bit worse for the wear. She was sweet-tea cool, edge-of-her-seat energized, and didn't appear to have a care in the world.

"They're going to make mistakes? Right, Bianca? I say let them learn their lessons?"

Missy Jennings blinked inquisitively while waiting for me to agree with her. We were having lunch in a small private dining room at Wasabi, the upscale Asian-fare restaurant on the mezzanine level. I ordered a Mandarin mixed green salad with ginger lime dressing, and Missy was picking through a square platter piled so high with sweet and sour shrimp noodle salad it could feed a family of five.

She was wearing art. I'd never seen anything like it. You could hang her from a hook on the wall of a contemporary art museum between a sculpture fashioned from soup cans and an abstract painted by a manor of meerkats, and people would gawk and sketch. The top and the pants were boxy-cut silk, both cropped, revealing a wide band of dance-toned tanning-bed-bronzed midriff, with the matching cropped silk pants hitting just below her knees.

The whole ensemble was made of a futuristic crazy metallic print—copper, gold, silver, pewter—abstract shapes going in every direction, and it was making me dizzy. She was wearing so much jewelry, if she walked by a magnet it would suck her in.

"Red and I are so happy Quinn didn't get caught up in that witch-hunt sting your boy got caught up in? Whew!" Jazz hands. "I believe Red might kill him if he screwed up and didn't graduate?" She took a long noisy pull from her large Coke, light ice, two straws. "Not that we know what we're going to do with him hanging around night and day when he does graduate, right?" She bounced the entire conversation ball solo. I nodded along. "You know how some kids just aren't college material? Right? That's Quinn?" I felt sorry for the four pounds of finger-licking good shrimp she was picking out of the salad and popping in her mouth between words. "He knows he's headed home to take over the family business, right?" She held up and shook her tumbler of light ice. Another liter of Coke, right? "Red hasn't worked himself half near to death so Quinn can goof off and party at some college, right?" Jazz hands. "'Course if he played football? That'd be another story, right? Go Big Red Alabama Crimson Tide? Am I right?"

I opened my mouth to speak too late.

"I'm gonna tell you a trick?" She leaned in. (#Shrimp) "If you and your husband would grease a palm or two? You know what I mean? It might *go away*," she stage-whispered the last two words. "Right?"

I sucked in a breath to get a word in, again, too late.

"These kids, you know? They're gonna drink their beer, right? And they're gonna smoke a little weed, right? And they're gonna sit on the floor and play their stupid games, right?" Three more shrimps down the hatch. "Seems like the school could cut them some slack?"

Games. Sit on the floor. Play their stupid games. I reached for my purse. That's what else boys have in their dorm rooms. I scooted for the door. Several times today, I made a checklist inventory of boys' dorm rooms: bed, desk, books, backpacks, clothes. I stood. I'd forgotten Xbox. They all had Xbox. Every single one of them. #PoorPlayStation

"Missy? I need to run."

"Hey? Bianca?" Shrimp. "Good to see you?"

"Good luck tonight at Strike." (Right?)

"Girl? I got that covered?"

Shrimp, shrimp, shrimp.

Head down, hiding behind Fendi sunglasses, I took the long and winding road around the mile of mezzanine. The kid casino, Gamer, was packed. Why weren't these kids in school? (Right?) I slowed down at Shakes, the ice cream shop, looked both ways, then slipped through the unmarked door. I pulled off the sunglasses to scan myself into the elevator with the facial-recognition panel, rode down, then ran down the dark hall. Fantasy and Baylor jumped when I threw open the office door. "I need a knife!"

"Are you going to stab somebody?" Fantasy, bathrobe over bikini, sat up and yawned, arms wide and high.

Baylor muted the television, then dug in the pocket of his jeans and passed me a folding knife. I opened the coat closet, grabbed a handful of beanbag chair and lobbed it in the middle of the floor. I popped open the three-inch blade, speared then sawed through the fabric, stuck my hand in, dug, dug more, and pulled out a shrink-wrapped five-pound brick of marijuana.

*   *   *

A pattern was developing in which Thomas Sanders, though not innocent, was never guilty. He *was* a little pothead, the extent of which I didn't know and didn't want to. But after meeting with the authorities and the school's administration, Richard Sanders smoothed everything over for his son, and he did way more than the heavy lifting, with the school apologizing profusely to them both. Little Dude would be right back in Calculus I on Monday morning without so much as a scratch. Not that he needed to go down for possession with intent, be kicked out of school and have a record, but it seemed to me like he needed to learn some sort of lessons, somewhere, sometime. He hadn't taken a lick of heat over driving a car through the casino, smoking pot and letting a hooker in our office, and now this. An hour ago, in the middle of the frenzy started when I found two five-pound bricks of marijuana in the closet, one of the many phone conversations I'd had was with Little Sanders.

"Thomas, did you have any idea Quinn was giving people bean bag chairs loaded with drugs?"

"Dude. No."

See? This may or may not be true.

"Did you ask him for one?"

"No, dude. They're in that plane. He says have at it."

"You know, Thomas, if you say anything to anyone, it will get back to Quinn Jennings and he can't know. Lives are at stake, Thomas."

"Dude. I'm on lockdown."

I didn't want to bother her, but I called Brianna Strother, who, according to my calendar, should have returned from Elspeth's funeral today.

"Bean bag chairs," she said. "I can't believe it."

"And the Jennings kid passes them out like Halloween candy," I said. "We've had two in our offices this whole time. The takedown is tomorrow night, Brianna. Are you up for it?"

"No, Davis," she said. "Thanks for the invitation, but my plans are to brief my bosses, then take some time off. I'm moving to Florida to be closer to Elspeth's family, then taking an extended maternity leave. At least a year."

She asked that I contact her immediately when Elspeth's killer was identified.

Of course.

She thanked me for our help.

I wished her very, very well.

No Hair did the Bianca honors, giving her the light and fluffy headlines version: Your son isn't guilty; your husband will be home after the red tape. Fantasy, at my side, both of us working the phones and computers non-stop, still in a bathrobe over a bikini, asked him how it went.

No Hair pulled up a chair. "She honestly can't talk about anything but the fur coat." Then, "Davis? Do you have that shit on your head again?"

"She's killing me." Fantasy waved a hand in front of her face.

I was affronted. "If you two don't mind, I'd like to get married at some point. And I'd like to have some hair on my head when I do."

"Well, cover it up more," No Hair said.

"I can't. It's too hot. It melts and drips and burns when it gets hot."

Fantasy's eyes popped open. "That must be what's making it work! You're getting it on your head, then cooking it! Davis! Cover it up! You know what you need?"

I shook my bull-goo head no.

"Plastic wrap. You need to wrap it up in plastic. It'll heat it up good."

"Popeye told me to keep it *cold*."

"Who?"

"Besides," I said, "we don't have any plastic."

Fantasy pushed away from the desk and returned with one of the bricks of marijuana. It was wrapped in layer upon layer of blue cellophane. Ten minutes later, when Bea Crawford called, we had a big chunk of raw pot on a desk and I had a blue plastic turban on my head.

It was five o'clock. I let Bea's call go to voicemail because I needed to hit the showers for shampoo, rinse, repeat, shampoo, rinse, repeat. No Hair and Fantasy took off for Strike. Tomorrow morning we would meet with representatives from the Department of Justice and the Bureau of Alcohol, Tobacco, Firearms, and conference with a SWAT team who would conduct the Alabama raids at Jennings Tree Farm and Have A Seat. We'd oversee the takedown here. Instead of winning the million dollar Strike jackpot, Missy Jennings would win a pair of shiny new handcuffs. Along with her husband, her sister, the bartender, the Strike IT guys, and our new casino manager.

It was all coming together in a nice, neat package, and tomorrow, we'd wrap it up and put a bow on it.

Then I'd get married.

*   *   *

"It took days, *days*, David, to replace my wardrobe. And you want me to just *give* you a valuable portion of it after what happened the last time I let you wear something of mine?"

"Mrs. Sanders, it's Davis." I peeled a layer of blue Saran wrap off my head, trying to hold the phone and mop my face at the same time. "And if you'll remember, you've had *my* clothes since the morning after the fire. I need something to wear to the Strike casino tonight and I have nothing. I'll be attending as you again and I know you'd like me to look presentable." I eyed a small metal garbage can and wondered what would happen if I burned the stinky blue plastic. I could barely breathe for it. "Mrs. Sanders? Are you still there?"

"I've decided to redecorate, David. The white is damaging my eyesight. You'll need to be here all day tomorrow to meet with the decorators. I need several options."

"Fine," I said. (#NeverGonnaHappen) "But for tonight, would you mind buzzing Angela up and giving her a few wardrobe choices for me?"

She hung up.

Thirty minutes later, Angela and I were eyeing the few wardrobe choices Bianca sent. She was so, so mad at me. Both were from the new Gucci Spring Collection (it wasn't even winter yet), and both were hideous. There was a black lamé jumpsuit that looked like a black silk pajama parachute clown suit and a small, shapeless leopard brocade shift dress that would look like a mini leopard pillowcase on me. She sent one pair of shoes: six-inch spike heeled open-toe boots consisting entirely of straps of metal-studded leather. #Ridiculous

I wore the Santa's Helper outfit.

(No, I didn't.)

"Oh, good grief." Angela pulled the towel off my head. "You have bangs."

* * *

One last call.

"Daddy."

"Punkin."

"I feel like I haven't seen you in a month." I dug through the accessory drawer and added bright clunky jewelry to the mix. There wasn't enough bright clunky jewelry in the drawer to distract from the Big Fat Fashion Disaster I was wearing. "Catch me up."

My sister Meredith had been on a second and third date with the doctor. She told Mother and Daddy if all continued going well, she'd think about introducing him to my niece Riley. Not anytime soon. No need to rush things. My grandmother and her husband found a home for Cyril's "mangy mutt who had onion breath," and rented a thirty-foot travel camper. They were leaving for a weekend Senior Couples Counseling Retreat in DeSoto State Park.

"Who's driving?" I asked. "Granny can't push a grocery buggy and Cyril can't see his hand in front of his face." My father skipped enough of a beat for me to know who they'd roped into driving. My rat-rat ex-ex husband. Who'd drive the devil around for ten bucks and a forty-ounce Colt 45.

"That's not the worst of it, Davis, and you might as well hear it from me."

Dr. Crazy Kizzy was back at his prescription pad and had written Cyril one for, what my father called, a "marital aid."

#SomeoneShootMe

"How about you, honey?"

Was my father asking me if Bradley took "marital aids"? We weren't even married!

"Your situation with the marriage license."

#DodgedThatBullet

"Believe it or not, Daddy, Bea went to the courthouse, straightened it out, and we got the golden ticket in the mail yesterday."

"You're free and clear?"

"I am done with Eddie and his mother forever, Daddy. For. Ev. Er."

Total silence on my father's end.

"Daddy?"

"Honey. You'd better sit down."

I absolutely hate those words.

"Have you heard from Bea?"

"Yes and no. She called; I wasn't in the mood to answer."

The "favor" Bea had done me, having her snake-in-the-grass son drop the suit against me, had been part of a deal she'd made with Smerle T. He agreed to drop Eddie's lawsuit without a fuss, but only if she'd agree to provide him with another bone to chew. He couldn't sit around twiddling his thumbs in today's economy, because it looked like his other big divorce (Granny and Cyril) might fall through too. Surely she could come up with something. Bea told him she did have a little problem he could nose into, have arrested, then show up at the jail to save. He tracked down Bea's little problem, and instead of helping Bea out of the fire, he threw me into it. Smerle T. was naming me as defendant, Daddy said, in a lawsuit he would file on Monday, because Bea let it slip (all over town) that I was now the proud owner of Mel's. (No, I'm not. I dumped money in her checking account to be rid of her rotten son. I hadn't signed a thing. And didn't intend to.)

"Who's suing me now, Daddy?"

"Danielle Sparks."

I'm thirty-three years old. Barely thirty-three. And my past came back and slapped me stupid every ten minutes. I'm really not old enough to have so much bad history. I wonder if Bradley Cole would consider moving to a deserted island somewhere so no one could find me and ask me to pay for my old sins.

Danielle Sparks and I went back, all the way back. She hated me on the playground, even more on the football field at halftime when we twirled fire batons for the Pine Apple Pulps, and even more than that in the courtroom, as she sat beside her boyfriend Eddie the Ass during our second divorce. She'd been a cashier at the Piggly Wiggly in Pine Apple where she'd sneaky smashed every loaf of bread I'd ever bought, and all this ill will culminated in me accidently shooting her—all her fault—yet *I* was the one who got in trouble. I was a cop at the time, on duty, and maybe she wasn't holding a shotgun on me, but in my defense, I simply misfired. I'd been aiming for Eddie the Stupid Crawford and shot her totally and completely by mistake.

#AccidentsHappen

#Don'tFireOffRoundsInTheDark

"What? What, Daddy, could Danielle possibly sue me for?"

"Honey, she's claiming it's your fault she's a prostitute."

"How can she be a prostitute when she gives it away, Daddy, and how can I possibly be responsible?"

It was the most frivolous of all frivolous lawsuits. Danielle went to Dr. Crazy Kizzy complaining her mouth felt like it was full of thumbtacks and her legs felt like cooked spaghetti. Kizzy said it sounded like either a prolapsed uterus or mercury poisoning to him. Danielle went with mercury poisoning and blamed it on Mel's Diner. Specifically All-You-Can-Eat Fried Catfish Fridays at Mel's Diner. (That fish was carp, all day every day, including Friday.) Her chances at a happy marriage and an honest income were gone. Who'd marry a woman with a mouth full of thumbtacks? And spaghetti legs couldn't very well stand up at the cash register for eight hour shifts at the Pig. (And how is it that spaghetti legs and thumbtacks in your mouth don't interfere with prostitution?) She was forced to turn to the entertainment industry for employment, and all because of Mel's Diner. Which I owned. (I do not.) She took her diagnosis across the street to Smerle T. Webb, Esq., who told her it was a slam-dunk personal injury civil suit. I asked Daddy how much. Sixteen thousand for two years of lost income at the Pig, and three million for pain and suffering. Not to mention Bea Crawford throwing me under the bus for the millionth time in my life. I could hear it now. "Well, Davis, I only meant for him to get Danielle off my back. I didn't tell Smerle T. to go and sue you. That's your fault. I can't help it Danielle hates you."

"If you could slow down long enough to replace Smerle T.'s car, it would go a long way in smoothing his ruffled feathers."

Might as well buy Danielle and Kizzy cars too. I'd buy cars for everyone in Pine Apple if they'd all sign a waiver to leave me the hell alone.

It was closing in on seven o'clock. I needed to scoot to the casino. I was armed and ready in my silk pajama parachute jumpsuit and studded leather shoes. After the scenic route, Daddy and I finally arrived in Lickskillet.

"The Scottsboro crew and their arsenal are camping along the entrance of the property," Daddy said, "and the Jennings's residence has a domestic employee who arrives at nine every morning and stays until four. From the satellite feed, the only other signs of life are in the airplane hangar, and from what I can determine, honey, that's where your man is. And speaking of the airplane hangar, an odd thing popped up."

"What?"

"I found forty-thousand dollars of excavation work when the hangar was built, along with fifty-thousand dollars of concrete hauled in. You don't have to do forty-thousand dollars of digging to put a metal building on top of the ground," he said, "and fifty-thousand dollars of concrete is double what they would need for the square footage."

That's because they'd built an underground bunker beneath the airplane hangar. Walter Shaefer had most likely not seen the light of day in five years.

*   *   *

@StrikePlayers They're dropping like flies! After 4 hrs of play only 4 players left! #iHotGaming #OneMillionBigOnes

TWENTY

I tackled a Bianca Sanders chore last summer that had served me well: I worked with a dialect coach from a New Orleans film company to teach me Bianca Speak. I already deserved an Academy Award for my dramatic portrayal, but always with limited lines. Bianca Casimiro Sanders's parents were born-and-bred Italians, so there's that, and she was raised in the Midwest, and there's that. I'm Alabama through and through. You see the problem.

The dialect coach, a woman named CeeCee, about my age but a foot taller, had spa music going in the background as she "tapped the Broca's region of my frontal lobe" with "auditory feedback" and "repetitive tongue thrust" exercises, and after six weeks, I could turn it on and off like a faucet.

The addition of Hair and Makeup Angela helped close the gap between me and Bianca even more. Bianca was a big believer in Botox, while I'd never even dreamed of having poison hypodermically injected in my face. With a needle. So when Angela waved her wand over me—Bibbity Bobbity Boo—her base was the cosmetic equivalent of Elmer's Rubber Cement, the thick first-grade clear glue in the brown bottle that smelled so good, to keep my facial expressions tight and partially frozen, especially around my mouth and forehead. Then Angela "contoured" a lot. Then she "smoky eyed" me.

Her final Bianca touch was always lip filler to plump me (tingled), a needle sharp pencil outline, then red/black lipstick, so everyone could take one look at me and see just how mean I was based on my lipstick shade.

If ever I needed to fool someone into believing I was Bianca, it was tonight.

He eyed me suspiciously. He definitely didn't want to piss Bianca off, but absolutely didn't want fake Bianca, the Bellissimo's bumbling security screw-up, in his casino as his plans, years in making, stretching from Vegas to northeast Alabama to Biloxi, involving dozens of people, millions upon millions of dollars, and a murder was coming to fruition.

I crossed one pajama jumpsuit leg over the other and cut my eyes at Levi Hasselhoff.

"Well well well." He said it sing-song. "Bianca."

I turned my head slowly. "Can I help you?"

He rocked on his heels.

"Do you *need* something, Mr. Newman?"

He looked me over, head to shoes-made-of-dog-collars.

"I'd like to welcome you to Strike."

"And I'd like some privacy. And a cocktail. Send someone." He battled with himself, eyes narrowed to snake slits, and finally decided I was Bianca. He half bowed, then backed away.

#Whew

Baylor and Fantasy had set me up at dormant iGaming kiosk three, with a sliver of a view of Crazy Pants Missy Jennings in front of me (who hadn't changed from her art deco lunch outfit) (I'm one to talk about Crazy Pants), and a black granite wall at my back. They would stay close, to cater to Bianca's each and every whim and make sure no one ambushed her from behind.

"I fell out of my bikini." Fantasy sat a glass of wine down beside me.

"You did not!"

"I did," she said. "Flashed everybody a tata for ten minutes. Baylor saw me and fell on the floor laughing, or I'd have never known."

"He needs to grow up," I said. "Did anyone take a picture? I'll Snapchat it."

She took my wine and held it hostage until I said I was sorry.

"I told No Hair I'm done with this." She tugged at her bikini top to make sure she was still wearing it. "I'm sick of the allergy shots and I'm freezing to death. Tomorrow night, I'm in street clothes, not poking these brown things in my eyes even one more time, and these extensions," she displayed a handful of Halle Berry hair, "are coming off tonight."

"Is there any way to turn off this chocolate chip cookie?" I was in a fog of it.

Fantasy nodded at the flat screen in front of me. "Ask your buddy."

The chair, welcoming me with fragrance, was also asking for my thumbprint.

Hello, Walter.

The screen blazed with fireworks.

I was glad to see him too.

* * *

@StrikePlayer   Congrats   finalists   @DanceMamaMissy   and @love2win. Open play for eliminated Strike contestants noon till 6, showdown tomorrow night. #Don'tMissIt

* * *

By agreeing to allow unlimited social media access, all fifty Strike contestants had allowed the central processing unit—which we now knew wasn't in a room just through a door behind the small casino, but in a Lickskillet, Alabama, deep in a bunker—full access to their cyber lives. The game knew what time the players woke up and how they liked their eggs. The game knew what the players pinned on Pinterest and what they ordered from Amazon. The game knew the details and to whom the players private-room chatted. The game knew checking account balances, favorite books, the music the players listened to, and what they watched on television. The game knew the make and model of car the players drove, because somewhere on Facebook, everyone's posted a picture of themselves dangling the keys to a new car.

A hard truth: If you put it on the Internet, the Walter Shaefers of the world can see it.

The game knew and catered, immediately and specifically, to the needs and desires of the person behind the thumbprint.

I logged on and the screen flashed a huge pineapple. I smiled behind my hand.

Options popped up, and I watched as Walter Shaefer chose for me. No, I didn't want to participate in the community jackpot, and no, I didn't want to compete with any other players. Just me and the game. The screen asked if I was ready, and Walter answered for me—yes. Five slot reels popped up with five lines each. Randomly placed in the twenty-five squares were police badges, black Volkswagen Bugs, white saucers with two strawberry-frosted Pop Tarts, and double black-eyed mug shots of my rotten, rotten ex-ex-husband from an old DUI, that flashed, then faded to sun-kissed Bradley Coles.

I tried not to squeal.

A column ran down the right screen, like stacked ads, displaying live iGaming going on around me. Someone in one of these kiosks was playing a slot football game, Bears versus Giants, someone else was trying to line up ingredients for a chocolate ganache, and another someone was scrapbooking, trying to land Disney characters on the correct backgrounds. The right screen also contained a pay table, showing me what I'd win if all the black VWs lined up, or if I spun Bradley's into a diagonal line. Below that was a help screen I could access, and at the bottom, my instructions to unlock bigger and better games with bigger and better jackpots and the best, the sought-after bonus rounds. Missy Jennings had been "miraculously" advancing, then landing and winning bonus rounds since the Strike doors opened.

Not such a miracle after all.

Show me a bonus round, Walter.

I pushed the play button and was awed with visual and audio effects. When my car landed on a reel, it did a wheelie, wiggling its front wheels, flashed its lights, then honked. The police badge hit play spaces and spun itself into a rotating siren light, bright red, pull over now. The Pop Tarts burst out of a toaster, twisted in the air, sprinkles flying, then landed stacked on the plate. The mug shot of Eddie the Ass got a baseball bat to the face, complete with dizzying stars, then became a bonus space, turning into Bradley Cole. Every space with Bradley zoomed out and became a beach scene with a wedding ring twirling through the air and landing in his open palm. I hit the jackpot on my first spin (never ever ever ever happens in real life), five Bradleys on the beach, advancing me to the next level of play, compliments of the man under the airplane hangar in Lickskillet.

Scary, how much Walter knew about me in a day. Scary.

The next game Walter had for me was a calendar. My gaming options on the first screen asked me to choose a day. I chose tomorrow and the game broke out into thundering applause, then advanced to the next level. The screen filled with a clock face, and a small bundle of dynamite in the lower left corner. I hit the play button repeatedly until I worked the clock to early evening, I chose seven-thirty, then engaged the dynamite option. The fuse lit, then the dynamite exploded. I did squeal this time.

Now Walter knew when we were coming for him tomorrow evening.

You've unlocked film clips, the message center said. *Enjoy*.

I watched Jim Carrey in the role of Truman Burbank in *The Truman Show* escape fictional Seahaven. Next I watched a clip of Tim Robbins as Andy Dufresne crawl to muddy freedom in *The Shawshank Redemption*. Then *Star Wars* music came through the surround sound speakers at my head as Hans Solo and gang were rescued from the garbage compacter by trusty, ever handy droids.

Me too, Walter. I'm very happy for you.

The next movie clip cued—*Escape to Witch Mountain*? *The Great Escape*?—but flashed to black before it could begin, immediately replaced with fifty beasty little Yorkshire Terriers all over the screen, violently barking their little heads off at me.

Walter could see me. Walter could see *behind* me.

Levi Newman Hasselhoff appeared at my right arm. "I trust you're enjoying yourself, Mrs. Sanders?"

I tried to kill him with my smoky-eyed stare for a long hard minute, then turned back to the game, where a blinking envelope popped up in the lower right-hand corner of the main screen. I waited until the coast was clear, then clicked the communication open. A small photograph of a dark-haired girl smiled at me from a porch swing. A young Walter Shaefer sat beside her. The girl's feet didn't quite reach the ground. A tabby cat was curled in her lap and they both held mason jars full of lemonade. Above her, a black metal mailbox to the right of the front door displayed a Lickskillet, Alabama address.

Got it, Walter. We'll secure this girl first.

*   *   *

We convened in 3B at 3 a.m.

"Are we ever going to get any sleep?" Fantasy was wearing people clothes.

"One more word out of you and we'll go right back to ballet." Baylor looked at his watch. "In three hours."

"You know, Baylor," she poked him in the arm, "you don't get employee loyalty by making threats. You (poke) are (poke) not (poke) management (poke) material."

"And you are?"

"Kids." I covered my eyes with a hand, blocking the light. I was so tired I couldn't feel my legs. "Don't make me stop this car." I heard the beeps of the door being coded. "There's your dad. Now straighten up."

No Hair sank onto the sofa beside me. "Let's have it. Baylor, you go first."

"I've got two waitresses we need to take a look at."

"By my count," Fantasy said, "you've slept with half of them. So you've already had a good look at one, if not both of them."

I told No Hair they'd been fussing since we got here. He growled at Baylor, who turned beet red. So he had slept with at least one of them, and probably on the clock, since we'd all been on the clock for a solid week.

"Which girls?" No Hair asked.

"Seriously? You need a list?"

No Hair closed his eyes and explained that he didn't want the names of women Baylor had personal relationships with, but, however, if he wouldn't mind, he would like to know how to identify the two women in question. Baylor coughed up the names of his gold bikini friends who'd strayed from their normal routines tonight. The first he noticed passing notes between Wesley the bald brother bartender and Red Jennings, picking up from one and dropping off to the other, and the second bikini girl went to the ladies lounge with Missy Jennings for four long visits, and Baylor added she was jumpy, spilled drinks, mixed up orders. I said I'd run them through the wringer in the morning and see what squeezed out.

"Tomorrow night," No Hair said, "when we cast the net, we need to catch everyone. Anyone we let slip will disappear." He turned to Baylor. "Where do these girls live?"

"They're in a townhouse on Dismuke Avenue. Fifteen A."

"And you just knew that off the top of your head, Baylor?" Fantasy kicked him. "How many bedrooms?"

"Three."

"Good grief, Baylor." I could hear myself whining, weary-mother style. "Learn how to keep a secret or at least how to lie." The boy didn't know the word discretion. "Although," I uncovered my eyes, "the whole IT department lives in townhouses on Dismuke too." No Hair opened his mouth to bark out an order and I waved him off. If he'd let me get some rest, I'd run every resident in every unit in the townhouse complex and if they'd ever uttered the word "strike" they were going down.

"Now, Davis," No Hair said. "Go."

"Walter is running the system alone," I said. "Wherever they have him, there's no escape route or he'd have found it by now, but he doesn't have anyone looking over his shoulder."

"If he doesn't have anyone looking over his shoulder, then why isn't he out?" No Hair asked. "He could've waved a computer flag five years ago."

"Because there's a girl." Ten minutes earlier, I'd run the address. Her name is Cecelia Kelsey, she was Walter's high school sweetheart, she still lives at the address in the photograph, and her welfare must be what's kept Walter in a bunker for five years.

"How do you know all this?" No Hair was tugging at the knot of his tie.

"He communicated directly with me, which is how I know he's alone. He sent a picture of a girl, which is how I know there's someone else involved. The threat against the girl must be so great that no one has to stand over Walter with an assault rifle. If that were the case, he wouldn't have been able to talk to me. I'm not saying busting him out will be a cake walk in the park. No doubt there's an army to wade through to get to Walter," I came up for a breath of air, "but thankfully, that's up to the feds and out of our hands."

"Godspeed to them," Fantasy said.

No Hair asked if there was anything else. There were a million other things, and they'd all be waiting on us when the sun rose, but nothing else to go over tonight. "Let's run through our game plan for tomorrow," he said, "then get some sleep."

#Sleep

"I've got ten sets of eyes on Levi Newman," No Hair said. "He's upstairs in his suite and he's not going to sneeze that we won't know about it before he can even wipe his nose. We have eyes on the Jennings, Cassidy Williams, plus the bartender," he said, "and we'll stay on every one of them until we get them in the Strike doors tomorrow night. At which point," No Hair said, "we'll lock it down."

"We need to get a few cars on the ones living in the

townhouses." I rubbed my Bianca green eyes. "And not one of us."

"I don't know if I can even drive home," Fantasy said. "I know I'm not up for a stakeout."

"I could watch those girls," Baylor said.

We all stared at him.

"What?"

No Hair stood. "Go home. Get some sleep. We're going hot tomorrow," he said, "everyone packing and ready."

"I can't get a gun in my bikini, No Hair. I'll be in street clothes."

Fantasy and I held up fists and air bumped. I was tired of her being gold and naked too. Her legs are so damn long.

"We get this done or we're all in street clothes," No Hair said. "*On* the street. Us and the four thousand other people who work here." He made it to the door in one step. "Up," he said. "Go home. Get some sleep. Richard will be back in the morning. This will all be over tomorrow."

* * *

The sun came into our bedroom through a wall of windows looking out over the Gulf at a low morning angle, caught a crystal lamp base, and projected a chandelier starburst all over the room. This was maybe the third time we'd seen this show. Like the other two times, we didn't move until the sun did. Or in today's case, when a thick line of dark clouds crossed the sky.

"Davis?"

"Hmmm?"

Bradley stretched and rolled my way. "I signed for two court summons yesterday."

I pulled a pillow over my head.

He lifted it. "Why are two people suing you?"

"I only know of one person suing me, Bradley, and she's suing me because she's a prostitute."

"How is that your fault?"

"Exactly."

He dropped the pillow back on my head. It's so loud under a pillow. I could hear my own heartbeat. "Who else is suing me?"

"The Pine Apple lawyer. Smerle."

"He's suing me because I stole his car." Loud and dark under the pillow. I could stay here. "Bradley?"

"Hmmm?"

I came out from under the pillow to a different day. No starburst show, no sunshine, no hope of escaping my past. "You're a lawyer. Can you fix it?"

"It depends."

"On what?"

"If you want to move back to Pine Apple," he said. "I don't have a license to practice in Alabama. We'd have to move."

I wish I had Bradley's patience.

*　*　*

@StrikePlayers T-minus 6 hrs. till doors open for the last time. Open play for Strike contestants. Don't miss it! #Fireworks #ShinyNewCar #AMillionBigOnes

TWENTY-ONE

A tropical disturbance for us is a thunderstorm for everyone else. When the I states—Iowa, Irving, Indiana—forecast a weather event dumping seven to eight inches of rain in an hour, they say extremely heavy rain, thunder and lightning, sustained winds, flash-flooding likely. Here, everything's tropical, so for the same weather event, they say, "Run! Run for your lives! Make parking lots of the interstates! Jam the phone lines with preemptive calls to your insurance carriers! Get out!" In addition to the land-based frenzied panic, a forecast of tropical rain on the Gulf is accompanied by small-craft advisories, coastal flood warnings, and air-travel paralysis—nothing taking off, nothing landing.

Fantasy, Baylor, and I were deep in 3B watching surveillance feed at nine on Friday morning. Baylor won the sleep award, having logged five hours. I'd driven to work in rain heavy enough to have my windshield wipers on the top notch, but as deep in the building as we were, the streets could be flooded, with convenience stores floating up and down Beach Boulevard, and we wouldn't know it. No Hair called to say Mr. Sanders's plane couldn't land because of the storm. (What storm? Did he mean the rain? The plane couldn't land in the rain?) The pilots were trying to fly west of it and land at Lakefront Airport in New Orleans, but a thick line of squalls was diverting flights trying to land everywhere from Galveston to Panama City, and the Bellissimo Gulfstream 650 was one of the few misdirected flights with enough fuel onboard for a week of hold pattern. It might be awhile. Then, Davis, get up here for our conference call.

Fantasy pulled up a weather map. "It's coming down." She whistled. "But it will pass straight through." She read, "'Wide area of organized thunderstorms with frequent lightning and sustained winds between forty and fifty-two miles per hour.' It's nothing," she said. "It'll be over before lunch." Fantasy had a baby, K3, the youngest K son, at home with no electricity and no running water eight days after Hurricane Katrina hit in 2005. It took a lot more than a tropical storm to rattle her.

I stared at the weather model. "Yeah, but look where it's going."

A severe thunderstorm watch had been issued for the entire state of Alabama. When the storm blew past the Welcome to Mississippi sign, twenty miles east of Biloxi, it would visit Mobile, Alabama, then head straight up the state, where it would no longer be a tropical disturbance. It would be a severe thunderstorm. Warnings and watches had been issued.

The storm was forty-five miles wide, moving at fifty miles per hour with forecasted wind gusts up to sixty miles an hour, small-cell cyclones possible, likely to spawn up to thirty small tornadoes across the state, and it would continue a zigzag path of destruction until it reached the southern tip of the Appalachian mountain chain, where it would become stationary. And dump twelve inches of rain and hell. On DeKalb County, Alabama.

Fantasy patted my arm. Pat, pat. "That storm won't get there until ten o'clock tonight, Davis. They'll be in and out of there by then."

* * *

Richard Sanders's office, like half my home and so many other beachfront properties, had a wall made up entirely of glass—the magic real estate words for where I worked and lived, Gulf View! The view today was blue-black, with sheets of rain colliding on the impact-resistant hurricane glass.

No Hair and I were waiting on Felton Parham from the

Department of Justice, who was caught in the storm. I guess so.

I waited patiently, drumming my fingers to the beat of the weather. No Hair paced back and forth in front of the Gulf View! storm. When he paused, he scratched the top of his head with four crooked fingers at lightning speed like he was trying to find his tickle spot. It's his nervous move.

"Settle down, No Hair."

He looked at his watch. "He's late."

"Right," I said, "because he's swimming here."

The countdown had begun.

In the casino business, if takedowns weren't clean and quiet, operations were disrupted on the gaming floor. When that happened, the place cleared out. When gamblers left the casino in droves, profits tanked. When we stopped generating vast amounts of revenues, word got out. When the media got a hold of it, the headlines read "Trouble in Paradise?" When the Associated and United Presses spread it like wildfire, the only way the Bellissimo could get gamblers and their money back in the door was to let them drive away in shiny new cars. And we just weren't up for a shiny new car giveaway. At least until we could all get some decent sleep and married.

Individual, solo-act misdemeanors were kicked out daily. And on my watch, we'd busted groups several times—a false-shuffle gang, a color-up roulette ring, a pimp booking gigs and passing out room keys to his girls (and two boys) from a circular corner booth in Ivories, the piano bar just inside the casino—but this one was all ours. Both ways. Dissention within the ranks. Implosion. Bad apples in the Bellissimo barrel. With the exceptions of Missy and Red Jennings, the thieves were on our payroll. We had to outsmart and outmuscle the smartest and strongest criminals yet—our own.

The door opened and Felton Parham was ushered in. He had the same shock of white hair he'd had the day we'd processed Elspeth Raiffe's body, the same steel-gray eyes, the same Drew Carey eyeglasses, and I think he was wearing the same navy suit. The cuffs of his pants were dark where they'd sopped up the tropical storm and his shoes were still wet from the rain. Otherwise, he looked like he could have been sitting outside Mr. Sanders's door since the last time we'd seen him.

"Jeremy, Miss Way."

"Have a seat, Felton." No Hair swept an arm.

Felton commented about the weather; we all agreed it was a gully washer.

He told us we'd done a good job. The man's white hair was so thick, I wondered if he knew about bull juice. He was quite and pleasantly surprised we'd pulled it off. He asked where Mr. Sanders was.

"Trying to get here." No Hair gave the storm a nod.

Felton Parham nodded.

A representative from the ATF, one from the DEA, plus a SWAT guy, all in uniform and all out of Birmingham, Alabama, joined us by video conference from the Fort Payne police station. The men represented the agencies leading the joint task force moving in on Lickskillet and Have A Seat later today, and everyone at the table wanted it to be a successful mission—we'd like to keep our jobs, and government agencies can't buy the kind of goodwill shutting down a homeland drug cartel provides. Personally, I wanted Walter Shaefer busted out. The very reason I'd been invited to this all-male acronym review.

Too soon, the meeting was turned over to me. My knees were knocking under the table. I introduced Walter—his background, his role, his captivity, his suspected location, his high-school girlfriend, and how vital it was (to Apple, IBM, Google, and Microsoft) that he be protected. In the end, it was just a "Don't Shoot Walter" sermon, and my congregation agreed; they all said amen.

#SaveWalter

"Have you made provisions for the weather?" I asked the split screen of faces. The big burly men assured me they weren't worried about a little rain. We saluted each other and signed off. Before No Hair hit the stop button, we heard the ATF guy talking to the SWAT guy off-camera. "What did they say the woman's name is? The

redhead? David?" I caught my breath. They were talking about me.
And we could hear them. (I could have said something really
stupid. I could have said several really stupid things. These boys
were about to rip me a new one. In front of my boss. And a
Department of Justice man.) No Hair's thumb hovered over the
stop button as he leaned in to listen. So did Felton Parham. I
covered my eyes and held my breath. "Is she one of ours?" another
one asked. "She works for the casino." "Oh, hell, no. She's CIA."
"That woman is from Pine Apple in Wilcox County. Her name is
Davis and she's with the casino." There was a pause, then one
asked, "Are they hiring?"

No Hair pushed stop. Mr. Parham turned to me. "If you ever
decide to leave the casino industry, Miss Way, I'd like for you to
give me a call." He placed his business card in front of me and
stood. He wished us luck. He disappeared.

The dust settled. "You done good, kiddo."

"Thank you, No Hair."

A ray of sunshine cut across the floor as the storm finally
moved on. To Alabama.

* * *

It was like watching trees grow. The next two hours lasted twenty.
Fantasy, Baylor, and I stared at surveillance monitors until we
thought we'd go blind. When Baylor gets bored, he makes machine-
gun noises. When he gets bored with machine guns, he makes
aliens-at-war-while-driving-spaceships noises. He was driving us
crazy.

Of the ten people who would be turned over to the authorities
tonight, half were in-house, and we'd gone over every inch of
surveillance video twice from the time they'd gone to their rooms
after Strike closed. We had live feed aimed on their doors now. The
Jennings poked their heads out at noon, had lunch at Bones (ribs,
fries, slaw, and peach cobbler with vanilla ice cream), then right
back. Cassidy Banking had a pedicure in the salon on the

mezzanine at eleven-thirty, then back to her room. Hope she enjoyed it; it would be ten to twenty before her toes looked that good again. Bald bartender brother Wesley left his room at ten wearing jeans and a ball cap pulled low over his eyes, played three-card poker until eleven thirty, then back to his room. Levi Newman hadn't, that we could see, even rolled over.

"He probably takes Ambien," Fantasy said.

"Maybe he's washing his wig."

I had a laptop at my left elbow streaming live satellite radar of my home state—watching, waiting, praying. I talked to my father. "What's going on, Daddy?" "Wearing my flippers, Punkin." I talked to Bradley; we had a valid marriage license. (!) We had three quiet, simple wedding options we could choose from tomorrow: the Biloxi courthouse, Borrowed and Blue Wedding Chapel in New Orleans, or hop a plane to anywhere and come home married. Lunch came and went, and Baylor was the only one with an appetite. Fantasy and I were too full of coffee to be hungry, we didn't want anything from Taco Bell, we never want anything from Taco Bell, we were sick to death of Taco Bell. Finally, the clock ticked around to two, and Angela texted. *Let me in.*

At ten till three, I had my hand on the door to leave for Strike when it burst open from the other side. No Hair almost knocked me down rushing in, quickly followed by Mr. Sanders. No one spoke. (What is going on?) No Hair held up Mr. Sanders's phone and poked the arrow. Levi Newman's face filled the screen.

"Richard, Jeremy, any other assholes to whom it may concern, listen up. I'm not going down for the lesbian's murder. I'm not going down for the pot farm. I'm not going down for Strike. If I do, she's going with me." A wild-eyed, gagged, blonde head was shoved into the tiny display screen, then quickly shoved off camera. Flashes of phone fumbling, and then Levi Newman's face again. "If you think you're coming after me, think again. I've got your Inspector Lucille Ball Clouseau."

Except he didn't have Lucille Ball Clouseau. He had Bianca Casimiro Sanders.

* * *

Baylor's assignment was the Strike Casino. Stay there, don't move. You're the manager, a bartender, a waiter, and security. Keep things as normal as absolutely possible.

Mr. Sanders stopped speaking after the first thirty minutes, not that he was able to form complete sentences before he grew quiet. ("*How—? Why—? When—? How—?*")

Fantasy worked Security. She hand-picked them off the floor to work with us and called in subs to take their places. She briefed Biloxi Police Chief Michael Dawson, and he dispatched six officers and two detectives to the Bellissimo. At four o'clock we quietly raided Strike. Wesley Bartender, Cassidy Banking, all five IT guys, two waitresses, and the Jennings were walked out of the Strike casino and downstairs, where no one wants to go, without incident. Wesley Bartender was the only one we had to cuff. Cassidy Banking and her sister Missy Jennings were hysterical, and they had been from the moment they realized they weren't in the service hall behind Strike because they'd received emergency phone calls. We had the Jennings separated and in individual interview rooms, Wesley Bartender in a third, who had bloody busted knuckles from punching the concrete wall, and Cassidy Banking in the fourth and last room breaking the sound barrier. The IT guys and the waitresses were piled into the drunk tank, across the hall from the interview rooms, and the gold, naked bikini waitresses had been given blankets they were wearing like capes.

No Hair and I split them up: he took the boys and I took the girls.

I let the door slam behind me and slapped a file down in front of Missy Jennings. There was mascara. Everywhere. A hard set to her jaw. Evil in her eyes.

"You sneaky bitch."

No jazz hands.

"Shut up, Missy." I pulled up a chair. "Tell me where Levi is."

* * *

The call from Levi Newman's to Richard Sanders's phone traced local—it bounced off one of three cell towers within a rock's throw of the Bellissimo, so we didn't take the time to narrow it down to the specific tower. It pinged at one eighteen, but Mr. Sanders didn't listen to the message until two thirty-seven. By five o'clock, a team of forty-two plainclothes Biloxi police, along with as much of our staff as could be spared (as much of our staff as could be trusted), had systematically searched the three million square feet of casino and hotel without turning up a trace of Levi Newman. Or his hostage. The Sanders residence was perfectly intact. We went back over the surveillance video of his movement and activity from when he entered the casino manager's residence (down the hall from Jay Leno's place) twelve minutes after Strike closed, and watched, frame-by-frame, as room service had been delivered forty minutes later—the single, solitary activity between him entering the room and Mr. Sanders receiving the call. We found the room service waiter in his boxers, bound and gagged, in the bathtub of Levi Newman's suite. Which meant he abducted Bianca sometime after four a.m. this morning, made the call to Mr. Sanders from at least fifty feet outside one of the Bellissimo doors at one this afternoon, and by now they could be hundreds of miles from here. Or out to sea. Or landing in Phoenix.

Richard Sanders went to his office without a word. No Hair briefed him every thirty minutes or as needed. Mr. Sanders didn't respond or even acknowledge he was listening. No Hair said, "When I stop talking, he hangs up."

We convened in the hall outside of the four interview rooms that were doubling as holding cells. Fantasy turned the corner and joined us.

"Missy Jennings isn't giving me anything," I said. "Nothing."

"Her husband isn't giving it up, either. All he wants is his lawyer and the DEA," No Hair said. "He's spouting off names of dealers in three states, and throwing Wesley Shaefer under the bus.

It's the other side of the coin with Wesley Shaefer, trying to cut a deal and offering up Red Jennings. I've got someone from the DOJ coming in to talk to both of them. I'd gladly authorize an exchange of immunity for Bianca, but I don't think either of them has a clue as to where Levi is."

"What about Cassidy Banking?" Fantasy asked.

"She's wailing," I said. "On and on about how they made her do it. She's innocent. I can hardly make out a word she's saying. Honestly," I surrendered, "she's going to pass out any minute from screaming."

Fantasy pushed up the sleeves of the hoodie she was wearing. "Let me take a crack at her."

No Hair and I watched from the central observation room as Fantasy stepped in. A new audience had Cassidy cranking it up. No Hair reached for the dial on the volume box to squelch the screaming. Fantasy circled her screaming prey, holding her chin, tapping her cheek, and with each of Fantasy's steps, Cassidy screamed louder. In one motion, Fantasy jerked Cassidy up by a handful of black sweater and gold chains. The chair went skidding across the floor and hit the wall. Cassidy screamed loud enough to wake the dead in three counties. Fantasy, holding the shrieking woman up by her clothes, raised her right hand, then slapped the holy shit out of Cassidy Banking. And the girl finally shut up.

#Don'tMessWithFormerPrisonGuards

No Hair glanced at his buzzing phone. The calls were coming in too quickly for him to take any but the most urgent, but this one he took. "It's Baylor." He listened, hung up, then said, "The game's down. All of Strike gaming has gone black."

It was ten till six. The raid on Lickskillet had been set for seven. If all went perfectly, it should still take at least an hour to get to Walter, at which point, I fully expected the game to go down. The game would go down when Walter came up. It was happening too early. If they had changed the timeline to sidestep the weather, surely they'd have notified us. What had gone wrong in Lickskillet?

Fantasy came in the door shaking the stinging hand she'd used to smack the living daylights out of Cassidy. "Did you hear her? Levi Newman took off after the computer guy in Alabama. Walter. And he has Bianca with him."

TWENTY-TWO

The four Bellissimo jets were no help at all. The only airport that could accommodate even the smallest of the planes was forty miles from mountainous northeast Alabama. That meant thirty minutes of getting in the air, forty-four minutes of flight, landing in a storm, then having to arrange ground transportation in a monsoon rain. No Hair challenged the pilots, and they suggested he call the governor of Alabama and ask him to shut down Interstate 59; they could possibly put a plane down on it, which would be the only way to get anywhere near Fort Payne. The Bellissimo also owned two EC35 Eurocopters insured for four-dot-two million each, and they weren't any help either. The pilots wouldn't do it. The pilots couldn't do it. They'd never get clearance with the FAA because of the weather. The only option was to fly in Class G uncontrolled airspace under VFR, Visual Flight Rules. "Through storms? At night? Are you familiar with the term kamikaze mission?"

It took Felton Parham from the Department of Justice to authorize the task force schedule change. Move in. Now. He made the call at six fifteen, as Mr. Sanders, No Hair, and a Biloxi police officer boarded the best travel option we had: the Bellissimo Eclipse 550, a small fast jet used to shuffle high rollers short distances. No Hair was right back at the Bellissimo. Because of how the plane was equipped, it wouldn't hold him. The six-seater had been reoutfitted for two passengers plus pilot and steward, with luxurious amenities, and No Hair, the size of a refrigerator, tipped its luxurious scale. The choices were to rip out the kitchenette and restroom, leave them in a pile on the tarmac, or take off without No

Hair. There was no guarantee they'd be able to land anywhere near Lickskillet; there was no guarantee Bianca was even there; Mr. Sanders would not sit at his desk for one more minute.

No Hair looked at me. "Sometimes I'm just too tall."

That's it, No Hair. You're too tall.

Fantasy, No Hair, and I set up camp in the observation room in the middle of the interview rooms below the casino. We watched Missy Jennings, head on the table, periodically pounding it—why, oh, why—with her fists. Several times she rose and beat on the glass separating us. Calling us ugly, ugly names. Sailor language. Bad stuff. We turned off the volume.

The observation room door was wide open to the hallway, and someone had rolled in a cart of coffee and whiskey. I fixed myself an Arnold Palmer—half and half. Baylor called at six-thirty-two to say the natives were getting restless. He'd had to snag two bartenders from the main casino floor to help with the drunks, and one of the bartenders had walked off, refusing to work under the gold glass spikes above the bar. (I don't blame him.) Baylor called Chops and had them bring platters of lobster and thinly sliced tenderloin, then he called Seven, one of the three Bellissimo nightclubs, and brought in a small band to play Luther Vandross music and hopefully put all the players to sleep (didn't work), and he had no other tricks up his sleeve. We were on the verge of a Strike Casino riot. I marched across the hall and keyed myself into the drunk tank. The five IT guys and two waitresses looked up. I asked, "Who is Doug Engelbart?"

A man in his mid-forties who had a wiry goatee and wore frameless eyeglasses was stretched out on one of the metal benches. He said, "Doug Engelbart invented the first computer mouse in nineteen sixty-four."

"Get up," I said. "You're coming with me."

We climbed the service steps to the hallway behind the east wall of the casino and made our way to Strike. I turned to him. "What's your name?"

"Bobby Tobey."

"Do you have any way of communicating with Walter?"

He opened his mouth to lie. He snapped it closed. "No."

"Can you get the game up?"

"Probably, but I'll have no control over it. Whoever wins wins," he said, "and whoever loses loses."

Which is all we ever wanted from the Strike Casino.

I pushed through the small hallway. After you, Bobby Tobey. I pointed to the computer room. "Do it."

I pulled my phone out of my pocket.

@StrikePlayers Game back up in 30. Sorry. #OurBad #PatiencePAYS #LastNight #Enjoy!

* * *

Alabama Governor Harris Lee declared DeKalb County to be in a state of emergency at six-thirty. Emergency Management, the Red Cross, and a Weather Channel guy in waders up to his neck were on the way. Mandatory evacuations were being executed for residents of all populated places in and around Fort Payne; the water was pouring off the mountains and flooding the city.

A rockslide had closed both lanes of Greenhill Boulevard. Shelters were slapped together at the high school gymnasium and in Fort Payne First Lutheran's sanctuary. No power anywhere except generator. The storm had churned its way upstate and was parked over Fort Payne, with dry air wrapping around it, creating intense levels of atmospheric instability. In other words, the storm wasn't going anywhere anytime soon, and for the next hour, lightning strikes could be as many as 158 an hour per square kilometer.

"If nothing else," Governor Lee said, "get in your bathtub and pull a mattress over your head."

The storm knocked out our cell phone communication with the task force ten minutes after they entered the Jennings Tree Farm compound. Mr. Sanders and crew radioed they were approaching the Northeast Alabama Regional Airport in Gadsden, forty-eight miles from Lickskillet, and they'd keep us posted. It was fifty-fifty, they might have to push back, they'd let us know.

We sat around a steel table, the three of us, barely breathing, for the next thirty two minutes. No Hair took the call that Mr. Sanders had landed safely in Gadsden, but was going nowhere because I-59 was closed. He had his buddy, Vernon Rider Wilson, the governor of Mississippi, on the phone with Governor Lee of Alabama, requesting state troopers. He'd let us know. Fantasy quietly checked in with her family, I checked in with mine. Everything was A-OK and soggy in Pine Apple, and Bradley had made his way to Strike, where he was helping tend bar. "On the other side," he said, not the side of the bar where Elspeth lost her life. He liked making martinis, there was a bit of art to it, and he'd be right here should we need him for anything. There wasn't much Bradley couldn't do in a casino.

The task force contacted us by satellite radio at seven-twenty-two.

"We have everyone in custody. We moved them out in Humvees. We're down the mountain and we're not going back up for a second sweep until daylight or the weather breaks."

Walter Shaefer's fifty square feet of prison under a ten-by-ten steel grate in the southeast corner of the airplane hangar/marijuana processing plant, we were told, was open and empty.

"You have to go back in," I said to the radio. "You have to go back."

"We have secured the area, Miss Way. We have two dozen people in custody. My orders are to clear out. I couldn't go back in if I wanted to, and truthfully, only an idiot would drive up that mountain in this storm."

After five minutes of total silence, I looked at No Hair and Fantasy. "If you all will excuse me, I have to call an idiot."

I walked slowly to the end of the hallway, where I fell against the wall, then slid down to the linoleum floor. I dug my phone from my pocket, looked to heaven above for help, and dialed.

He answered. "This better be good."

"Where is my grandmother?"

"What's it to you?"

"She's my grandmother, Eddie. Answer the question."

He huffed. "They had a group seminar on the art of love," he said. "She's in the lodge with no clothes on doing body painting with twenty other old fat people. It's the nastiest thing I've ever seen."

"How did you see it, you pervert?"

"I'm their pizza delivery boy, thank you. I got a large meat lover's for myself and can't even eat it after what I saw. I'm thinking about washing my eyes out with battery acid. It's raining like a mother here, Davis. Do you need something, or are you just calling to bitch at me because your grandmother's such a Koo-Koo bird?"

"You listen up, Eddie, and you listen good."

"I don't know who you think you're talking to—"

"Shut up." I knew exactly who I was talking to. "I'm sending you an address. Plug it in the GPS of that thing you're driving, and you haul ass."

"I'm not driving this tank in this weather. You're like a dumb blonde with red hair, Davis. You're a dumb red."

"That it's a tank is the very reason you can drive in this weather."

"What?"

"Eddie, I swear to you, I will hunt your sorry ass down and kill you with my bare hands if you don't do this right here, right now, this minute."

My bare hands were shaking.

"Why should I? Why should I do *anything* for you?"

"It's not for me," I said. "It's for Bianca."

I heard the engine turn over. "Where am I going?"

"You're driving eight miles to Fort Payne. Take a right behind the McDonald's, then seven miles up a mountain to a tree farm. You're looking for a paved road on the left about halfway up. It will lead you to the big house where owners live. Don't miss it. If you get to the top you've gone too far and you probably won't be able to turn around. Find the house. Bianca's in it somewhere."

He hung up.

I cried.

Twenty-eight minutes later, my cell phone, in the middle of the table, buzzed. A picture of a rattlesnake, teeth bared, flashed on the screen. I answered it in speaker mode. Eddie raised his voice over the background noise of pelting rain on the aluminum siding of the RV.

"Davis? I didn't have any trouble finding the house," he yelled. "I'm looking at it. It's burning down to the ground. Lightning must have got it. What do you want me to do?"

We looked at each other over the rattlesnake.

"Stay there. I'll call you back."

* * *

I called in the fire to the emergency responders in Fort Payne. They said too bad and don't worry, a fire won't last ten minutes in this rain. I poured myself another Arnold Palmer.

"We can't ask him to go into a burning house, Davis." No Hair had taken off his tie, a goose sitting on a golden egg.

"Sure we can." I paced. I stopped. I paced. I stopped so fast I almost tripped over myself. "Who talked to the waiter who was tied up in Levi Newman's room?"

"I did," Fantasy said, "on the fly, earlier. Why?"

"What'd he say?"

"He said he'd own this place next week."

He might be right.

"Why?" No Hair asked.

"Because." I took a deep breath. "Levi Newman had to know he could fit into the waiter's uniform. And if—"

No Hair stopped listening, took a corner, and started dialing.

Five minutes later, a Biloxi police officer walked the waiter to us; they'd been taking his statement in the banquet hall on the conference level above the casino—temporary staging for Bellissimo Mayhem Round Two—first the lightning strike and evacuation, now this.

I offered the waiter coffee or whiskey. He couldn't decide, so I made him an Arnold Palmer, then sat down across from him.

"What's your name?"

"Scott Rosenburg."

"When did you meet Levi Newman?"

His right eye twitched.

#Gotcha

"How much did he pay you for the uniform and a few hours in the tub?"

The whole right side of his face twitched.

"Come on, Scott. Whatever he paid you, we'll pay you twice that."

No Hair, against a wall, cleared his throat.

"I want immunization."

"Do you mean immunity?"

"Right." Left eye joined in on the twitching.

"Of course, Scott. We're on the same team. Just one question before you go. We need to cover all our bases. Who else have you seen in his room? Anyone, anytime."

(Please don't say Bianca. Please don't say Bianca. Please don't say Bianca.)

"A blonde woman," he said.

Oh, holy shit.

"What about that immunization?"

"You're going to walk out of here free as a bird, Scott, with as much money as we can stuff in your pockets."

"A tall woman with long blonde hair who wears a lot of jewelry."

"Thank you, Scott." I tipped my chair back on two legs. "Officer?"

The patrolman stuck his head in.

"Book him," I said. "Conspiracy, withholding evidence, aiding and abetting."

Scott had himself a little fit. "That's enticement! You tricked me!"

"I can entice you all I want, Scott. I'm not an officer of the law, and you're a dumbass."

No Hair and I looked at Fantasy. She said, "Let's go have another little chat with the tall blonde who wears a lot of jewelry."

We entered the room and closed the door. Cassidy took one look at Fantasy and started whimpering.

"Cassidy?" Fantasy perched herself on the table next to her. "You sure have pretty teeth."

Cassidy, pale and trembling, shaky-whispered, "Thank you."

"Braces in middle school?"

Cassidy shook yes.

"Laser whitening," Fantasy tipped Cassidy's chin up with one finger and examined her, "oh, every six months?"

The pretty white teeth chattered.

Fantasy leaned in. "Do you want to keep them in your head?"

Cassidy froze.

"Tell us what Levi Newman knows about your sister's property and where he would go to hide."

Ten minutes later I stuck my head in the door and was warmly welcomed (not) by Missy Jennings. "The school needs Quinn's birthdate, Missy."

The question caught Missy off guard, and she auto-answered. "December twenty-sixth. Ninety six."

I ducked out. Two seconds later, Missy realized the school knew Quinn's birthdate. Aunt Cassidy might not have it on the tip of her tongue, but the school had it handy.

#MajorScreaming

The Jennings had a safe room. Of course they did, the Yankees were coming. It was behind the back wall of the detached four-car garage. I dialed Eddie's number.

The storm had broken; the house was gone.

There's a safe room, Eddie.

Cool. Next up on his to-do list: build a safe room under his mobile home.

Great, Eddie. Shut up, Eddie.

He was going in. To save Bianca.

TWENTY-THREE

"Dammit, Davis."

My only sibling. And she talks to me this way all the time.

"I have company!" she whispered.

"Oh, the doctor! I heard about that. Are you sleeping with him? Did I call at a bad time? Meredith, you just met him! Hey," I said, "send me a picture."

"What, Davis, do you want?"

"Oh, right. You've got to go get Granny. She's at DeSoto State Park. In the lodge. You should take towels."

"Why?"

"Because they've been body painting."

"Dammit, Davis, no. Why do I have to go get her? Eddie's supposed to be with Granny. What'd he do now?"

It was nine o'clock. It felt like ninety o'clock. I was under the gold glass spiked murderous light fixture in Strike. The bartender under the golden glow was crazy hot—sleeves rolled up, messy hair, snapping a bar towel with a loud pop when he wasn't mixing drinks—honestly, I might just marry him. When I sat down (more like fell down), he reached for my hand, gave it a squeeze, then pointed to the phone. At my ear. I whispered, *Meredith*. Bradley held up a wait-a-minute finger. He winked. He carefully mixed and poured me a martini, then gently pushed it along the granite. It was a chocolate milkshake in a martini glass.

"Eddie got caught up in a big mess of ours, Meredith." My gorgeous bartender's head jerked. "And Granny's up there without a ride."

"I wasn't really ready to introduce Corey to everyone just yet, Davis. And I don't really want to start with Granny and Cyril when I do. Did you say body paint?"

"Edible body paint, Meredith. Edible."

My bartender laughed.

Debris was cleared from Interstate 59 between Gadsden and Fort Payne, and Richard Sanders rode shotgun with a state trooper to retrieve his rescued wife. He talked to No Hair for two minutes, then asked for me.

"Mr. Sanders?"

"Give it to me straight, Davis."

I'd walked out of the observation room to the hallway. Missy Jennings, cuffed, led by a female officer and on her way to central booking, stepped into the hall. I held the phone to my ear with my shoulder and waved bye. Jazz hands.

"Davis?"

"Sorry."

"Tell me now."

I could hear the crackle of the trooper's radio.

"She wasn't involved, Mr. Sanders. Levi Newman truly thought he had me. I can look into it quietly for you, but I don't think Bianca had a thing to do with it."

"Not a word to anyone," he said.

"Of course."

I wonder if the day will come when her husband really trusted her. He loved her, of that there wasn't much doubt, but he didn't trust her. With good reason.

The holding cells were cleared at eight thirty. Everyone was transferred from the luxurious Bellissimo to the luxurious prisoner intake of the city jail. The Bellissimo Eclipse 550 took off from Gadsden at eight forty-five and would be back in Biloxi in less than an hour. I hoped they had Xanax or a two-by-four on that plane for Bianca.

Fantasy, No Hair, and I made our way to Strike for a few (dozen) hard-earned chocolate shake martinis. I poked my head in the IT door, where Bobby with the goatee was chain smoking, drinking straight from a bottle of Jack Daniels, and rolling a chair between terminals. "Hey." He looked up. "Do any of you guys know anything about computers? Just anyone who can even hit enter who could help me?"

"No."

"Damn."

"At ten o'clock, I need you to switch the game over to tournament mode," I said.

"I can't do that by myself."

"Find a way, Bobby, or you'll be joining your buddies downtown." I closed the door, and said to the Biloxi policeman who was babysitting, "Watch him. Don't let him leave that room."

I made my way to the bar. Bradley. And it was then I remembered the loose string that was my grandmother. Eddie had destroyed the RV, and it didn't sound like he had any desire to leave Fort Payne Police Station until he'd exhausted everyone with his heroics. "Does he ever stop talking?" the chief asked me.

"No."

The Strike Casino, on its last night of operation, was a happy place. It was beautiful, the gaming was extraordinary, and finally, it was operating by the book. It was packed, with only two empty gaming kiosks. And those two players were never coming back. No Hair stepped away, Scotch on the rocks in hand, to take a call from a Biloxi PD homicide detective. He returned ten minutes later and sat down beside me to tell me the police had received the forensics results from the feds. They'd recovered two different blood samples from the glass icicle murder weapon. One the victim's, the other, scant and unknown, but surely the assailant's. So our perp didn't drive the stake into Elspeth's heart without shedding a drop of their own, which was good news for us, if we could get blood samples from everyone who'd ever entered the Strike doors.

"And a partial latent print," No Hair said, "but not enough to run."

A latent fingerprint, different from a patent or impressed

print, is made when body fluids or other substances transfer an image onto a surface. It's dusted, photographed, then lifted, and can often point directly to the killer. Latent prints might show up in bacon drippings, buttercream frosting, or huckleberry-scented wax. If so, look at the butcher, the baker, or the candlestick maker. If they come back Triple Sec, gin, and draft beer, look at the bartender.

Wesley Shaefer.

"He'll lawyer up, Davis." No Hair had run out of Scotch. "We won't get a blood sample from him for six months." He rattled the ice in his glass. "But at least we know."

"We already have a blood sample, No Hair. He punched the wall downstairs. We have his DNA all over the interview room."

It would take time to know the details, but if I had to guess, I'd say Wesley Shaefer heard every word before he busted up mine and Elspeth's special moment in the liquor closet and he killed her for it.

A sobering thought: If things had gone right for him, mine would have been the next name on his list.

I looked up to see Mr. Sanders, as crisp and fresh as if he'd just returned from vacation, step into Strike. With him, a pale smiling man who had a dark ponytail halfway down his back.

Walter Shaefer.

*   *   *

I took a deep breath before I stepped off the elevator. I can do this. I've been through worse.

"DAVID!"

Cue the dogs.

Bianca was freshly showered and wearing a floor-length, sheer, black gossamer robe. Very loosely belted.

Pass the battery acid.

I tried not to step on her little beasts, who were trying to kill me, as I fell into a white wingback chair. I was too tired to get chewed out by a naked woman while standing. Bianca parked herself opposite me, a table holding ivory candlesticks between us, should I need a weapon.

Bianca lit, then took a long drag from her old bad habit. Next, she had a coughing fit. She put out the cigarette, guzzled half a martini (not chocolate) (clear) (vodka), then patted her chest. She dabbed at her eyes with a lapel of the robe. I looked up; I looked down; I looked sideways.

Drumming her fingers on the arms of the chair, she started her speech. "I've been good to you, David."

"It's Davis."

"Don't interrupt me."

Sorry.

"Richard has been good to you."

I nodded.

"I realize," she eyed the pack of cigarettes, thinking about giving them another try, changing her mind, "the casino business is difficult. I've grown up in it. You know that, right, David? My father *owns* the Las Vegas Strip. So I realize situations arise with no warning. And you are one of the people Richard and I count on to keep things running smoothly, and we count on you to *protect* us, and to protect our *son*."

She was up now, and I got a clear shot of her backside on display thanks to her see-through robe. I thought of everyone downstairs at Strike, relaxing, listening to Walter stories, and me up here with Exhibitionist taking the blame for everything. She padded barefoot to a table, picked something up, padded back, and threw it at me.

"Explain this to me this minute, or I will have Richard fire you."

It was an eight-by-ten glossy of me flying through the air, cannonball style, hair on fire.

＊ ＊ ＊

We promised them a tournament and we gave them one.

"I can run it with my eyes closed," Walter Shaefer said. "Point the way."

"No, Walter." No Hair was Not Sober. "You sthay right here." He lobbed a big arm across Walter's shoulders and almost crushed him to death. We booked Walter in Jay Leno's suite upstairs, gave him free run of the place for as long as he wanted to stay, and offered him every delicacy the twelve Bellissimo restaurants had to offer. He asked if we minded him making a long-distance call to an old friend; he ordered a cheeseburger, fries, and a Coke.

Fantasy texted Mrs. No Hair to explain the Dewar's White Label situation we had going on with her husband while I was upstairs getting my ass chewed out by Bianca, asking if she'd like to pick him up or if she'd rather us send him home in a Bellissimo limo. She said neither. She'd join us. Another thing that had happened while I was upstairs with Naked was a venue change. Our party had moved to the sunken-seating leather-chair area of Strike with a panoramic view of the gaming. Bradley had given up his bartending duties after four hundred dollars in tips, spilling from his every pocket like a stripper boy's, and was at my side. Baylor had taken off his gold bowtie and cuffs, and had his gold cowboy boots up and crossed at the ankles on a million-dollar table.

At ten, the gaming went into tournament mode. The Strike player sweepstake points were reset to zero: everyone's in, everyone has the same chance of winning the million, go! At eleven, the most points wins a million big ones.

"Davis."

I stopped my chocolate shake midair. "Yes, sir?"

"I offered your ex-ex-husband a job."

Everyone stopped their drinks midair and stared at Mr. Sanders.

"In Tunica."

It was the sigh of relief heard round the world.

"You know what?" Richard Sanders loosened his tie. "We forgot the car. The Mercedes. We're supposed to be giving it away too."

"We replathed it, Richard." No Hair tipped his glass. "We're giving away a..." he thought long and hard, "something else."

"A Porsche," I supplied. "A gold Porsche."

"Where's the Mercedes?" Mr. Sanders asked.

"Special order thires," No Hair said. "We couldn't get replacement thires on it in time."

"What happened to the original tires?"

No Hair unloaded gun fingers on Mr. Sanders.

Fantasy and I hid behind our drinks so we could laugh at Drunk No Hair.

"Who shot out the tires on the Mercedes?" Mr. Sanders asked. He didn't wait for an answer before he turned to Walter. "Do you need a car, Walter?"

"Yes." Walter grinned from ear-to-ear. "I want a hybrid. A Prius!"

I raised a finger. "I could use that Mercedes, Mr. Sanders."

"Done," he said to Walter, then to me, "done."

"Are you giving up the Bug, Davis?" Fantasy asked.

"No. I'm sending that Mercedes to Pine Apple."

Tammy Cotton, founder of the Cotton Animal Shelter in Geneva, Illinois, won the million. Second place, and a gold Porsche, went to Denise Horn, an Entomologist from Allentown, Pennsylvania.

The clock struck midnight. It was my wedding day.

*   *   *

We were married at five in the afternoon on Saturday, October twenty-second, in the white-wedding living room of the Sanders's residence at the Bellissimo. My parents drove down, my sister brought a doctor date, and Bradley's mother was picked up by limo at her front door and flown in by Bellissimo jet. She told my mother she was very afraid that her son would starve to death being married to me and asked my mother why she hadn't taught me to cook. They were in opposite corners of the white room.

My father gave me away with a kiss to my forehead.

Bianca was bored out of her skull, and dressed in head-to-toe black. Her dogs wore black silk scarves.

Fantasy's husband and three K children were chasing my niece Riley around, marring all the white.

No Hair was holding his hand out for Aleve every ten minutes. His wife Grace shook them into his open palm.

We sat around an enormous glass banquet table after the quick ceremony. There were toasts and there were tears, all mine. I honestly couldn't stop leaking. Forks and knives clinked. I couldn't taste a thing. Mr. Sanders was at the head of the table, No Hair on one elbow, Bradley on the other.

"Bradley," our host said. "I need a new casino manager. You're on my short list. In fact," Mr. Sanders said, "yours is the only name on the list."

#UhOh

Gretchen Archer

Gretchen Archer is a Tennessee housewife who began writing when her daughters, seeking higher educations, ran off and left her. She lives on Lookout Mountain with her husband, son, and a Yorkie named Bently. *Double Strike* is the third Davis Way crime caper. You can visit her at www.gretchenarcher.com.

In Case You Missed the 1st Book in the Series

DOUBLE WHAMMY

Gretchen Archer

A Davis Way Crime Caper (#1)

Davis Way thinks she's hit the jackpot when she lands a job as the fifth wheel on an elite security team at the fabulous Bellissimo Resort and Casino in Biloxi, Mississippi. But once there, she runs straight into her ex-ex husband, a rigged slot machine, her evil twin, and a trail of dead bodies. Davis learns the truth and it does not set her free—in fact, it lands her in the pokey.

Buried under a mistaken identity, unable to seek help from her family, her hot streak runs cold until her landlord Bradley Cole steps in. Make that her landlord, lawyer, and love interest. With his help, Davis must win this high stakes game before her luck runs out.

Available at booksellers nationwide and online

Visit www.henerypress.com for details

Don't Miss the 2nd Book in the Series

DOUBLE DIP

Gretchen Archer

A Davis Way Crime Caper (#2)

Davis Way's beginner's luck may have run out. Her professional life is dicey and she's on a losing streak at home. She can't find her gun, her evil twin's personal assistant has disappeared, Bellissimo's Master of Ceremonies won't leave her alone, and her boyfriend Bradley Cole thinks three's a crowd.

Meanwhile, she's following a slot tournament trail that leads to Beehive, Alabama, where the So Help Me God Pentecostal Church is swallowing up Bellissimo's high rollers. The worst? Davis doesn't feel so hot. It could be the banana pudding, but it might be the pending pitter patter of little feet.

DOUBLE DIP is a reckless ride in the fast lane, and Davis Way can't find the brakes.

Available at booksellers nationwide and online

Visit www.henerypress.com for details

Henery Press Mystery Books

And finally, before you go...
Here are a few other mysteries
you might enjoy:

DINERS, DIVES & DEAD ENDS

Terri L. Austin

A Rose Strickland Mystery (#1)

As a struggling waitress and part-time college student, Rose Strickland's life is stalled in the slow lane. But when her close friend, Axton, disappears, Rose suddenly finds herself serving up more than hot coffee and flapjacks. Now she's hashing it out with sexy bad guys and scrambling to find clues in a race to save Axton before his time runs out.

With her anime-loving bestie, her septuagenarian boss, and a pair of IT wise men along for the ride, Rose discovers political corruption, illegal gambling, and shady corporations. She's gone from zero to sixty and quickly learns when you're speeding down the fast lane, it's easy to crash and burn.

Available at booksellers nationwide and online

Visit www.henerypress.com for details

BET YOUR BOTTOM DOLLAR

Karin Gillespie

The Bottom Dollar Series (#1)

(from the Henery Press Chick Lit Collection)

Welcome to the Bottom Dollar Emporium in Cayboo Creek, South Carolina, where everything from coconut mallow cookies to Clabber Girl Baking Powder costs a dollar but the coffee and gossip are free. For the Bottom Dollar gals, work time is sisterhood time.

When news gets out that a corporate dollar store is coming to town, the women are thrown into a tizzy, hoping to save their beloved store as well their friendships. Meanwhile the manager is canoodling with the town's wealthiest bachelor and their romance unearths some startling family secrets.

The first in a series, *Bet Your Bottom Dollar* serves up a heaping portion of small town Southern life and introduces readers to a cast of eccentric characters. Pull up a wicker chair, set out a tall glass of Cheer Wine, and immerse yourself in the adventures of a group of women whom the *Atlanta Journal Constitution* calls, "... the kind of steel magnolias who would make Scarlett O'Hara envious."

Available at booksellers nationwide and online

Visit www.henerypress.com for details

THE BREAKUP DOCTOR

Phoebe Fox

The Breakup Doctor Series (#1)

(from the Henery Press Chick Lit Collection)

Call Brook Ogden a matchmaker-in-reverse. Let others bring people together; Brook, licensed mental health counselor, picks up the pieces after things come apart. When her own therapy practice collapses, she maintains perfect control: landing on her feet with a weekly advice-to-the-lovelorn column and a successful consulting service as the Breakup Doctor: on call to help you shape up after you breakup.

Then her relationship suddenly crumbles and Brook finds herself engaging in almost every bad-breakup behavior she preaches against. And worse, she starts a rebound relationship with the most inappropriate of men: a dangerously sexy bartender with anger-management issues—who also happens to be a former patient.

As her increasingly out-of-control behavior lands her at rock-bottom, Brook realizes you can't always handle a messy breakup neatly—and that sometimes you can't pull yourself together until you let yourself fall apart.

MACDEATH

Cindy Brown

An Ivy Meadows Mystery (#1)

Like every actor, Ivy Meadows knows that *Macbeth* is cursed. But she's finally scored her big break, cast as an acrobatic witch in a circus-themed production of *Macbeth* in Phoenix, Arizona. And though it may not be Broadway, nothing can dampen her enthusiasm—not her flying caldron, too-tight leotard, or carrot-wielding dictator of a director.

But when one of the cast dies on opening night, Ivy is sure the seeming accident is "murder most foul" and that she's the perfect person to solve the crime (after all, she does work part-time in her uncle's detective agency). Undeterred by a poisoned Big Gulp, the threat of being blackballed, and the suddenly too-real curse, Ivy pursues the truth at the risk of her hard-won career—and her life.

Available at booksellers nationwide and online

Visit www.henerypress.com for details

CPSIA information can be obtained
at www.ICGtesting.com
Printed in the USA
LVOW13s1524150617
538255LV00009B/549/P

9 781940 976334